BLACK RIVER FALLS

BLACK RIVER FALLS

A NOVEL BY

JEFF HIRSCH

CLARION BOOKS | HOUGHTON MIFFLIN HARCOURT | BOSTON NEW YORK

CLARION BOOKS
3 Park Avenue, New York, New York 10016

Clarion Books is an imprint of
Houghton Mifflin Harcourt Publishing Company.

www.hmhco.com

The text was set in Minion Pro.
Book design by Sharismar Rodriguez

Library of Congress Cataloging-in-Publication Data
Names: Hirsch, Jeff, author.
Title: Black River falls / Jeff Hirsch.
Description: Boston ; New York : Clarion Books/Houghton Mifflin Harcourt,
  [2016] | Summary: "Seventeen-year-old Cardinal has escaped the virus that
  ravaged his town, leaving its victims alive but without their memories"—
  Provided by publisher.
Identifiers: LCCN 2015036597 | ISBN 9780544390997 (hardback)
Subjects: | CYAC: Virus diseases—Fiction. | Memory—Fiction. |
  Survival—Fiction. | BISAC: JUVENILE FICTION / Action & Adventure /
  Survival Stories. | JUVENILE FICTION / Science & Technology. | JUVENILE
  FICTION / Science Fiction.
Classification: LCC PZ7.H59787 Bl 2016 | DDC [Fic]—dc23
LC record available at http://lccn.loc.gov/2015036597

Manufactured in the United States of America
DOC 10 9 8 7 6 5 4 3 2 1
4500596989

THE

TORGOTTEN CITY

I'S FUNNY the things that get stuck in your head. Little things, I mean. Like the woman who gave me this notebook. I never knew her name, barely even saw her face, but I remember her so clearly it's like she's sitting across from me as I write this.

She wasn't National Guard or CDC. Red Cross is a possibility, but the cut-rate hazmat suit she was wearing makes me think she was from one of the smalltime charities that flooded the Quarantine Zone right after the outbreak. The October Sixteenth Fund, maybe, or Remember Black River. They'd show up in Monument Park with backpacks stuffed full of clean socks, toothbrushes, and soap. Some candy for the kids. Others, like the Remember people, brought Facebook profiles, old yearbooks, and printouts from the DMV, promising to "help reunite you with you."

This woman was different. All she had was notebooks.

"We thought some of you might want one," she said. "So you can record things about yourself or your family, or what's been happening here since the quarantine. That way if you get, you know, infected, it could be like your memory."

That was almost a year ago. I've been carrying one of her

notebooks around in my backpack this whole time, but I've never even opened it until tonight. To tell you the truth, I'm not sure what made me do it now. The last thing I need is help remembering. I remember everything, it's just that it's all so jumbled up in my head. Maybe I'm hoping that if I spill it out in front of me like this, it'll finally line up in a way that makes some kind of sense. Maybe then I'll know what to do.

Dad told me once that when he knew a story was going to be hard to write, he'd pretend he was telling it to just one person, like he was writing them a letter. That way, no matter how tough it got, he'd never feel alone. The only trick, he said, was choosing the right person. For me, that part's easy.

I choose you.

1

I T ALL STARTED with a fight Greer and I had one morning up on Lucy's Promise.

This was eight months after the outbreak. I was walking through the woods, gathering branches for a project I had in mind. Once the quarantine cut Black River off from the rest of the world, we had to rely on the National Guard for just about everything — food, clothes, medicine, mail deliveries — so every other week they brought in a shipment and handed it out in Monument Park. In one of the last ones there were a few packets of seeds, and they got me thinking I could start a small garden in this clearing not far from my tent.

The only problem was the hundreds of deer and squirrels that lived on the mountain with us. They'd devour anything I planted as soon as it came out of the ground. I'd been about to ditch the whole idea until Gonzalez — that's Hector Gonzalez, the National Guard lieutenant who checks on us every once in a while — figured out how I could make an enclosure for it. He sketched it out and even hauled a roll of chicken wire all the way up the mountain for me.

So that's what I was doing that morning. Looking for

branches I could use as a framework to hang the fence on. I'd collected about half of what I needed when I heard Greer's voice coming along the trail that ran up the mountain from his camp.

"Yo! Cardinal Cassidy! Where you at?"

"Over here!"

Snow Cone and Hershey Bar came bounding through the woods just ahead of Greer and plowed into me. Hershey Bar was a black and tan German shepherd, and Snow Cone was this huge white pit bull, terrifying-looking if you didn't know she was a total pushover. They'd limped up to Lucy's Promise a few months earlier, half starved and bitten bloody by fleas. The fleas were gone, and the dogs had filled out a little, but there was still this red, hairless patch on Snow Cone's side. I'd hoped it would clear up on its own without a trip to town to see the doc, but that wasn't looking very likely.

There was a rustle out in the trees. Greer was getting closer. I left the dogs and went to my backpack to grab my mask and gloves.

"It's okay, man. I'll keep my distance."

Greer kneeled down by an old tree stump and started petting the dogs. I gauged the space between us. It was something I'd gotten pretty good at over the last few months. He was five feet away, maybe six. The virus — technically, it was called Lassiter's Viral Amnesia, but most of us just called it Lassiter's — worked like an especially contagious strain of the flu, and you caught it the same way. Once you did, you had maybe ten hours before it took effect. You know how if you put a really big magnet against a computer's hard drive it'll delete everything on it? Well Lassiter's does the same thing, only to people. Who you are, where you're from, your family, your friends, your whole history—wiped out. Anyway. Like I said, it spreads like the flu. Even without any protection, staying four or five feet away from someone who was infected was generally considered safe. But I hadn't stayed uninfected as long as I had by taking chances. I took a last breath of the woodsy air, then pulled my mask down over my mouth and nose, cinching the rubber straps tight to make sure I had a good seal. The air that made it through the charcoal filters tasted like hot rubber and sweat. I put on my gloves and started gathering up the branches I'd dropped.

"Did I ever tell you I'm pretty sure I was a professional golfer before the outbreak?" Greer was sitting at the edge of the clearing now, a blade of grass stuck between his teeth.

"Nope," I said. "Don't think you mentioned that."

Luckily, Gonzalez had been able to score me one of the newer masks, so I didn't sound like Darth Vader with a mouth full of cotton balls when I talked.

"Oh yeah," Greer said. "Isaac found this old set of clubs in the supply shed. All we had for a ball was a walnut, but — man, when I hit that thing? It just felt *right*, you know? Like I've been doing it my whole life. Do pro golfers make good money?"

"Yeah, but they have to wear weird pants. I thought you were getting the kids ready to go on the supply run."

Greer picked up an acorn and chucked it into the woods. "Yeah, but I had to get out of there. Breakfast time? Those kids turn into a bunch of piranhas. I try to tell them that I'm, like, their savior. That we both are. That if it wasn't for us, they'd all be fending off the gropers in that Guard shelter in town."

"Please tell me you don't let Benny and DeShaun hear you say things like that."

He waved me off. "Ah, they're fine. All I'm saying is you'd think after all we've done for them, I'd rate an extra helping of reconstituted powdered egg product in the morning."

"World's not a fair place, I guess."

"Amen, brother. A-men. But don't worry. Your old buddy Greer hasn't forgotten you. Despite being weak with hunger, I managed to score you some grub before I left."

He pulled something out of the pocket of his sweatshirt and pitched it to me. Two biscuits wrapped up in a red bandanna. They were craggy and golden brown. I tossed them back and returned to my work.

"Nah, you go ahead."

"Dude, these are *Tomiko's* biscuits we're talking about here. If the gods had biscuits, they would be these very biscuits. What? Are you sick?"

"Not hungry."

"You ate already?"

"Yep."

"Are you lying to me?"

Those piranhas Greer was talking about? They were this group of infected kids who had been orphaned by the outbreak. Usually the only choice for kids like that was to stay in this crappy shelter the Guard built, but Greer hated the place so much he grabbed a bunch of them and brought them up to Lucy's Promise instead. Their time together had turned him into a total mother hen. Usually all it took to make him back off was a good hard glare. I gave him one, and he threw up his hands in surrender.

"Hey, it's your loss. I'll just have to eat them myself." He slipped the bundle back into his pocket. "So what's going on, anyway? You starting up the Farmer Cardinal project?"

"Gathering branches to make the fence."

Greer dug around in the leaves and presented a branch the size of his pinkie.

"Little bigger than that."

He jumped to his feet. "Good thing I also used to be an expert finder of branches! Come on, fellas!"

The dogs dashed along beside us as we went tromping through the woods.

"So, for real," I said. "How's everybody doing this morning?"

He tossed aside a half-rotten log. "Fine. It's the usual chaos. *You stole my hairbrush. That's my shirt. You're stupid. No you're stupid!*"

"You make sure everyone took their meds?"

"Yeah, right," he said. "Like I'd go anywhere with those kids if half of them weren't hopped up on happy pills."

"Oh, hey. I fixed Crystal's backpack and sewed that button on Ren's shirt. Left them by their cabins last night. Tell Eliot his shoes are probably a lost cause, though."

"We'll try to find him a new pair today." Greer held up another branch. "How's this?"

"That'll work. DeShaun and Benny doing okay?"

He shrugged. "Better, maybe? I don't know. They're still not talking much, but they ate breakfast with everybody this morning, so — you know, baby steps."

"If you think they can't handle going to town —"

"They'll be all right. Hell, it'll probably be good for them."

He kicked through a pile of brush, sending Snow Cone into a frenzy. She jumped into the air and did a 360, chomping at the flying leaves.

"I think it's time to go talk to the doc about her," I said. "Her side's not getting better."

"Ugh. Seriously, dude? That guy *hates* me."

"He doesn't hate you."

"He does too! You remember that time I asked him to get us that flea stuff for Hershey Bar? He said I should try using some on myself."

I laughed. "Send one of the kids to talk to him, then. Send Makela!"

"Ha! Yeah, right. By the time she's done with him, he'll be so terrified he'll hand over the entire pharmacy."

"And maybe a Guard helicopter."

Greer shook his head. "Nah, the poor guy doesn't deserve that. I'll take care of it. I'll just add it to Greer's eternal to-do list, won't I, Snow Cone?"

The dog gave an excited woof. Greer dropped the branch he was carrying, and they started to wrestle. As soon as Greer got the upper hand, Hershey Bar joined in, flattening him onto his back.

"Help! I'm being attacked by a rabid bear! Help!"

Hershey Bar pawed at Greer's shoulder, pulling the collar of his shirt down enough to expose the corner of one of his tattoos. A chill crept up my spine.

This is probably a good time to mention that, yes, when I say Greer, I mean *that* Greer. Trust me, I find the amount of time I spent hanging out with Greer Larson just as strange as I'm sure you would. Even after all those months, whenever I looked at him, it was like I was seeing two Greers at the same time: the Greer of Lucy's Promise and that scowling kid at the bus stop with the shaved head and the grubby denim jacket. The one whose big brother gave him his first tattoos in the seventh grade with a ballpoint pen and a sharpened paper clip. What happened to that Greer? Same thing that happened to all of us, I guess. October Sixteenth.

Once we got the branches I needed, we headed over to the clearing. Greer and the dogs flopped down by a stand of mountain laurel while I started digging four holes for the main posts that would hold up the fence. It was sweaty work, made sweatier by the leather gloves and the rubber and plastic mask.

"So I was talking to Eliot this morning."

I muscled out a shovelful of dirt and rock. "Oh yeah? He decided whose heart he's going to break yet? Astrid's or Makela's?"

"Jury's still out on that one," Greer said. "No, you know Jen and Marty? They have that cabin over near Mantel Rock? Eliot was talking to them the other day, and they said they'd heard about a couple kids living on their own out on Joseph's Point."

"Why would anybody live on Joseph's Point?" I asked. "The place is nothing but a swamp."

"Marty says they've been there since the outbreak."

I stopped digging. "You serious?"

Greer shrugged. "That's what he said."

"How old?"

"He says six. A boy and a girl."

I pushed the blade of the shovel back into the hole. "No way. Two kids that age couldn't make it alone on Joseph's Point all this time."

"Word is they come out for the supply drop, grab what

they need, and then go right back. Marty said he even saw them once. Looked pretty bad off."

I thought about that for a second, then tossed the shovel aside and grabbed one of the larger branches. "Okay, well, find Gonzalez when you get to the supply line. He'll get his guys to look into it."

"Absolutely. Good plan. *Or* I could just go down to Joseph's Point and get them myself."

"Seems like a waste of time, going to get them just to hand them over to Gonzalez."

When Greer didn't say anything, I turned around to find him grinning at me in that slightly maniacal way of his.

"No way, man," I said. "You know the deal."

"But —"

"We don't bring anyone else up here, and the Guard leaves us alone."

"Oh, come on," Greer said. "Gonzalez was totally winking when he said that."

"He was not winking! The only reason we even got to *make* that deal —"

"Is because Gonzalez is a comic book nerd who's obsessed with your dad."

"— is because we keep to ourselves and the Guard's got bigger things to deal with. Bringing more people up here changes that."

"How?" Greer asked. "It's two kids. Little ones. They're probably adorable."

"If you want to go look for them, fine. But if you find them, you have to hand them over to Gonzalez."

"And what's *he* going to do with them?"

"He'll find their families or something."

"Dude!" Greer said. "They've been out there for *eight months.* That means no one's looking for them. So what're Gonzalez and his guys going to do? Stick them in that stupid shelter of theirs? How do you think *that's* going to turn out?"

"Greer, I *promised* him."

He jumped to his feet. "Well, what the hell did you do that for? It's not like you talked to me about it. Like you talked to *any* of us about it. These are two little kids! Alone!"

"What did you want me to do? Go to war with the National Guard? Take the chance of screwing over everybody here just because *you* want to play superhero again?"

"I'm not trying to play—"

"You think they'll just ignore this? Why? Because we're a bunch of kids?"

"We're supposed to be helping!"

"We *are* helping!"

"Card!"

"The answer is no!"

Suddenly Makela called out from down in the camp. "Greer, come on! It's time to go!"

I snapped back to reality, surprised to find Greer and me squaring off with each other, panting as if we'd just run a mile flat out. His gray eyes had gone stormy and were locked on mine. My throat ached from shouting I didn't really remember doing.

"*Gre-er!*" she called again.

"I'll be right there!" he yelled back over his shoulder.

But he didn't move. He stared at the ground, fists clenched, shoulders hunched. The silence between us was heavy and strange. It was like when a storm tears through a summer day and then retreats so fast it's hard to believe it ever really happened.

I took a shaky step toward him. "Greer, listen . . ."

He turned away and started down the trail. "Forget it, man. Good luck with your gardening."

The dogs followed him as he headed back to camp. Soon their footsteps faded, and I was alone again. I tore off my mask and dropped it. My hands were ice-cold and shaking bad, so I curled them into fists and squeezed until I felt as if a bone was about to pop. There was an angry buzz in the back of my skull.

Everything was so damn simple to Greer. A couple kids might be in trouble? Go get them! Who cares that there might be a price to pay? Who cares that one wrong move could lead to everything we'd built being taken away? And the thing was, it wasn't just Greer. All the infected lived in a world that, as far as they knew, was unbreakable. Every betrayal they'd ever felt? Every disappointment? Every failure? Every disaster?

Gone. That's why they needed me. I remembered how fast the world could fall apart, and I remembered what it was like when it did.

I kicked at one of the branches and started back to my tent. I wasn't going to be able to get any more work done that morning. As I stepped through the woods, a flash of red caught my eye. Greer's bandanna. He'd left it sitting on a rock by the trail. Right where he knew I wouldn't miss it. I knelt and untied the bundle. The two biscuits were still there. Golden. Untouched.

When *had* I eaten last? Not that morning. The night before? Sometime earlier the previous day? That was the thing about Greer. He was never more annoying than when he was right. Kind of like you.

I took the biscuits off the rock and devoured them.

2

BY THE TIME I made it down to Greer's camp, it was in full-on riot mode.

"Let's not forget our ponchos, people!" Greer shouted as the kids sprinted from cabin to cabin, getting ready. "Radio says rain later on, and I don't want a repeat of last time. Let's move! We don't have all day!"

There were eleven of them, five boys and six girls, ranging in age from seven to fifteen. They all lived on the grounds of the old summer camp about a quarter mile down the mountain from my tent. I had lived there myself for a while, but once Greer and the kids showed up, I'd grabbed some camping gear and found a place of my own closer to the peak of Lucy's Promise.

Greer caught sight of me and planted himself a few feet away, his arms crossed over his chest. "What's up, Cassidy? You forget something?"

"I'm coming with you."

"Coming with me where?"

I stared at Greer until it dawned on him.

"What? No. Card, that's not —"

"I'll get Snow Cone's meds, and then I'll talk to Gonzalez about those two kids. We'll work something out."

"Work something out so you can bring them up here?"

"So we can find them a good home."

"Card—"

The buzz in my head started up again, but I forced it down. "If we bring more people up here, Gonzalez can't protect us. That's it. Game over. Benny and DeShaun and all the others get stuck in that National Guard shelter. You want to take that chance?"

Greer looked away, his eyes narrowing on Eliot and Ren, who were play wrestling in the dirt by the main lodge while the girls cheered them on.

"We protect who's here now."

His jaw tensed, as if he were gnawing on a scrap of leather. "You haven't been in town since—"

He cut himself off. No one liked to mention the night of the sixteenth, especially to me. To tell you the truth, I hated it—the way they tiptoed around me like that.

"Look, I've got my mask and my gloves. And it's not like I'm going to stand in the middle of Monument Park. I'll go see the doc, talk to Gonzalez, and come right back."

"But—"

"Can we just go? Please? Seriously, Greer, we don't have all day."

Greer spun away from me and headed back to the kids. I

hadn't meant to snap at him. I'd apologize later. I just wanted to get this over with.

"Yo!" Greer called out. "Rugrats! Anyone not with me in five seconds stays here and cleans bathrooms! Five — four — three — two — one!"

The chaos stopped at once, and everyone snapped into a single-file line at the head of the trail that led off the mountain. As always, Carrie was in the lead, since that meant she got to be closest to Greer. She stared up at him adoringly as he gave the group their final inspection. He sent Astrid back to her cabin to put on more sunscreen and told Isaac to get a bigger backpack. Once they returned and Greer double-checked the four wagons they used to haul things up the mountain, it was time to go.

"Okay, troops! Let's move out!"

I started to follow, but stopped when I saw Benny standing off by himself a few feet from the trail. He was all hunched up, head down, skinny arms hugging his chest. It was like he thought that if he tried hard enough, he might be able to make himself disappear.

Lassiter's didn't have any after-effects. Once it did its work erasing someone's memories, it left them perfectly healthy. Unfortunately, that rarely meant they were okay.

At seven, Benny was one of the youngest kids in camp. From what we could figure out, he got separated from his mom and dad when they were all infected on the night of the sixteenth. Once the quarantine was in place, the Guard tried to reunite him with his folks, but as far as Benny was concerned they were trying to make him live with two complete strangers who acted like they were his parents. He ran away. The Guard dragged him back. He ran away again. Greer found him nearly a month later, hiding out in an old muffler shop. He'd been living on creek water and a vending machine he'd smashed open with a brick. Greer brought him up to Lucy's Promise and, I don't know, I guess the Guard finally decided they had bigger things to do than chase around one pissed-off seven-year-old.

The rest of the kids on Lucy's Promise had similar stories. Families that fell apart when the memories that bound them together were gone. Parents who died in the chaos of the sixteenth. Parents of kids who never got infected and left the Quarantine Zone to keep it that way. Some of them just couldn't stand living with all the other infected down in Black River. You remember that animated *Rudolph the Red-Nosed Reindeer* movie we used to watch when we were little? The one with the Island of Misfit Toys? I guess that's what the sixteenth had turned them into. Misfit toys. Lucy's Promise was their island.

"What's going on, Ben?" I asked.

He scrunched up his face, still not looking at me. At first I thought he wasn't going to answer at all, but then I got a dry little whisper.

"Isaac and Eliot say there are ghosts."

"What? Where?"

Benny pointed his chin toward the trail that led to Black River.

"In all those houses down there," he said. "And up here too. In the trees and stuff. They say if you're not careful, the ghosts'll reach out and —"

"Isaac and Eliot were teasing." I made a mental note to have Greer give them a talking-to. A vigorous one. "There aren't any ghosts."

He gave me a deeply skeptical look. "How do *you* know?"

"Because I know."

"But, well, what if I get lost? Or somebody grabs me, or they make me go back to that shelter —"

"Do you think any of us would let somebody grab you?" I said. "Or let you go back to that place?"

His forehead wrinkled as he considered it, but clearly he wasn't convinced. I checked behind me and found the trail deserted. The rest of the group was already past the first turn. I squatted down so I could look Benny in the eye.

"You know, when I was your age, I had nightmares a lot."

Benny cocked his head. "You did?"

"Oh yeah. Bad ones, too. They'd wake me up in the middle of the night, and then I'd be too scared to go back to sleep. And since I shared a room with my big brother, that meant he couldn't go back to sleep either. So he came up with this thing to help me get over being scared."

"I'm not —"

"No, I know. You're not scared. But still . . . you wanna try it?"

The way Benny looked at me it was clear that every atom in his body was primed for some kind of trick. But in the end, he nodded.

"What's the happiest thing you can remember?"

The question took him by surprise, but then he thought about it for a second and said it was one day last month when he and DeShaun — the camp's other seven-year-old and Benny's best friend — were walking through the woods and found a bird's nest. It was small, he said, the size of two hands cupped together, made out of twigs and leaves and bits of plastic. Each of the four eggs inside it, snow white and speckled with blue, was hardly larger than his thumb. Benny said that he and DeShaun stood there for the longest time, not saying anything, just staring at those tiny eggs until it was like they were the biggest things in the whole world.

"Okay," I said. "Now, close your eyes."

He did.

"I want you to see those eggs again," I said. "Not like you're looking at a picture, but like they're really there in front of you. Do you see them?"

Benny nodded slowly.

"Now I want you to feel how warm the sun is on your skin and how the pollen tickles your nose. Now smell the honeysuckle and the dogwoods and that musty smell that comes from all those old decaying leaves on the ground. I bet there are birds up in the trees too, right?"

Benny nodded again.

"You can hear them singing and DeShaun's breathing beside you and your own heartbeat."

Benny's shoulders relaxed and his mouth fell open, his bottom lip fluttering in and out as he breathed. It was almost as if he were on the edge of sleep.

"Open your eyes."

When he did, they were steady and bright. Calm.

"No matter what happens, no matter what you see, that moment is locked up inside you. So if you ever get scared, that's where you go. Deal?"

He nodded solemnly, never taking his eyes off mine. "But nothing bad's going to happen, right?"

I raised my hand. "I swear. There's nothing to be afraid of."

It was as if the chains holding him back snapped. He went shooting off after the others, kicking up a cloud of dust as he went. I knelt there in the quiet of the camp, staring at the trail and thinking about walking the streets of Black River for the first time in eight months. It had to have been eighty degrees that day, but I felt as if I'd swallowed a bucket full of ice.

Once Benny was out of sight, I went back to my own campsite. I dropped to my knees and hunted around inside my tent until I found what I was looking for: a T-shirt–wrapped bundle hidden under my sleeping bag.

From time to time we traded with the other groups that were scattered throughout the woods and hills surrounding Lucy's Promise. Not long after I moved up to the mountain, I sought out one of them, and swapped almost everything I had for the one thing I wanted.

I unfolded the T-shirt. Inside was a six-inch hunting knife with a leather-wrapped handle. All along the top of the blade there were these rat's teeth serrations, the kind you'd use to saw through thick branches. The cutting edge itself was so sharp it seemed to hum.

I tested the edge with a finger. It whispered through the skin, sending a pinprick of blood curling into my palm. The world became a little brighter and a little more clear. I smeared the blood off on my jeans, then sheathed the knife and threaded it onto my belt. I left camp and started down the trail toward Black River.

3

I SAW THE RIVER first. I'd come around the second-to-last switchback and the trees had started to thin. The Black River cut the Quarantine Zone roughly in half, with the mountains on one side and the town on the other. From up on Lucy's Promise it looked like a dark ribbon. The only bright spot along its course was where the water ran fast over the falls, turning to white foam as it slipped beneath the stone bridge.

The town appeared next. From where I stood it was just trees mixed with black and russet-colored roofs and a few lines for roads. It grew larger with every step, until I could pick out the red brick of Black River High at the south end of Main Street and the crown of mansions way up at the north end. As soon as we came off the mountain, the kids sprinted down Route 9. Greer chased after them, but my legs wouldn't move. I stood there, one foot on the asphalt, one on the grass, looking down the road at what had become of Black River.

The last time I'd been off the mountain was just after the sixteenth, when the QZ had been packed with people. Infected. Uninfected. National and local news teams. Ten different charities. Eight different government agencies.

The uninfected went first. They were released from quarantine around Thanksgiving. Once another month or two passed without any real developments — no cure or vaccine, no culprit, no other outbreaks — the news vans left skid marks on their way out of town. The Red Cross and the Salvation Army were next, followed by the Gates people and the Clinton people and the World Health Organization. The CDC, USAMRIID, and the rest of the government agencies hung in there until early March. After they left it was just us, a dwindling force of National Guardsmen, and the occasional smalltime charity — a bunch of losers shuffling around an empty dance floor long after the cool kids had found someplace better to be.

It was the silence that tripped me up the most. The chaos of those early days was long gone, but there was nothing to take its place. There were none of those old summer afternoon sounds. The pre-outbreak sounds. No whirring lawnmowers or blaring radios. No hissing hoses as people washed their cars or watered their lawns. Just wind moving down empty streets and in and out of the open windows of abandoned houses.

Months of neglect had led to overgrown yards and weed-cracked sidewalks. Roofs with missing shingles. Shutters hanging from broken windows. A family of white-tailed deer, two adults and two fawns, stood on someone's front walk, nibbling at the grass. Another house seemed completely untouched, except that the front door was hanging open, exposing the empty throat of the hallway and shiny hard-wood floors.

"Yo! Cardinal!"

Greer had stopped in the middle of the street and was waving me forward. Benny was standing next to him, looking back, curious, as if maybe I'd forgotten something. Of course it was also possible that he was wondering why a seventeen-year-old kid couldn't just walk down an empty street. I took a deep breath and then I forced one foot in front of the other.

Every few blocks there were reminders of the night of the sixteenth. Empty lots where, instead of a house, there was a pile of ash and charred wood. Two police cars, burned black with smashed windows, sat in the cul-de-sac at the end of Elm Street. Spent tear gas canisters, mixed in with trash and fallen leaves in the gutter, made bonelike sounds as I kicked through them. A rat's nest of zip-tie handcuffs lay bleaching in the sun.

I stepped up onto the cobblestone bridge that spanned Black River Falls. My shoulders tensed. Forty feet below me, the water crashed against jagged slate-gray boulders. The sound was like a wave of static. I looked over my shoulder, up toward the peak of Lucy's Promise. The trail I had walked on only minutes before had vanished into the trees. It felt like a hand had grabbed hold of my guts and twisted.

"Hey. Take a look."

Greer had stopped the kids at the far side of the bridge. He nodded up the street as a large black pickup truck came rolling toward the intersection. The back of it was open, packed with ten or fifteen men wearing bright blue hazmat suits. Black rifles hung from their shoulders. The men turned to face us as they passed. The eyeholes in their suits were shiny plastic, blankly white in the sun's glare. The air filters that grew out of their masks looked like the jaws of huge insects. I stepped back, my hand automatically going to the knife at my side.

"Easy," Greer said. "They're just passing by."

They picked up speed as they crossed Route 9 and headed toward Main Street. Just before they disappeared, I saw a logo on the tailgate — a globe pierced by a sword. Beneath it were the words MARTINSON/VINE.

Greer stepped into the street to watch them go. "Dude, who the hell is Martinson Vine?"

I didn't know, but something about them made me feel my heartbeat pulse in my throat. "Come on. Let's just get this over with."

Greer and the kids had a quick huddle, and then they were on the move again. I followed along, and pretty soon the heart of Black River came into view. This is where most of the infected lived. Thousands of them. They slouched against the walls of boarded-up shops or lounged in the tall grass around abandoned houses and apartment buildings, eyeing us as we moved down the street. I'd heard that there were infected with enough money hoarded away from before the outbreak that they could make a life in the QZ that was almost normal, but they were a minority. Most everybody lived like these people, jobless and adrift.

See, as soon as the quarantine came down, Black River became like a body that was dying one organ at a time. The tourist shops and art galleries closed first, then the grocery stores and the drug stores and the all-night diners. Last to go were the schools and churches. The National Guard and the charities had tried various kinds of resuscitation, but none of them worked. We were too far gone. No wonder Benny believed Isaac and Eliot when they told him Black River was haunted. In a town like this, there were bound to be ghosts somewhere.

By the time we hit Main, small bands of infected were coming out of every alleyway and side street, merging into a flood of people as they funneled toward the park. I tightened the straps of my mask and tried to get Greer's attention, but he was talking to Astrid and Ren and they were laughing. How was that possible? How could they laugh in the middle of this?

It didn't matter. I spun around, looking for the street that would take me away from the gathering mob, but was surprised to find myself lost. Hundreds of shifting bodies made streets and storefronts that had once been so familiar seem strange and distorted. My only choice was to fight against the tide and get someplace where I could think and breathe.

There was a split-second shift, and I saw through a gap in

the crowd that Oak Street was practically deserted. I pressed the mask to my face and ran for it. The second I made it out of the throng, there was the blast of a horn, and then the same black truck from earlier came barreling down the street, inches from flattening me. I fell and my elbow crashed into the sidewalk, sending a thunderclap of pain up my arm. A man shouted at me from the back of the truck, and another laughed.

When they were gone, a second wave of infected rushed past, jostling and shouting. The world spun as I got up and stumbled away from them. I saw flashes of bodies, broken glass, cracked asphalt. I smelled smoke and heard what I thought were bells ringing. The next thing I knew, the crowds were gone and I was on my ass in an alleyway, bent knees in front of me, a greasy Dumpster wedged into my shoulder. Out on the street, teakettle voices screeched and wailed. I pushed myself deeper into the alley and tore off my mask so I could breathe. The air tasted sour and vinegary. My stomach flipped. I remembered what I told Benny, and I clawed through my memories, looking for someplace safe to hide. Most of them slipped away too quickly to get ahold of, but then I felt a snag.

Me and you. Our old bedroom in Brooklyn. Snow falling on the fire escape outside our window. Mom and Dad had gone to bed hours earlier. Once you were sure they were asleep, you slipped out into the living room. I lay there watching the snow and listening to the sound of you padding around in your socks. A desk drawer opened and closed, and then you flung yourself back into the room and shut the door.

"Tennant, what were you doing in Dad's desk? He'll freak if he finds out."

"Dude!" you hissed. "Shut. Up."

You fell into bed beside me, and a flashlight flared to life, moving down the length of your arm to the pages you held in your hand. The title was in black letters across the top.

CARDINAL AND THE
BROTHERHOOD OF WINGS.

"Whoa. Tenn, those are — we can't."

"It's just us," you said. "Besides, Mom and Dad named you after the main character. That gives you, like, a legal right to read it."

I was about to refuse, but then you handed me the first page and it was like everything in the room vanished except for that rectangle of black and white. There they were. The towers of Liberty City shining in the sun. The Brotherhood's Aerie. Sally Sparrow and Rex Raven soaring through a cloudless sky. We worked through that first issue page by page, warm under the covers while the snow piled up outside. We met Madame Night. Penny Dreadful. Kirzon Sloat and the Emerald Horde. It was like watching a whole new universe explode into existence right before our eyes.

"Hey! You all right?"

A woman's voice tugged me back toward the alley. I didn't open my eyes, didn't look up. Whoever she was, I hoped she'd just go away. I wanted to be left alone, wanted to stay where I was, with you, but she didn't leave.

"Kid?"

"I'm fine," I said.

"Funny. You don't look fine, hon."

That voice. I lifted my head and opened my eyes. Sunlight poured around the silhouette of a woman standing at the mouth of the alley. She took a step forward.

It was Mom.

4

I SAT UP SLOWLY and flattened my back against the wall. My mask was sitting beside me, but something stopped me from putting it on.

"I'm okay," I said. "Thanks."

I'd spent three days after the outbreak searching for her, but this was the first time I'd actually seen her since that night. She was thinner than she used to be, and her skin was a deeper brown, as if she'd been spending a lot of time outside. I looked at her left hand and saw that her wedding band was gone. I tried to remember if she'd already stopped wearing it before the sixteenth.

The biggest change was her hair. Remember how when we were kids she'd always talk about ditching the chemicals and going natural? Well, she'd finally done it. It looked like she'd chopped it down to her scalp before letting it grow back. Since she was a quarantine away from any relaxer, it was coming in as a half-inch halo of tiny curls. It suited her, highlighting her big eyes and the sharp angles of her face.

"Well, if you're sure you're okay . . ."

Mom turned toward the wave of people heading for the park.

I scrambled to my feet, resisting the urge to close the distance between us. "Maybe I'm just hungry."

I glanced at a big straw bag hanging from her shoulder. When we were kids, she never left the house without a snack in her purse. Apples. Rice cakes slathered with peanut butter. Remember how she said low blood sugar turned us into monsters? Mom dipped one hand into her bag. My heart leaped a little when she drew out a granola bar and tossed it to me. I rechecked the distance between us and then moved into the sunlight near the mouth of the alley.

"My name's Cardinal," I said. "Cardinal Cassidy."

Once the Guard got the town under control, their first order of business had been to try to put everything back the way it was. Tell people their names. Reintroduce them to their families. But when I said my name, there wasn't so much as a wrinkled eyebrow to suggest that Mom recognized it. Had they missed her?

There was a shout from somewhere in the crowd. She turned toward it.

"Nice to meet you, Cardinal. But I better get going."

"No, wait a second. Please. I have to —"

The sound of engines cut me off. Three Guard trucks rumbled by. Mom mixed in with the few infected still on the street as the rest ran out ahead of the trucks. I called out to her again, but if she heard me, she didn't turn around. The last thing I saw was a flash of her short dark hair as she melted into the crowd.

The next thing I remember is sitting on the hill overlooking Monument Park. My mask was strapped on tight and my hands were sweating inside my gloves.

By then a few thousand infected were pressed shoulder to shoulder behind the National Guard trucks. They moved in swells, surging forward and then just as suddenly pulling back. I dropped my head onto my bent knees and squeezed my eyes shut.

As soon as I did, I was right back in our living room in Brooklyn before we'd moved to Black River. It was a typical Saturday morning. You and I on the floor mashing buttons on the controllers of a beat-up old Xbox. Dad behind us, hunching his giant frame over that tiny desk in the corner he called his office. He'd be sketching furiously and bouncing his head to The Clash so hard that his mane of blond hair danced over his shoulders.

Mom was sprawled out on our worn-out blue couch, exhausted from a night of dance rehearsals followed by a late shift at that hipster bar with the fifteen-dollar hamburgers. She had a book tented on her chest, but like always, she was watching us play and enthusiastically yelling out useless bits of advice.

"Go over there! Now kill that guy! No! Not that guy, *that* guy! Tennant, come on. *Just kill. All. The. Guys!*"

"Shut *up*, Mom!"

My eyes popped open at a series of shouts down in the park. An old man with white hair and a tattered black overcoat was elbowing his way through the crowd, picking up speed as he moved away from the trucks. He turned to look behind him and slammed into the postal table, sending stacks of letters flying into the air like confetti. Everyone reared back in anger as he righted himself, but he ignored them and ran on. I looked closer. The black coat and filthy clothes. The scraggly beard. It had to be Freeman Wayne, Black River's self-proclaimed town librarian. I'd never seen the guy before, but he matched Greer's description exactly. What was he doing?

Whatever it was, it had attracted the attention of the Guard. They started moving toward him but stopped suddenly when they saw five of the men in the blue hazmat suits approaching him as well. A few words were exchanged and the guardsmen backed off, allowing the strangers in blue to take hold of Freeman. Why would the Guard do that? As Freeman was led away, the crowd pulsed and squirmed like a nest of bees that'd just been poked.

I couldn't stand it another minute, so I went down the opposite side of the hill, ending up on an empty two-lane road. Even with a barrier between me and the park, the air still pulsed with the energy of the crowd. I passed a rusty playground and the old ice-cream shop and then crossed over into a warren of boarded-up houses.

The yards were overrun, choked with weeds and wild-flowers in red and yellow and blue. Honeysuckle spilled out onto sidewalks, filling the air with a sweetness so syrupy it smelled like rot. I pictured Mom in her sun hat and gloves, gardening manual in hand, ordering the two of us around that first year in Black River. *Cut this! Water that! Fertilize over here!* She'd spent weeks making fun of our yard-obsessed neighbors, but there we were, beating back the sprawl of weeds to make room for roses and lavender and that yellow spidery thing that nearly took over the entire lawn. After years of living in Brooklyn, it seemed that having soil under our feet instead of grease-shellacked concrete had made Mom deranged. What would she think if she knew how useless all of it had been?

I turned down streets at random, following some internal compass with a needle that spun and spun. Soon the sounds of the park were gone, replaced by wind blowing through untended grass and down empty streets. I passed our high school and the library and the now abandoned vintage store where Mom used to go.

I knew I couldn't blame the infected for not remembering. But how many times had I seen lightning flashes of the person Greer used to be? Like when some random guardsman was giving him a hassle and he'd clench his fists and grit his teeth. For a second he was that kid from the bus stop all over again. Didn't there have to be places like that within all the infected? Like knots in a length of wood that could be sanded down but never erased completely. And if there were, how was it possible that *I* wasn't one of those places for Mom?

As I came around a corner, a crow shot out of a tree with a shriek. Startled, I jumped back. That's when I realized I was standing on our front lawn.

I hadn't been back to the house since the sixteenth. It had almost entirely escaped the chaos that raged through town that night. A few soot marks marred the white porch columns, and the attic window was broken, but other than that, it was unchanged.

A bank of clouds passed over the sun, sending a pins-and-needles chill up my spine. I scanned the yards around me and peered down the gaps between the houses across the street. They were empty. I was alone.

A voice in the back of my head, yours, told me to turn around and leave, but I didn't — couldn't, it felt like. It was as if I'd wandered into a stream and the current was dragging me along. I placed one foot on the bottom step and took hold of the railing, then climbed up to the porch. The floor seemed like it was moving beneath me in rounded swells. I steadied myself by staring at the end of a single brass nail hammered into the door, the one Mom used to hang Christmas wreaths and Halloween skeletons. I heard her singing "The Little Drummer Boy."

I staggered backward. Something brushed against my leg. I looked down and was surprised to see that I was clutching the hunting knife. I didn't remember pulling it out of its sheath, but there was something about that slab of metal in my hand, with its jagged rat's teeth and cutting edge, that made the pitching feel of the floor beneath me go still. I moved down to the kitchen windows. I told myself not to look inside, but even as the thought went through my head, I was lifting my hand to wipe the dust away from the glass.

I could make out the edge of the coffeemaker sitting beside the sink, and the turquoise tops of the chairs that surrounded the marble kitchen island. I remembered Mom spending an entire weekend with those chairs after she brought them home from some secondhand store. Cleaning them, sanding them, coating them with layer after layer of spray paint, and then polishing them until they glowed.

I leaned my forehead against the window and yanked my mask down so I could breathe. Sometimes it seems that all the good things and all the bad things are like vines growing up the side of the same house. There are so many of them, and they're all so tangled up that it's impossible to tell one from the other. It's easy to think you've been saved when really you've been doomed all along.

I should have left right then. I should have turned around and run, but I didn't. I peered inside again. Light from the windows filled that wide-open first floor Mom and Dad loved so much. I could see from the kitchen to the dining room table and beyond, to the stairs at the edge of the living room that went up to the second floor.

I turned and pressed my cheek against the glass. The wall

by the front door was marked by streaks of shadow that gleamed thickly as they ran down to the floor and spread out in dark pools. I stared at them for a long time, long enough to realize that they weren't really shadows at all.

I heard bells ringing somewhere out in the neighborhood. No, not bells. Wind chimes.

The inside of the house swirled into streaks of turquoise and white. My knife hit the ground and the next thing I knew my knees crumpled and my stomach seized, folding me in half. I vomited acid onto the porch and then fell onto my side and buried my head in my hands. I grasped for the hush of the snowfall and the rustle of pages as they went from your hand to mine, but every time I thought I had it, my fingers slipped and the memory went hurtling away. The last thing I saw before darkness rushed in was the silver blade of a knife.

THE GIRL WITH THE GREEN HAIR

5

DUDE! **CARDINAL!** Slow down!"

"Leave me *alone!*"

I was running down Water Street toward Brooklyn Bridge Park, and you were struggling to catch up. I hadn't stopped or slowed down since Mom and Dad announced our impending move to Black River.

"You totally freaked out Mom and Dad!"

"Good!"

"Cardinal!"

"They freaked *me* out, Tennant! Didn't they freak you out?"

"No!"

I stopped and turned around. You tried to hold on to the lie, but it took only a couple seconds of being stared at by a pissed-off thirteen-year-old before you threw up your hands.

"All right! Fine! So maybe it was a little abrupt."

"A *little?* They looked like crazy people!"

You laughed. "They aren't crazy. They're just excited. This is *huge* for them. Dad's wanted to quit that stupid advertising job for years. Selling the Brotherhood to Marvel means he can!"

"But what about Mom?"

"What has she wanted to do ever since she had to stop dancing? Open her own studio. She can do that up there."

I crossed my arms and scowled at the sidewalk. We were just a couple blocks from the park. I could hear kids screaming and the ice-cream truck's jingle.

"Look," you said with a sigh. "You're freaked. I get it. How about you let me buy you an ice-cream cone —"

"I'm not *nine*, Tennant."

"I know you're not nine, Card. *I* want a cone. Okay? Let's get a couple, then we'll sit down and figure this out."

I looked over my shoulder to where the East River appeared and disappeared between the buildings at the edge of the park. What choice did I have? If I started running again, pretty soon we'd both be swimming.

Minutes later we were sitting on a bench watching the skateboarders whiz by while tourists snapped pictures of the bridge. I worked on my soft serve while you ticked off the pros.

"No more bedbugs. No more roaches. No more getting packed into subway cars with busted air conditioners in the middle of summer."

"What about our friends?"

"Black River is only two hours away," you said. "We'll see them whenever we want. And besides, when we start at Black River High, we'll be the cool and mysterious kids from Brooklyn, so we'll make tons of new friends. Hot girls will *literally* swoon."

"Hmm."

"And there are bike trails," you continued. "And rivers, and mountains. And people go out and pick their own apples and pumpkins in the fall. We can learn to kayak!"

"Since when do you want to learn to kayak?"

"Since right now! I just decided. I'm gonna be Kayak Guy. Oh! And maybe Snowboarding Guy. Wouldn't that be awesome?"

"Yeah," I said. "Awesome."

"I can see you're a tough sell, kid. That's why I saved the best for last. This house Mom and Dad are buying? We'll have our *own rooms.*"

I didn't say anything, but all I could think was that I didn't *want* my own room. You and I had been sharing a room since *birth.* The idea of being locked up in some room all on my own made me feel like I'd just been tossed into the East River with a sack of concrete tied to my ankle. I dumped the dregs of my ice-cream cone in the trash.

You nudged my shoulder with yours. "Think about it this way, bro. What would have happened to Kal-El if he'd grown up on Krypton instead of Earth?"

"Uh, he would've died when the planet exploded?"

"Okay. Fine. But forget that for a second. If Kal-El had grown up on Krypton, he'd have ended up just like everybody else. Dude had to move to *Earth* to be Superman."

You turned to me on the bench and leaned in closer.

"Just think about it. There's a whole new world out there,

and we can make it into anything we want. We can make *us* into anything we want."

Across the river the sun streamed down over the sky-scrapers of Manhattan. I imagined a streak of blue and red soaring over the city and smiled despite myself.

"Yeah," I said. "Maybe that is kind of awesome."

I woke with a start and found myself still on the porch. I sat up, groaning, and put my back against the railing. The world was hazy and smelled of sweat and vomit. Dark clouds had spread over the town, and the air had that heavy, charged feeling that comes just before a storm. Once my head stopped pounding, I gathered my things, then staggered down toward the street.

As soon as I hit the sidewalk, I thought I heard someone call my name. I spun around, but didn't see anyone. Just the house, towering over me. I thought about all the rooms sitting side by side within its walls — my bedroom, yours, Mom and Dad's. They seemed like those chambers they find hidden inside pyramids, sealed up for a thousand years, airless. I felt a pull to go inside — to climb the stairs, to lie in my old bed — but I pushed it away. I strapped on my mask and started the walk back to Lucy's Promise.

The supply drop must have ended hours earlier. The streets were empty and Black River was quiet. I could've believed I was the only one left in town until I heard the sound of someone running on the cross street up ahead. Whoever it was, they were moving fast and heading my way. I slipped behind a row of hedges and waited for them to pass.

The footfalls got louder, and then a girl with emerald green hair appeared, sprinting down the sidewalk. She made it to a brick house across the street from where I was hiding and collapsed against a telephone pole, head down, panting. The pale blue button-down she was wearing was dark with sweat. Her cutoff jeans and boots were splashed with mud.

The girl caught her breath, then looked back the way she'd come. That's when I saw her clearly for the first time. As soon as I did, the world went a little bit still.

She was about my age, with a heart-shaped face and pale, lightly freckled skin that had gone pink from running. She was obviously scared, but she surveyed the road behind her with a fierceness that was so intense it seemed to make the air around her shimmer.

I started around the hedge, but before I could take more than a step, she was off again. At the end of the street she cut right and disappeared. By the time I came out into the road, it was empty in both directions. Whoever or whatever she'd been looking for was nowhere in sight.

I turned to where the peak of Lucy's Promise rose over the neighborhood. The clouds above it were low and heavy. It took only a few seconds for a storm to turn the trail up the mountain into a river of rocks and mud. I told myself that the girl wasn't my problem, that I needed to get back home before the rain started. But when I got moving, it wasn't toward the mountain, it was to follow her.

When I rounded the corner, I saw her dodging into the driveway of a blue house halfway down the block. A second later, two figures appeared at the far end of the street, racing toward the same house. They hadn't seen me yet. I wasn't sure why, but I thought I shouldn't let them. I hid until they were out of sight and then quietly followed.

A rusty pickup truck was parked at the end of the driveway. I moved behind it and looked through the windshield into the fenced-in backyard. It was small and overgrown with weeds. A pile of construction debris — lengths of two-by-fours, a box of nails — sat beside a half-built shed in the corner. Two men were squatting in the grass between the house and the shed, looking into the space beneath the back porch.

One of them was young, in his twenties maybe. Skinny, with shaggy brown hair and a beard. The other man was older. His father? He was thick-chested, with a sizable gut and a sunburned bald patch on top of his head. He looked familiar, but I couldn't put my finger on who he was until he pulled a pair of large gold-framed glasses out of his breast pocket and put them on. Mr. Tommasulo. You remember him? The crossing guard for the elementary school down the street? The one who always waved and told us it was a blessed morning as we walked past him on our way to school.

The younger man inched forward, tilting his head toward

the space beneath the porch. "We know you're confused. You have every right to be. There's a virus. You caught it. That's why you've lost your memory."

"Dale's right," Mr. Tommasulo said in that same bright voice I remembered. "But everything will be better if you come out of there. I promise."

I eased down the side of the truck and crouched by the front tires to get a better view of the porch. The area beneath it was thick with shadows, but I could just make out the girl. She'd wedged herself in, her back to the house's concrete foundation. One arm was out in front of her, as stiff as a lance. A shard of broken glass was in her hand.

"Your name is Myra," the younger man — Dale — continued, loud and slow, like he was talking to someone who barely understood English. "You and I were married last spring in Hudson. We went to Barcelona for our honeymoon. It cost us an arm and a leg, but we went because it's been your dream since high school."

"You read a book about that architect fella," Tommasulo said. "The one who made all those weird buildings."

"Gaudí," Dale said. "God, it kills me that you don't remember, but I know it isn't your fault. You're sick. That's all. But we can explain if you come with us."

Everything suddenly became clear. I'd always known that I wasn't the only uninfected person in Black River. Just as there were people who refused to leave their beach houses when a hurricane was bearing down on them, some uninfected had

49

chosen to stay despite Lassiter's. They were pretty strict about keeping to themselves, but I'd heard that every now and then one of them got careless and ended up infected. Looked like it'd happened again.

"We've got the photo albums at home," Tommasulo said. "Wouldn't you like to see pictures of your wedding?"

Myra didn't answer. There was a rumble in the sky, and a light rain began to fall. Before I left, I took a last look. The girl had ventured closer to the lip of the porch. I could see the blue of her shirt and her hand clutching that shard of glass, but everything else was still in the shadows. I felt strangely disappointed not to see her face again. Why? She was just some careless infected girl. I didn't know her. Had barely even seen her.

There was another crack of thunder. I started back down the driveway, heading for the street.

"We can't wait," Tommasulo continued behind me. "This thing you have, this virus — it doesn't just take your memory."

I stopped where I was. Raindrops pattered on my shoulders.

"That's right," Dale said. "Pretty soon it goes to the next stage and makes you sicker. You could die!"

"But it's okay. We have the cure at home. It'll be like this never happened. You just have to come with us."

"That's right," Dale agreed, an oily laugh dribbling out between the words. "Just come on out and we'll take you home and give you *exactly* what you need."

I turned and looked through the truck's windshield. Dale was approaching the edge of the porch, reaching into his back pocket as he did. There was a glint of steel as a pair of hand-cuffs emerged.

Time jumped forward. I was in the driveway, and then I was in the yard running flat out. Dale turned, his eyes going wide as I drew my knife. But then there was a crash and the world cut to black. The next thing I knew, I was on the ground near the shed and Tommasulo was on top of me, scrambling for my throat. I thrashed underneath him, managing to get my knife hand free. I swung blindly and Tommasulo leaped back, one hand pressed into his thigh.

I got to my feet. The rain was heavier now, soaking my clothes, weighing me down. I saw a blur off to my left, and then a fist plowed into my ribs. The knife shot out of my hand and I stumbled, barely catching myself before I fell into the pile of debris. Dale growled and came at me again. I scooped up a two-by-four and swung, connecting with his shoulder. He groaned in pain and I charged again, aiming for his head this time. There was a crack, but I didn't let up. I swung again, harder, feeling like I was tearing the muscles in my arms, but not caring. There was another crack, and then the sound of a body falling into the mud.

Movement to my right. Tommasulo was coming at me again. I pivoted toward him, but a wave of exhaustion made me slow. Before I could swing, he buried his fist in my stom-ach, once and then again. It was like getting hit with a baseball bat. The air shot out of me. I dropped the plank and slumped to the ground. The rain had become an angry squall. I tried to get up, but my legs wouldn't move. Tommasulo loomed over me.

I looked behind him but the space beneath the porch was empty. The girl was gone.

Tommasulo darted forward and ripped off my mask. He threw it into the mud and smiled, exposing crooked yellow teeth.

"You know," he said, "one of my great disappointments is that I never had a son. I think maybe it's time to change that."

"Mr. Tommasulo, wait! I —"

He reached for me, but I kicked at the mud, pushing myself away until my spine slammed into the fence. He'd maneuvered me into a corner; there was nowhere else to go. Tommasulo leaned down. I clapped my hand over my mouth and nose and shut my eyes, willing myself away from that muddy yard, away from Black River.

A street in Brooklyn. A summer night. I'm seven and you're ten and Mom is walking us back from a school concert. Out of nowhere, she bounds into the light of a nearby pawnshop. She lifts her arms over her head and does a single perfect pirouette, then stretches out into an impossibly long arabesque, her dark, slender arms reaching out in front of her, one leg reaching back. The universe's spin slows and comes to a halt.

I hear your breath hitch, then stop. Your mouth is hanging open. Mine is too.

I opened my eyes. Mr. Tommasulo was gone.

The girl with the green hair had taken his place. All I could make out through the curtain of rain was her silhouette and the two-by-four in her hand. Mr. Tommasulo was on the ground at her feet, his eyes closed. His skin was as pale as cotton.

The girl whipped around, thrusting the club in front of her. Dale stood there cringing. His face was a mess of bruises. He nodded toward his friend and she stepped away, careful to keep the two-by-four between them. Dale shook Tommasulo until his eyes opened, and then he hooked his hands under Tommasulo's armpits and hauled him up. Together, the two of them lurched out of the yard and down the driveway. Seconds later they were gone.

I looked at the girl and she looked at me. Something glinted in the hollow of her throat. A silver key hung from a leather cord around her neck.

"Who are you?" I asked.

She dropped the board and ran.

6

BY THE TIME I dug my knife and mask out of the mud and made it to the street, she was gone. I twisted through the neighborhood, searching every side street, yard, and alley, but came up empty.

No matter where I went, I could see the peak of Lucy's Promise and the arrow-shaped notch in the trees that marked Greer's camp. They were probably already back there, safe and dry in their cabins. I thought about giving up, telling myself that the girl would eventually run into a guardsman who would help her, but I knew that the other, more likely possibility was that she'd be found by Tommasulo or one of his friends, so I kept going.

I'd just passed the high school and was heading back toward Monument Park when I finally saw her.

An hour had passed, maybe two. The rain had stopped, leaving a junglelike fog. She was on Elm Street, drenched and panting, barely managing to run the length of a few houses before she had to stop and catch her breath. I trailed her until she fell against the stone wall at the edge of the park. She slid down it and collapsed over her knees.

I was half a block away when she saw me. Her exhaustion vanished in a flash. There was a softball-size chunk of rock sitting by the wall. She grabbed it and jumped to her feet.

"It's okay! I'm not with them. My name's Cardinal. Cardinal Cassidy."

"You called that man by *name*," she shouted. "I heard you."

I took a step toward her and she hoisted the rock, ready to swing at my head. I stopped and raised my hands in front of me.

"I know his name. That's all. I promise. I was trying to help you."

The girl kept the rock hoisted, ready to swing, as she put more distance between us and searched the surrounding streets.

"Where am I?"

"A town called Black River."

"How did I get here?"

"You live here," I said. "I know. It sounds crazy. Just listen. This town has been quarantined for months because of a virus called Lassiter's. It makes people lose their memories. That's what happened to you."

"Those men said I was going to get sicker. They said —"

"They were lying. The virus makes you lose your memory, that's all. I promise."

There was a snap behind me. I whirled around, one hand dropping to the hilt of my knife, but no one was there. I told myself it was a branch knocked loose by the storm, nothing else.

"Look," I said, trying to keep the nerves out of my voice. "There's a National Guard shelter just a few blocks from here. I can take you there. They'll let you stay with them while they figure out who you are and where your family is."

The girl considered. Her fingers had gone white on the rock. She searched the park and the hill above it.

"But those men who attacked us, they live here too. Don't they?"

"There are people running the shelter. Soldiers. They can protect you."

"So I'll be safe there."

The voice in my head said yes, but I couldn't get the words out. In the first weeks of the quarantine the Guard had hundreds of men, but their numbers had gradually dwindled until there were only forty or fifty for the whole town. There were never enough of them to keep an eye on everything, not even at their own shelter. If I left the girl there, it would only be a matter of time before Tommasulo and his friends found her. And then, as soon as one of the guardsmen turned his back . . .

I scrambled for options, but they all came to dead ends. All except for one. I drew in a shaky breath.

"No," I said. "You won't. But I think I know somewhere you will be."

I nodded toward Lucy's Promise.

"Me and my friends live up there. In a camp on the mountain. You can stay with us until we find out where you belong."

By then the girl's arm had started shaking. She was having trouble holding up the rock. Having trouble standing, it seemed. Still, she didn't say anything and she didn't move. Who could blame her? Minutes earlier she'd nearly been kidnapped by two strangers, and now another one wanted to take her away to an isolated mountaintop. As far as she knew, Tommasulo and I were just using slightly different versions of the same con.

Voices came from somewhere in the neighborhood. Men's voices. Three or four of them, shouting to one another. Tommasulo's friends, no doubt. They were a few blocks away, but closing in fast. I did the only thing I could think of.

The girl jumped back when I pulled my knife from its sheath. She was about to run, but I flipped it so the blade was in my palm and the hilt was facing her.

"Take it," I said. "This way you'll be the only one who's armed."

She didn't make a move. I set the knife on the ground and backed away.

"If I try anything, you have my permission to stab me." I forced a nervous laugh. "You can even kick me a few times while I bleed out on the trail. Okay?"

Footsteps and shouts echoed among the houses, growing louder as they closed in. The girl dropped the rock and snatched up the knife, holding it out between us. The key around her neck glistened. She nodded toward the mountain without taking her eyes off me.

"You first."

The tip of the knife hovered near the base of my spine the whole way up the mountain. We never slowed down and the girl never spoke. When we came around the final bend in the trail, Greer's voice boomed through the trees.

"Throw, DeShaun! Throw the ball! No! To Carrie!"

He was watching the kids crash into one another in the space between the cabins. DeShaun threw the football to Carrie, who was brutally tackled by Makela. A whistle blew.

"Okay, everybody! That was an awesome first half! Let's all go get hydrated. Astrid, your team is in the lead, so when we get back, you'll start the dance-off."

We'd stopped at the edge of the camp. "That's Greer," I said over my shoulder. "The halftime dance-off is one of his innovations. Funny thing is, we actually have a rule book. He just thinks it's more fun to —"

I turned around, but the girl was gone. I thought maybe she'd run off, but then I caught a flicker of movement in the trees. While I'd been watching the game, she'd slipped into the woods and hidden herself behind a boulder.

"It's all right," I said. "You don't have to hide. We —"

"Yo! Cassidy! Where the hell have you been, man? The

kids were about to send out a search party." Greer was jogging toward me.

"Sorry. I, uh — I got sidetracked."

"Sidetracked? Dude, you left before the big announcement!"

"What announcement?"

"The one about the Marvins."

"What? Who are the Marvins?"

"Those guys we saw with the blue hazmat suits," said Greer. "Martinson Vine? Mar Vin? The Marvins? Kids all thought it was pretty inspired. Anyway, the Guard announced that they're going to —"

He cut himself off.

"What?" I asked. "The Guard is going to what?"

Something had caught Greer's eye, and he was looking into the woods behind me. "Uh, buddy? Is it just me or is there a green-haired girl with a big knife hiding behind that rock?"

I turned and called back through the trees. "You can come out. Greer's a friend."

There was a pause, and then she came out from behind the boulder. The knife was at her side, but she was gripping it tightly enough to make the tendons in her hand stand out in sharp ridges.

"I found her on my way back," I said. "She's just been infected. A couple guys were running the lost wife scam on her."

Greer leaned to the side to address the girl. "Hi. Welcome." He held up one finger. "Can you excuse us for just one tiny second?"

"Greer, I . . ."

He marched off. I motioned for the girl to wait where she was, and then I followed him.

"Look, Greer —"

"You know what's weird?" he said when we were a safe distance away. "I keep having crazy flashbacks to a conversation you and I were having just this morning."

"What was I supposed to do? You know what those guys would have done to her."

"What did Gonzalez say about it?"

My stomach flipped. "I, uh, I didn't see him."

"You didn't *see* him? That was the whole point of you — what about how bringing anyone else up here jeopardizes all of us?"

"And what about *you* not giving a crap about that?"

"I care," Greer said. "But if we're going to ignore the rules, I'd kinda rather do it for a couple six-year-olds starving to death in a swamp than for some girl who looks like she'd like to knife us all in our sleep."

"She's just scared! And I get that you're pissed. But all we have to do is hide her until we figure out who her family is, and then we hand her over."

"Oh! Is that all? Well, if we can hide *her,* then I'm sure a couple little kids won't be a problem."

"Greer!"

"Either you want to help them or you don't."

"You know I do, but we can't —"

"I'm not asking anymore," he snapped. "I'm taking Ren and Makela, and I'm going after them first thing tomorrow morning."

"You can't just —"

But he was already moving away from me and toward the girl. She jumped back as he approached.

"That's Astrid's cabin," he said, stabbing a finger in the direction of the camp. "There's an extra cot in the back. If you want it, it's yours." He pointed across the field to the main lodge. "Bathrooms are over there, and so is the kitchen. There's running water, but the state only provides electricity from seven p.m. to twelve midnight. Ask Card if you need anything else."

He stomped off toward the playing field. "Wait!" I shouted. "Greer! What about the Guard? What was the big announcement?"

Greer spun around. "They're pulling out."

"What? Pulling out? Why?"

"Because they're handing control of the QZ over to the Marvins."

I stood there dumbstruck, my mouth hanging open, as Greer rejoined the kids.

"Okay, people! It's mambo time. Astrid, your team's up! Eliot! Let's get some music going!"

Eliot pressed play on the radio, but I could barely hear it. It was as if I were a mile underwater. The Guard was pulling out? Gonzalez was leaving? It didn't seem possible. He would have said something. He would have warned us. Greer must have misunderstood.

There was a rustle of tree branches as the green-haired girl left the woods and hurried past me toward the cabins.

"Hey, if you want some help getting settled, I can —"

Halfway there, she veered away and started up the trail that led into the woods above the camp. My knife was still in her hand, slicing at the air as her arm swung back and forth. A second later, she was gone.

Astrid called out over the music. "Ready, everybody? Let's go!"

The dance started. Greer had pulled Ren and Makela off to the side by the dining hall. He was down on one knee explaining something as the two kids nodded. When he was done, he sent them back to the game and looked at me across the camp. His gray eyes were icy.

7

SOMETIMES, WHEN I didn't know what else to do, I ran.

The first few weeks after the outbreak I felt like my head was going to explode right off my shoulders. But then I remembered something you said about being on the cross-country team. I'd asked if running that far hurt, and you said that was the point — that the pain wiped every other thought out of your head. Every worry. Every doubt. Every fear. As if the whole world fell away, and all that was left was you and the course.

It was three o'clock in the morning the first time I tried it. I grabbed a flashlight and left camp, running until my legs ached and my lungs burned. It was just like you said. The outbreak. Mom and Dad. You. It all left me in a rush. It was nearly dawn when I came back to my tent and collapsed, feet bleeding and body drenched in sweat. I slept through the night for the first time in weeks.

The night I brought the green-haired girl to camp I ran until the muscles in my legs felt like they were filled with broken glass. But no matter how hard I drove my feet into the ground, I couldn't knock everything that had happened that day out of my head. It was too much. Seeing Mom. Finding the girl. Fighting with Greer. The Guard leaving — actually *leaving* — and handing the QZ over to a bunch of strangers.

I pushed double hard up the last incline and made it to the reservoir, where I collapsed. Once I caught my breath, I cupped my hands and splashed water on my face and through my hair, then sat back on my heels. The reservoir was vast, with shimmers of moonlight skating across its surface. A fire from one of our neighbors' camps flickered on the opposite shore. The only sounds were the chittering of crickets and the lap of the water.

I swear to God, Tenn, I thought. *There isn't a single day, a single second, when I don't wish you were here. You'd know what to say to Greer, and what to do about the green-haired girl and the Guard and the kids at Joseph's Point.*

I picked up a rock and threw it out into the water. There was a soft splash and then quiet.

You'd know what to do about Mom.

I saw her standing in that alleyway again, the sunlight on her skin. I wondered where she was right then. It didn't look like anybody had been staying at our place. Was she at the Guard shelter, jammed together with men like Tommasulo? Squatting in some abandoned house? Wherever she was, could it be possible that she was staring into the dark and wondering about me, just like I was about her?

I threw another rock, harder this time. Even if she was, I thought, it wouldn't make any difference. The truth — the truth we all pretended not to know — was that Lassiter's was fatal in all cases. The woman I saw in that alley looked like Mom and sounded like Mom, but Mom was dead and gone. Even if she went to the Guard and got her name back, it wouldn't mean a damn thing to her.

The moon fell behind some clouds, turning the surface of the lake into a black plain. I thought about how cold it must be at the bottom, and how dark. I wondered what it would be like to be down there.

Would it be like that winter night in Brooklyn when the heat went out in our building? Remember? Mom and Dad dressed us in every stitch of clothing we owned and then buried us in blankets and quilts and old sweaters. At the bottom of all of that, there wasn't any sound and there wasn't any light, just this warm darkness wrapping itself around us. Would sinking to the bottom of the reservoir be like that? Peaceful and still?

An owl hooted, then flew from tree to tree. The moon had arced over my head and was starting to fall. How long had I been there? I took a last look at the water and then made my way through the dark to my tent.

When I got back, Greer was waiting for me.

8

WHAT'S GOING ON? Is everything okay?" I asked.

All Greer said was, "Gonzalez."

"Where?"

"Down the trail. And he's not alone. He's got a twitchy-looking Marvin with him."

Damn it. "The kids still asleep?"

Greer nodded. "You want me with you?"

"Yeah. Go ahead. I'll be right behind you."

He started to fade into the dark.

"Wait! We should talk about the —"

"Forget it," he said.

"But —"

"Don't worry," Greer said. "There's plenty of time for me to call you a jackass in the morning. Now let's get moving."

The dark swallowed him up as he moved down the trail. I changed out of my running clothes, trying to still the nervous tremors in my hands. Gonzalez and a Marvin showing up in the middle of the night on the day they announced that the Guard was bugging out. Whatever they wanted, it couldn't be good.

I found the three of them in a circle of light at the first

turn of the trail. Gonzalez was standing there with a flashlight, looking uncomfortable in his body armor, helmet, and mask. The Marvin was next to him.

He had on the same blue hazmat suit as the men in the truck, but sported a clear faceplate with a hose running to a tank on his back. It was overkill, but not unusual for someone new to the QZ. Through the faceplate I could make out dark eyes set in a slab-of-granite face. His gloved fingers were tapping against his biceps, which bulged beneath the blue plastic. By the time I joined them, Greer was doing a little song and dance in front of him.

". . . you should *totally* take off that mask, Marvin. Maybe you're immune! You'd be like a gift to science."

"Greer, could you please —"

"Hush, Gonzalez. Now, about the suits. Are you guys *trying* to look like giant blueberries or —"

"Cardinal!" Gonzalez edged Greer out of the way when he saw me coming. "This is Mr. Raney. He'll be handling security in the QZ once Martinson Vine takes over. I'm guessing Greer told you about today's announcement."

So it was really true. The Guard was bailing on us. I stopped a few feet away from them and crossed my arms.

"What can we do for you guys?"

Gonzalez started to speak, but Raney stepped out ahead of him. "Two gentlemen showed up at the doc's office earlier today. Both of them beat up pretty bad. Thought maybe you'd have an idea how they got that way."

"Why would I?"

"Said they ran into a girl with green hair and a skinny black kid wearing a Bio-Mask."

Greer let out a big laugh. "Well, that leaves Cardinal out, Marvin. My man here is *bi*-racial!"

"Greer," Gonzalez warned.

"We don't know any girls with green hair," I said. "And I'm not the only uninfected kid in town. I'm guessing one or two others might look like me."

"Really?"

I gave Raney the biggest, most innocent smile I could muster. "Well, sir, Black River has always prided itself on being a diverse community."

Greer cackled, earning himself an elbow in the ribs from Gonzalez. Raney stood perfectly still. There was a tense hush as he looked from me to Gonzalez to Greer. When he was done, he walked past me to take a higher position on the trail. He nodded up toward the camp.

"So, you guys have been living up here since the beginning, huh?"

I glanced over at Greer. "Uh . . . yeah. Just about."

"That's good," he said. "I got a couple nephews about your age. All they do is sit inside and play video games. I try to take them hiking or fishing, and they act like I'm suggesting we reenact the Bataan Death March." Raney chuckled to himself, then shifted so he was looking down at the three of us.

"Listen, fellas. I've been the new sheriff in town before.

Everybody thinks I'm planning to come in and declare that up is down and black is white. And I'm not saying there won't be changes — we'll be making sure you all start school again, for one thing — but at this point I see no reason to cancel Lieutenant Gonzalez's live-and-let-live policy when it comes to you-all. Sound good?"

He smiled, but there was something about it that made me think of the Terminator — like if I looked close enough, I'd see a titanium chassis behind his lips.

"And just between us," he said, lowering his voice like it was some big secret, "those guys getting stitched up in the doc's office? They look to me like the types that maybe could have used a good beating. So how about we just call that one even for now? If you should happen to hear anything more about it, or if you hear about anything else going on in the QZ you think I should know about, you'll come tell me. How's that for a deal?"

Raney stuck his blue-gloved hand out. Not seeing what choice I had, I shook it.

"Outstanding," he said. "And tell you what, to seal the deal — Salvation Army sent us a big shipment just the other day. Lots of kids' stuff in there. Clothes and whatnot. How about I send some of it up here with my guys?"

Greer jumped in from the sidelines. "That'd be great. Thanks."

I shot him a look and he mouthed, *What?*

"Not a problem," Raney said. "And listen. We've got some

good stuff planned for Black River. Some *fun* stuff. You guys could use a bit of fun, right?"

I gave him a tight smile and then he turned to Gonzalez. "Lieutenant?"

"I need to talk to Cardinal a minute," Gonzalez said. "Wait for me here?"

"I'm sure I can find my way. You boys have a good night now."

Raney pulled out a flashlight and strolled away down the mountain. Once he was out of sight, Gonzalez gave Greer a shove.

"Damn it, Larson! Why do you have to be like that? You just met the guy!"

Greer laughed. "I swear, Gonzalez, it's like you don't even know the most basic rules of warfare." Greer tapped at his temples with two fingers. "You gotta get inside the enemy's head."

"Raney's not your enemy."

"He's not *now*," Greer crowed. "Not after that expert-level intimidation."

Gonzalez rolled his eyes. "You got a minute, Card?"

I turned my back on him and started up the trail. "Later."

"Card. Seriously. A minute. Please?"

I stopped. Kicked at a pile of gravel. I was exhausted, pissed off too, but there was no mistaking the tone in his voice. I glanced at Greer. "See you in the morning, okay?"

As I said it, I flicked my eyes down the mountain, hoping he'd get the message: *Follow Raney. See what you can find out.*

Greer smiled. "Yeah, sure. Tomorrow." He threw Gonzalez a crisp salute. "Night, Lieutenant."

Greer bounded up the trail. Gonzalez glanced at me, then called after him.

"Yo! Larson! Going all the way up there just so you can double back and follow Raney as soon as I'm gone? Waste of time. You're gonna lose your target that way." Gonzalez jerked his thumb back over his shoulder into the woods. "I'd head that way. Follow the streambed. He'll never see you."

Greer reversed course, knocking Gonzalez on the arm as he passed by.

"Good tip, Lieutenant. Thanks!"

"I'm in your head, Larson! Never forget that."

Greer raised his middle finger over his shoulder as he left the trail. Gonzalez turned to me with a shake of his head, but I didn't feel like playing our usual game of *Wow, that Greer sure is crazy.* Whatever he had to say, I wanted to hear it and go. I blew past him, heading for the spot where we usually met.

When we got there, I expected Gonzalez to get right to explaining, but instead he stripped off his mask and knelt by a little stream that cut through the woods. He filled his palms and splashed water on his face.

"How could you not tell us?" I snapped. "You're bailing on us and *this* is how we find out?"

"I'm not bailing on you!"

"Oh, really?"

"I go where they send me, Card! And the Guard isn't set up for stuff like this. We've been here almost eight months!"

"And how long were you in Iraq?"

"That's different," he said. "This domestic stuff? We're supposed to be in and out. And I didn't tell you because the governor of the State of New York doesn't exactly check in with me when he's deciding how to deploy the National Guard. I found out like five minutes before you did."

I kicked at a root sticking up out of the ground. He was right, I knew he was right, but it didn't stop me from feeling like the blood in my veins had caught fire.

"When?"

"Haven't set a date yet," Gonzalez said. "A few weeks probably for the transition."

"Who the hell are they?"

"One of these megacorporations," he explained. "Into a little bit of everything. Private security. Pharmaceuticals. Construction. Hell, about half the guys I served with in Iraq were Martinson Vine contractors."

"And now they want to take over the QZ."

"Apparently they've been offering since the beginning, and the governor finally said yes."

"So what happens now?" I asked. "We all go live in some shelter? Get stuck with random families?"

"You heard what Raney said."

"*Live and let live?* You actually believe that? What's the real story, Hec?"

"Dude, it's not like they cc me on their emails."

"But you've gotta know *something.*"

Gonzalez sighed. He pulled off his helmet and ran his fingers through his sweaty hair.

"Look, the way I see it — me and my guys? We're Superman and the Justice League. Okay? We do what we do for Truth, Justice, and the American Way. Martinson Vine? They're more like Heroes for Hire."

"And what were they hired to do?"

He shook his head and scuffed his boot through the dirt.

"Gonzalez?"

"I don't know," he said. "But if I had to guess? It was to make a problem go away."

"What problem?"

He took a breath. "This whole damn place," he said. "Black River."

Whatever strength I had left flowed out of me. I dropped down next to the streambed. The water raced by, overloud, like crinkling cellophane. I rubbed at my temples, trying to get at an ache that had started deep inside.

"How?" I heard myself ask.

"I wish I knew, man. I really do."

I pulled off my mask and craned my neck to look up

through the trees. The way the wind bent the upper branches made it seem as if the whole earth was shaking. Like we were caught in an earthquake that wouldn't stop.

There was a nudge at my shoulder. Gonzalez was holding out his canteen. I took it from him but just sat there with it in my lap. Gonzalez slid down to sit beside me.

"I would have told you about all this sooner if I'd known," he said. "I promise."

I nodded. There was this rawness in my throat. I unscrewed the cap on the canteen and took a drink, but it didn't help.

"It just seems like every time we get used to something . . ."

"Yeah. I know."

Gonzalez leaned over the stream and stared down into the dark water.

The first time he came up to Lucy's Promise, the kids were so sick of seeing me and Greer that a new person was like a gift from God. Most anybody else would have run screaming the other way. Not Gonzalez, though. He just tightened the straps on his gas mask and played Santa, handing out bits of his equipment. Makela took apart and reassembled his radio. Ren played with his compass. Astrid found a tube of woodland camo face paint in his pack, and he showed her how to use it. If one of us had asked for an arm, he would have sawed it off and handed it over.

"Guess this means you'll be able to make it to Comic Con this year."

Gonzalez nodded, his head still down.

"You gonna do the portfolio review?"

"Don't know," he said. "Maybe."

"Maybe?" I swatted him on the shoulder. "Come on. Let's see the goods."

He looked up from the water. "Seriously?"

"You got it with you?"

Of course he did. He hustled the backpack off his shoulders and pulled out a big sketchpad.

"Who all did you end up putting in it?"

"Cloak and Dagger. Luke Cage." He snorted. "Wolverine, if you can believe that."

I rolled my eyes. "Everybody draws Wolverine."

"I know," Gonzalez said. "But I figure you gotta show the powers that be that you can draw the big boys. You sure you don't mind taking a look?"

"Yeah, but I'm telling you, it's not like I'm an expert or anything."

"Are you kidding me? Dude, you're —"

He cut himself off, but I knew what he was about to say. *You're Derrick Cassidy's son.* He recovered pretty quick.

"— someone who knows his stuff. Everybody back at the barracks, they go see a couple Captain America movies and they call themselves comic book nerds, you know?"

Gonzalez clicked on his flashlight and trained it on the pages as I moved through them. I'd never seen his drawings before, but he'd been talking about going to the Comic Con portfolio review practically since the day I met him. I have to say, I was impressed. The drawings were solid. More than solid. The faces were expressive, and he had this cool, sketchy style that made all his characters look like they were bursting with motion even when they were standing still. Kind of Ronin-era Frank Miller or maybe Bill Sienkiewicz.

"Don't be afraid to be honest, man. *Brutally.* Tear my guts out."

I flipped through the drawings. Wolverine. Luke Cage fighting the Absorbing Man. Cloak and Dagger right before teleporting. A really good Kitty Pryde with Lockheed. I made it all the way to the back and then turned to the last page. What I saw there froze the breath in my lungs.

Gonzalez reached for the sketchbook. "Oh. Crap. Right. Dude, I was going to mention that. I hope you don't mind."

"It's fine."

"You sure? I had a colorist take a whack at it since I thought it'd be my big finale and all."

His last drawing was of Cardinal. Of course it was. He was in a classic Cardinal pose, arms and wings outstretched as he soared over Liberty City, the noonday sun shining off his armor and the towers of the city below him. His wings extended out beyond the edge of the page, each feather meticulously detailed. His colors of scarlet, black, and white were rendered perfectly, deep but bright. The only real difference was that where Dad usually drew Cardinal as a kind of burlier Iron Man, Gonzalez had gone the other way. His drawings made Cardinal look leaner and more graceful, like a dancer.

"I guess it's kind of like a tribute," he said. "I can totally take it out if you think —"

"No," I said automatically, not really hearing him, or myself. "It's fine. Really."

"It's just that without your dad's stories I probably would've ended up another loser grinding it out in the Bronx, you know? I mean, I must have read those comics a thousand times. I had the single issues *and* all the trades. And I wasn't one of those poseurs who started reading after all the awards. I was there from the start! I've even got this guy in the city says he has a line on some of your dad's scripts for what would have been Volume Five."

"He's lying," I said. "There is no Volume Five."

Gonzalez kept going — talking about Dad and how his Cardinal stories had inspired him, first to join the Guard and then to be an artist — but I was too distracted by a twisted-up feeling in my gut to really hear him anymore. It was a strange thing, Tenn, to wish you could see your father the way a stranger did.

Gonzalez was interrupted by a burst of static from his radio, followed by a muffled voice.

"Surveyor One, this is Homeland. We need you back at the line, over."

"Ah, damn it. Duty calls." He grabbed the mic clipped to his shoulder. "Acknowledged, Homeland."

Gonzalez started gathering his things.

"Oh, hey," he said. "I gotta ask."

"Ask what?"

Gonzalez dipped his head and looked at me from beneath an arched eyebrow. "You get yourself a green-haired girlfriend and not tell me?"

Right. That. "She's just this girl. I came across a couple of guys trying to run the lost wife scam on her."

"So you strapped on your Cardinal wings and saved the day, huh?"

"Just in the wrong place at the wrong time, I guess."

"What were you doing in town anyway?"

"Snow Cone needed meds for that rash," I said. "Greer had enough to worry about."

Gonzalez nodded. "So you brought the girl up here?"

"Didn't see any other choice. That shelter of yours —"

"Yeah, I know. It sucks." He took a breath. "I can cover for you on the girl. With everything that's going on, Raney's probably going to be too busy to give a damn for a while anyway. Just keep her out of sight. No more Buffy the Pedophile Slayer."

I nodded.

"And for real," he said. "You guys keep your heads down. Whatever Raney's intentions are, tread lightly. You're not careful, the Eye of Sauron's gonna turn your way. Picture our Mr. Raney leading a platoon of orcs and wargs right up Lucy's Promise. You got me?"

"Yeah. I got you."

Gonzalez slipped into his backpack and helmet. I started to hand him the sketchbook but he waved it off. "It's okay. Spend some time with them. I'll be back before the pullout. You can give me your professional opinion then. All right?"

I nodded.

"I'll owe you, man. Ten percent of my millions. For life!"

We said good night, and then his boots crunched through the trees, slowly fading out until I was alone in the dark. Or until I *thought* I was.

"I swear, Cassidy, you kill me."

Greer was standing in a patch of moonlight on the other side of the stream, grinning. I set the sketchpad down and pulled my mask back on.

"*Black River has always prided itself on being a diverse community,*" he said, chuckling as he came through the trees. "I don't care what everybody says, you're funny."

"Anybody else out there?" I asked.

"Few other Marvins looking around near the base of the mountain."

"They see you?"

"Please. I got within five feet and they just stood there picking their noses. So! What did Lieutenant Supernerd have to say?"

"He can cover for us on the girl," I said. "Thinks Raney's probably too busy to worry about her right now anyway."

Greer plopped down on the streambed across from me. "So he didn't seem so bad, right? Raney?"

I looked over at him.

"What?" Greer said. "I'm serious. He said nothing's going to change."

"He said he saw no reason *right now* for anything to change," I corrected him. "It was a threat, Greer."

"Come on."

"He was making sure we knew he could change his mind anytime he wanted. I mean, seriously, didn't you think it was a little weird that he didn't come down on us at *all*? Why not?"

"Fine. Maybe it's weird. But the kids *could* use some fun. Not to mention new clothes."

"We don't know anything about him," I said. "We start taking favors from him now, then —"

"I know, I know. He's gonna turn out to be some kind of lizard person who wants to eat our faces off. But how about we deal with that *after* we get everybody some new underwear?"

Greer kept on chattering away, but his voice faded out just like Gonzalez's had. The sketchbook had fallen open to a drawing of Black Panther. I went to close it but ended up flipping ahead until I came to the end again, to Cardinal. The way the moonlight washed out the colors, it looked like those early pages, the ones you and I shared as the snow fell on the fire escape outside our window. I could almost feel you beside me as I traced the curve of Cardinal's wing with my fingertips.

"I'm coming with you," I said.

Greer stopped whatever he was saying and turned to me. "What?"

I looked up. "Tomorrow morning. To find those kids. I'm coming with you."

"Seriously?"

"There's a trail from here to Joseph's Point that doesn't go through town. We'll go first thing in the morning."

"But what about Gonzalez? And Raney?"

"As soon as we get those kids back here, we figure out where they belong and we get them there. Same with the green-haired girl."

"Uh, yeah. Great."

"Who knows," I said. "Maybe we'll get lucky and they'll all have family in town just dying to take them back."

Greer laced his fingers behind his head and lay back near the streambed.

"Us getting lucky," he said. "I wonder what that'll feel like."

By the time Greer and I made it back to camp, it was raining again. I stopped at the equipment shed to grab a few things before starting up the trail to look for the green-haired girl.

I found her not far from my own campsite. She was crouched between two boulders at the edge of the mountain. When I came out of the trees, she spun around, holding up one hand to ward off the glare of the flashlight. My knife was in her other hand. She held it just like she had held that shard of glass, marking out the borders of my world and hers with its tip.

"I brought you a tent," I said. "It's not much, but it'll keep the rain off."

The girl didn't say anything, so I backed away and started assembling it nearby. She didn't take her eyes off me the entire time. When I had it set up, I pulled the other things I'd brought her out of a backpack, holding up each one before putting it inside the tent.

"Flashlight. Dry sweatshirt and socks. One can of tuna and some crackers. Bottle of water." I pointed back the way I'd come. "My camp is just a couple minutes down that path. If you need anything else —"

"I won't."

There was nothing left to say, but I couldn't seem to leave. My eyes went to the knife in her hand. The rain splashed against it, sluicing down its sides and dripping off its row of teeth. I wanted it back, but the words wouldn't come. Maybe

I wanted her to feel the way I did when I held it, like I was anchored in place. Or maybe I just didn't want her to see how much I needed it.

"Try to get some sleep," I said. "Tomorrow we'll figure out where you belong."

There was a rumble of thunder. I turned to go. Her voice cut through the rain behind me.

"What if I don't belong anywhere?"

I stopped. Turned back. The silver key around her neck glinted in the flashlight's beam.

"Everybody belongs somewhere."

THE GREAT SECRET OF THE WORLD

9

THE NEXT MORNING, Greer and I found the boy and the girl cowering inside a shelter they'd constructed out of brush and a moldy tarp. They were all jutting bones and pale skin, livid with mosquito bites. The boy warned us away with a rusty butter knife, but after an hour or two of Greer's patient convincing the kid dropped it and they came with us.

When we got to the camp, they were both clearly overwhelmed, the boy most of all. He stood there rigid, his eyes wide. The girl went into big-sister mode. She grabbed his hand and drew him a little bit behind her, shielding his body with hers.

It was hard to blame him for being freaked out. The camp was in its usual state of semi-chaos. The kids were tearing from one end of the place to the other, cleaning cabins and hanging laundry on lines strung between the boys' cabin and the dining hall. Makela was running the show, like she always did. She stood on a chair at the center of camp, clipboard in hand, barking out instructions. Jenna and Crystal, her loyal minions and enforcers, flanked her.

Greer came up beside me. "Is it possible that Makela was the dictator of a small country in her past life?"

"What are they up to? It's not like them to clean without being asked."

"They are a constant source of mystery," Greer said. "Yo! Astrid!"

Greer whistled, and Astrid, Carrie, and Tomiko headed toward us. Dreamy girls with grubby hands and matted hair, they were the polar opposites of Makela and her friends.

Greer squatted down and drew the Joseph's Point kids close, one hand on each of their knobby shoulders. "My friends are going to find you some new clothes and something to eat. Okay?"

The boy looked at the girl, unsure until she nodded.

"Now, I'm going to warn you," Greer added with great seriousness. "These three girls are very, *very* weird. They might try to talk to you about your auras or make you fingerpaint your feelings."

"*Greer,*" Carrie complained, clearly loving that he was talking about her, even if it was to make fun.

Astrid lifted the hem of her long, flowery skirt and dropped to her knees in front of the two children. Her white-blond hair practically glowed under a pink handkerchief.

"I bet you two are hungry, right? Well, my friend Tomiko here just happens to be the best baker in the whole entire universe. Want her to make you something?"

The boy and girl looked to each other, then nodded

eagerly. Astrid beamed and took the girl's hand. The others followed suit, making a chain and snaking their way through the bustle of the camp.

"We'll wait a few days before we start figuring out who they are," Greer said. "Let 'em get settled. Gonzalez won't blow a gasket over that, right?"

I shook my head. Greer stood up and stretched.

"Well, that's two lives saved for the day. How about we shoot for the trifecta? I'll go see if I can find angry-girl-with-knife. Now *her* we can get moving along."

I jumped up. "It's okay. I'll find her."

He gave me a look.

"What?"

He smiled. "Nothing. You know what? You're absolutely right. You go after her. I'll grab my things and get set up."

Greer jogged off. I gathered some food into a paper bag and set out along the trail. It wasn't long before the noise of the camp receded behind me. The morning was warm and the rain clouds from the day before had passed, leaving the sky achingly blue.

I found the girl right where I'd left her the night before, sitting at the edge of the mountain wedged between two boulders. She had her back to me and was looking out at the valley below. Her shirt was drying on one of the rocks, leaving her in a gray tank top that exposed the curve of her shoulders, which were as taut as a strung bow. I'd barely made it into the clearing when she heard me and turned, knife in hand.

I lifted the bag. "Thought you could use something to eat."

She studied it like she was trying to decide if it contained a hidden explosive device.

"There's this girl in our camp," I said, stepping from the dirt trail to the grass. "Tomiko? She's twelve. Greer found her hiding out in the health-and-beauty aisle of a Rite Aid. Literally all he did was show her this cookbook he got from the library, and in no time she was making the most amazing biscuits ever. Cakes, too. You know, when we can get sugar and stuff. Which isn't very often, but —" I suddenly realized I was babbling. "Anyway, I managed to score you a few before the kids devoured them all."

I took another step toward her, and she jabbed the knife out into the space between us.

"Right. No problem. I'll just leave 'em here." I set the bag at the base of the boulders and retreated. "They're really at their best when they're warm, so you might wanna —"

The girl turned her back again. There was a clatter as she set the knife down within easy reach. It would have been nice if I'd had a plan at that point, but I didn't, so I just found a spot on the grass halfway between her and the tent and settled in to wait. The tent looked like it hadn't been slept in, and I saw through the flap that the clothes I'd brought were still in a neat pile right beside the uneaten food.

Greer was the master detective, but I couldn't resist starting to look for clues.

Her clothes were unremarkable. Cutoff shorts. Tank top

and an old button-down shirt. Black combat boots. It was the kind of thing anyone might have picked out of a Salvation Army delivery.

Her skin was pale, but there were traces of pink on her shoulders, which made me think she had been spending most of her time indoors until just recently. Not surprising, if she'd been hiding out in the QZ with a bunch of uninfected for the last year.

The only really odd thing was her hair. Fully dry, it was a lighter green, like leaves with the sun behind them. How could she have done that? Hair dye certainly didn't come in a Guard supply drop. A looted salon, maybe? There was a black market in town run by a couple of enterprising guardsmen, but it usually dealt in booze and cigarettes. Of course, I was pretty sure they'd supply green hair dye if the price was right. So, that was something. She must have had access to money or at least something worthwhile to trade.

I picked up an acorn and rolled it in my palm as a story started clicking together in my head. She's hidden away with her family since the outbreak, maybe in one of those mansions uptown. She gets bored. Dyes her hair green. It's not enough. One day when Mom and Dad aren't looking, she sneaks out of the house for a few thrills and gets careless. And then, boom. Here she is.

It was plausible. Probable, even. It was a little depressing, though, to feel the mystery of her drain away so easily. Surely there had to be more to her than that. Maybe —

"Why do I know how to tie my shoes?"

I looked up. The girl was leaning forward, elbows on her knees, knife in hand. Her eyes were wolflike.

In the universe of questions I thought she might ask, this one was nowhere to be found. "I don't under —"

"When I woke up this morning I bent over and tied my shoelaces without even thinking about it. How can I do that if the memory of learning *how* to tie my shoes has been erased?"

Luckily, months of living with Lassiter's had made us all experts on the subject of memory.

"Because different types of memory are stored in different parts of your brain," I said. "There's episodic memory, which is your memory of all the events in your life, kind of like your own personal autobiography. Semantic memory is general knowledge type stuff, basic things you know about yourself and the world. Cultural stuff, language and symbols, your name, where you're from. Procedural memory is like muscle memory: it's your memory of things you've learned to do through lots of practice."

"Like tying my shoes."

"Exactly."

"So the virus erases episodic and semantic memory."

"Mostly episodic," I said. "That's all gone. Some semantic memory is still left though. See, those two types of memory live right next to each other in the brain. They think that some pieces of your semantic memory — like your name or where you're from — are so connected to the autobiography in your head that they got wiped out right along with it. Other parts of your semantic memory that weren't as connected are still there."

"Like what?"

I had to chew on that one a second. "Oh! Okay. Who's Superman?"

The girl cocked her head. "He's a superhero."

"What's his costume look like?"

She shrugged. "Blue tights. Red cape. Big S on his chest."

"Now tell me about a time when you read a Superman comic book or saw a Superman movie."

The girl's eyes narrowed on the grass between us as she tried to remember. She shook her head.

"See? The idea is that a semantic memory like that survived because it wasn't as strongly linked to your personal story. It was just something you knew."

She lowered her head, nodding like she was filing it all away. "How did this happen? The virus."

"We don't know."

"You don't know, or nobody knows?"

There was something exciting about the way she talked. It made me think of a razor slashing through the air.

"Nobody knows exactly," I said. "There's this Founder's Day thing we used to have in the park every year. Practically the whole town went. They're pretty sure that was ground zero for the outbreak, but nobody knows where the virus actually came from."

The girl took that in; then she looked over her shoulder and nodded toward a wide black smudge in the woods out past the northside mansions. "I saw lots of places like that. Houses burned down. Broken windows."

"Half the people in town lost their memory on the sixteenth. It was"— I swallowed dryly —"a confusing night."

"*Half* the town lost its memory? The other half was immune?"

I shook my head. "They weren't exposed. As far as we know, no one's immune."

She looked away. Her grip on the knife tightened. It was a while before she spoke again, and when she did she said, "Am I ever going to get my memory back?"

For the first time, there was the slightest quiver in her voice. Greer told me that every time he'd come across someone who was recently infected, this was the question they circled back to again and again.

He'd usually tell them something vague and hopeful. *It's early yet. People are working on a cure all the time. We have to be patient.* I had those exact words all queued up, but when the time came to say them, I couldn't, not to her.

"There's a doctor in Manhattan," I said. "Evan Lassiter. He's the one they named the virus after. He's been studying it ever since the outbreak, trying to create a cure or a vaccine, but none of them have worked."

"So . . ."

"So you'll be able to make new memories, but no, your old ones aren't going to come back. I'm sorry."

The girl was absolutely still. I don't know what I expected. That she'd cry? Scream? Deny it? According to Greer, that was what most people did. But not her. Her eyes drifted away from me to a patch of grass between us. Her chest rose and fell evenly. I thought about how, over time, everything that happens to us—what we do and see and feel—comes together and makes what we think of as reality. What's possible. What isn't. Who we are. What we believe. It was as if the girl was bearing down and rewriting all of those things through force of will alone, finding a way to integrate Black River and Lassiter's and this new blank slate in her head.

It was pretty amazing.

When the process was done, the girl came out from between the boulders and opened the paper sack. She ate the biscuits and a green apple, right down to the core. I tossed her the bottle of water that was sitting inside her tent. She drained it in a single pull.

"How about some good news?" I asked.

I want to say she smiled then, but it wasn't quite a smile, more like the ghost of one.

"Somewhere at the bottom of this mountain you've got a family and friends waiting for you. You've got a name. A home."

I pointed at the key around her neck. "That probably unlocks the front door."

95

Her fingertips went to the key. She lifted it carefully, as if it were made of glass.

"My friend Greer, he's the best at figuring out who people are. With him on the case we can probably have you back in your own bed by tonight. Once you're there, well, you won't remember, but at least you'll *know*. You know? And hey, if nothing else, it'd be nice to call you something other than Green-Haired Girl."

She released the key, then moved away from the edge of the mountain. I backed off as she approached, but she stopped before she got too close. She looked curiously at my mask and then extended her hand.

My knife lay in her palm, the hilt facing me.

"I decided I'm probably not going to have to stab you."

She couldn't see it, but I smiled behind my mask.

"Thanks."

I took the knife, and then she stepped past me and through the veil of trees. I stood a moment in the quiet, looking at the blade and thinking about how its serrations reminded me of the teeth of a key. I slipped it back into its sheath and followed the green-haired girl down the trail.

10

WHEN WE FOUND Greer, I'm pretty sure she was having second thoughts about returning my knife. I couldn't blame her — the whole setup was pretty weird.

He was sitting in a small meadow halfway between camp and the reservoir. It was empty except for two straight-backed chairs facing each other a few feet apart. Greer sat in one of them with his eyes closed, his hands resting lightly on his thighs, taking slow, deep breaths.

Beside him there was a stack of books and an open cardboard box. Inside was a yo-yo, a pennywhistle, a baseball, a set of drumsticks, three large stuffed animals, a tape recorder, and multiple stacks of note cards covered with strings of words or pictures copied from the library.

"Greer just, uh . . . he takes this whole thing pretty seriously. Have a seat."

She must have decided it wasn't an elaborate trap, because she marched out into the meadow and deposited herself in the chair across from him. A minute or two passed. Then two more.

"Um . . . Greer? Buddy?"

He held up one finger, then rolled his neck in circles until it crackled. Who would have guessed that a master showman was trapped deep within his old scowling exterior?

Greer's eyes popped open. He rummaged in the box for a notebook and pencil and held them out to me. I took them and retreated to a spot by the trees. Taking notes on these sessions was my job.

He loudly cleared his throat, then sat forward in his chair, directing every iota of his attention on the green-haired girl.

"Has your nose been running?" he asked. "Are your eyes itchy?"

She looked at me.

I shrugged.

"Um. Maybe a little bit?"

"Any difficulty breathing? A cough? Weakness in your elbows, knees, or ankles?"

"No."

He popped out of his chair and began a series of slow revolutions around the girl, studying her from every angle as if she were a prized horse.

"Good muscle tone," he said. "Broad shoulders. Smile for me?"

What she managed was nearer to a grimace, but it was close enough.

"Straight teeth. No piercings of any kind. No visible tattoos. Hair is recently dyed and cut. Eyebrows indicate her natural color is brown." He reached out and tipped her head back into the sun. "A light, honey brown."

I struggled not to roll my eyes as I wrote. "Hair the color of honey. Got it."

Greer dropped to his knees and took both her hands.

"Small calluses on the fingertips of her left hand. Nails are short. Not cut, though. They look chewed. No indications of nail polish. No rings."

His eyes fixed on the key. He glanced over his shoulder. "Is it normal for people to wear these as jewelry?"

I shook my head. He turned back to the girl and reached for the key, but she smacked his hand away before he could touch it.

"Interesting," he said. "Take off your shoes, please."

"Why?"

"It is vitally important that I examine your toes."

The girl crossed her arms over her chest and glared at him. Perhaps realizing that discretion was the better part of valor, Greer backed off. He stood across from her, still staring intently, his chin balanced on his fist.

"What do you think?" he asked me.

I went over my notes. It wasn't a lot to go on. "I guess we do the whole thing."

Greer nodded solemnly. "Agreed."

He returned to his chair and pulled the cardboard box and note cards to him. Greer had tests designed for older kids and younger kids. Boys and girls. He flipped through the box, selected a packet, and laid it in his lap.

"Now! There are a few different types of memory —"

"Card went over that already."

He turned and glowered at me. I laughed. He hated having his thunder stolen.

"Okay, well, what we're going to do is try and get a sense of what kind of person you are by seeing what's in your procedural and semantic memory."

"I thought semantic memory was common knowledge type stuff. Stuff everybody knows."

"It is," I chimed in. "But what you've got in there depends on where you grew up and how. Like if I'd asked a kid from China who Superman was, they wouldn't necessarily know since he's not a big part of their culture."

"Right," Greer said. "An infected person who studied, like, birds all their life would be able to identify more birds than an infected person who hadn't. Someone who studied math would have absorbed more math."

"And doing this will help you figure out who I am."

"Exactly."

"So how will you —"

"Think fast!"

Greer scooped up the baseball and chucked it at her. She didn't even flinch. The ball sailed past her and into the trees.

"Interesting." He held up a card with pictures of Lebron James, Derrick Jeter, and Serena Williams on it. "Who are these people?"

"No idea."

"How many players are there on a football team?"

"Uh . . ."

"Don't think, just answer."

"Eight?"

"Finish this sentence: 'We've got spirit, yes we do, we've got spirit —'"

The girl tilted her head as if he were speaking Arabic.

"Can you describe how to play Quarters?"

She shook her head.

"How about beer pong? Flip cup? T-Rex arms?"

"Those are games?"

"If you wanted to buy beer and didn't know anyone over twenty-one, would you go to Black River Beverages, Quik Stop, or Harry's Gas?"

"I don't think I like beer."

Greer draped one arm over the back of his chair. "That's a hard *no* on cheerleader, party girl, and athlete."

I made a note. "Got it."

Greer did pop culture next. Not much help there. Beyond things that pretty much any teenager in America would know, she was kind of a blank slate. So not a huge movie or TV fan. As for physical abilities — she couldn't draw, sculpt, juggle, tie a trucker's hitch, or start a fire using two sticks and a length of shoelace. When Greer had her sing the Happy Birthday song, she was enthusiastic, but painfully out of tune.

After about an hour of this she started to get restless.

"Is this getting us anywhere?" she asked. "I mean besides establishing the fact that I don't know anything about anything."

"Finding out what you don't know is just as important as finding out what you do," Greer said. "Which means you're giving us a *ton* to go on."

She scowled at him. He grinned and held up another three-by-five note card.

"What does this say? Come on! Time's a'wasting."

The girl sighed, then sat up and squinted at the card. "E equals MC squared."

"Hey, you got one! And what does E equals MC squared mean?"

She gave him the same look she gave me when I asked about Superman. "Energy equals mass times the speed of light, squared."

"And what's the speed of light?"

"One hundred and eighty-six thousand miles per second," she said. "In a vacuum."

Greer looked back at me, impressed. He held up another card. The girl got it instantly.

"The Pythagorean theorem."

He held up another.

"Pi."

Another.

"Deoxyribonucleic acid."

Another.

"The War of 1812."

She got ten more right without a single miss. The girl wasn't bored anymore. She was teetering on the edge of her chair, practically trembling. Greer was too. He shuffled through his cards with unsteady hands.

"Quick, Greer! Give me another!"

"Uh . . . Okay! Literature. Finish this quote: 'All happy families are alike; each unhappy family . . .'"

"'Is unhappy in its own way.'"

"'It is a truth universally acknowledged that a single man in possession of a good fortune . . .'"

"'Must be in want of a wife!' Jane Austen. *Pride and Prejudice*. Oh! Give me another one!"

"What book includes the characters Ponyboy, Sodapop, and Cherry?"

"*The Outsiders!*"

"Merricat, Constance, and Julian?"

"*We Have Always Lived in the Castle.*"

"Aslan and Mr. Tumnus?"

"*The Lion, the Witch and the Wardrobe!*"

"Who killed James and Lily Potter?"

The girl shot to her feet, her arms raised in triumph. "Tom Marvolo Riddle, also known as Lord Voldemort!"

Greer and I broke into rowdy applause. The girl's cheeks reddened as she bowed grandly.

"So did that help?" she asked. "Do you guys know who I am now?"

Greer laughed. "Oh yeah," he said. "You, my friend, are what they call a big ol' nerd."

Minutes later Greer was sitting on the ground by his chair, sorting through towers of hardback books while the girl watched.

"You thinking St. Edwards?" I asked from my place a short distance away.

"Gotta be, right?"

"What are you guys talking about?" the girl asked.

Greer placed a hand on top of one of the stacks of books. "These are the yearbooks from every school in the area."

"Greer, uh, liberated them from the local library," I said.

"Anyone who went to a school anywhere near Black River is in one of these," Greer went on. "St. Edwards is the closest private school."

"Why do you think I went there?"

He gave a casual shrug. It was another part of his showmanship. Acting like the whole thing was a snap.

"Solid dental work, general physical health, what looks like professionally dyed hair. That probably means money. No piercings, tattoos, or jewelry says a fairly conservative family. Around here that generally means private school."

"That," I added, "and it *definitely* sounds like you studied a lot."

The girl sifted through the note cards in front of her. "So that's why I knew all this stuff? From studying?"

Greer tossed a book aside and grabbed another.

"If you drill facts into your head hard enough over a long enough period of time, they can move into your semantic memory, which you still have most of. Usually it happens with common-knowledge things, like the president's name or the fact that we live on Earth in the United States, but it can be other things too."

"Or in your case," I said, "everything."

"Lot of good it did me," she said. "I still don't know my own name."

"Yeah," Greer said. "That's because —"

"Card already told me."

Greer sputtered. The girl and I shared a hint of a smile before she turned again and slid a yearbook off one of the stacks. "So where did you two go to school?"

"Black River High," Greer said. "The school for weirdoes, morons, and troublemakers."

"Oh yeah? Which of those were you?"

"All of the above, probably."

"You don't know?"

Greer shook his head.

"But if you're so great at figuring out who people are, how come you don't know who *you* are?"

"We were able to figure out his name," I said. "But that was it."

Greer closed a book and opened another. "We know that me and the birdman here went to the same school. But we didn't know each other. And apparently everyone I *did* know is either infected, dead, or on the other side of that fence."

"But couldn't you just —"

"We better get back to it," I said. "Right, Greer?"

"Right. Sorry. You two hush. Work to do."

He leaned over his books. The girl left him alone, moving across the meadow to sit closer to me. I was backlit by the sun, so she raised her hand to shield her eyes, which cast a little mask of shadow across her face.

"So there'll be a picture of me in one of those? And my name?"

I picked a blade of grass and wound it around a fingertip. "That's the idea. But there are thousands of pictures, so knowing more about you narrows things down. Like for you, Greer will probably be looking at academic clubs, student government, library assistants."

"Nerd stuff!" Greer called out. "Somewhere in this stack I bet there's a picture of you and Card at some interschool dweeb mixer."

She laughed, which made her nose wrinkle prettily. "So you're a nerd too, huh?"

I shrugged. "Guess so. But I'm a sci-fi slash comic book nerd. Looks like you're more of an academic nerd."

"So if we met, we would've had to fight to the death."

"Probably."

The girl smiled again. It was like this weird drug. Every time I saw it, I tried to think of ways I could get her to do it again.

"Oh hey," I called out to Greer. "You should also check band. Jazz band maybe."

"Good thinking!"

"What? Why band?"

"You're a musician," I said. "You play guitar anyway."

"I do? How do you know that?"

I started to reach for her hand but pulled away at the last second. I pointed instead.

"Those calluses on your fingertips. You got them from holding down the strings of a guitar."

She held her fingers up before her eyes. "I was wondering where those came from."

"We've seen it before," I said. "Astrid plays a little too. Her calluses were fainter, though. Looks like you've been doing it longer."

"So wait, if I picked up a guitar right now . . ."

"You'd be able to play," I said. "Whole songs you wouldn't even remember learning."

"That is just . . . *spooky*."

"A lot of this is," I said. "You'll get used to it."

Greer raised his voice again. "Hush, nerds!"

The girl got up and moved closer, stretching out on the

grass in front of me. She was right on the line of too close, but I didn't move. I watched as she picked dandelions and gathered them into a bunch.

"I was wondering," she said. "Why did we stay? I mean, if my family and I weren't infected, why wouldn't we have just left?"

"Most everybody thought a cure was right around the corner," I said. "And when it wasn't, I don't know, I guess some had relatives who were infected and they didn't want to leave them. Others wanted to keep their eye on their houses or businesses or whatever. Maybe some people just didn't have anywhere else to go."

"Which one of those were you?"

Her eyes moved up and over the contours of my mask.

"I mean, you're not infected, right?"

I nodded.

"So why'd you stay?"

My face felt like it was burning. I scrambled for an answer, but then, just over her shoulder, I saw Greer slam a book shut and toss it aside.

"What's up, Greer?"

The girl turned around. "What's wrong?"

He was running his palm back and forth over the stubble on his head. "Nothing. It's just . . . you definitely weren't at Edwards, so I was thinking Perkins, but . . . sorry. It's tricky, since you probably looked a lot different then."

She returned to Greer's side. It was a little disappointing to have her suddenly gone. I watched from my spot as he went through one of the books a second time. When he came to the final page, he went back through St. Edwards and then all the others, one by one. After that he reached into the cardboard box and pulled out a sheaf of papers.

"What are those?" the girl asked.

"Missing posters."

She waited for more, but Greer was so absorbed in his work, I jumped in.

"Some people who got caught up in the outbreak didn't actually live here. The Guard took pictures and put them online so their families could identify them."

"But you said I just got infected — what? Yesterday?"

"That's what we thought, but . . ." Greer looked up from his pile of books. "What's the very first thing you remember?"

"Those two men," she said. "The ones who were chasing me."

"And you don't remember anything before that," I said. "Nothing at all."

"No. Why would I?"

I left my place by the trees and came into the meadow. "Once you're exposed to the virus it takes about ten hours to do its thing. The last couple hours of that, you're kind of going in and out. You know who you are one second, don't know the next."

"Sometimes people will remember bits and pieces from that time," Greer said. "Maybe one of them will mean something."

The girl bore down hard. It was as if there was a mountain in her path and she was scaling it one handhold at a time. "I remember standing beside a fence. It was low and black. And then . . . bells. I remember hearing bells."

"St. Stephen's," I said. "This was before the men found you?"

"I think so. I was hot. I smelled flowers. And then I turned around and they were there. Those two men."

"What did you do?"

"I ran. Oh! I think I dropped something."

"What was it?"

"I don't know," she said. "There were bells and then . . ." Her eyes went unfocused on the ground, and then she looked up suddenly. "It was a bag. Like a backpack. That's what I dropped when I ran. A backpack. It was green. I can see it in my hand and then hitting the ground next to —"

She shook her head.

"Next to what?" I asked.

"It doesn't make any sense."

"What doesn't?"

"I see a green bag on the ground next to a pink crocodile," she said. "I must have just been confused."

Greer and I locked eyes. "The sculpture garden," I said. "By City Hall."

"Guys, what is it? What's happening?"

Neither of us said anything for a second.

"Guys!"

"You're not in any of the yearbooks," Greer said. "Not one of them. And you aren't on any of the missing posters either."

"So? What does that mean?"

Greer turned to me. There was nothing left to do but tell her.

"It means we have no idea who you are."

11

WHOA!" GREER SHOUTED. "Hold on! Would you wait a second?"

"I'm not going to just sit there!"

The green-haired girl had left the meadow and was racing toward camp. Greer and I were struggling to keep up.

"You guys know where I dropped that bag, right?"

"Well, yeah, but —"

"So we'll find it," she said. "It'll be a clue."

I ran out ahead and blocked the way. "We're supposed to be keeping you under wraps, okay? And besides, those guys from yesterday are still down there."

"I don't care! I —"

"We have a friend in the Guard," I said. "We'll have him come up here and he'll be able to figure out who you are. You just have to be patient."

The girl whipped around, getting right in Greer's face. "If you thought there was something out there that could tell you who you really are, would *you* just sit around and wait?"

Greer glanced nervously over his shoulder at me. I mentally urged him to stay strong. "Absolutely! I would wait a reasonable amount of time and then go when all interested parties agreed that it was perfectly safe."

"*Liar.*"

She turned and ran on down the trail. Greer came up alongside me.

"Former Navy SEAL slash teen librarian," he said. "That's what I'm putting my money on. You're one day late returning a book and she punches you in the face."

Greer laughed, but I didn't join him.

"Hey, don't worry about it. I'll go with her and make sure she stays out of trouble."

"No," I said. "I brought her up here. It's my problem."

"Card —"

"I said I'll go."

By the time I got down to Greer's camp, the girl had passed through the cabins and was at the trailhead that led off the mountain. When she saw me coming, she pressed on, picking up speed. A familiar heat moved up through my stomach as I thought about being back on the streets of Black River. I grabbed hold of the knife to steady myself.

"You all right, man?"

Greer appeared beside me, stuffing some clothes into a backpack.

"You don't need to come. I can handle this."

His eyes narrowed. "Dude, do you really not understand how this works by now?"

"How what works?"

"If you're going to do something stupid, then so am I."

"Greer—"

He jogged past me, swinging the backpack onto his shoulders.

"Come on, birdman! Let's get stupid!"

Once we got down the mountain, I took the lead, with Greer in the back and the girl between us. My hand hovered by the hilt of the knife as I checked every overgrown yard and vacant house we passed — for infected, for Marvins, for Guard. I felt an edge of panic gathering from being back in town again, but I pushed it away as best I could and focused on what I was doing.

After we crossed the bridge, I led them down Harding Street to keep us away from the center of town for as long as possible. We'd be at the sculpture garden in ten or fifteen minutes and then back on Lucy's Promise a half hour after that. Easy. We just had to keep moving.

We came to the end of Harding and turned onto Warren. The boughs of the red maples on either side of the street met above us, making it feel as if we were in this shady tunnel. I felt something inside of me ease a little and I let my pace slacken. Soon the girl had drawn close, as close as I could let her anyway. The clothes I'd seen Greer stuffing into his backpack had been for her. She had her hair tucked up under a Yankees cap and she'd traded her old button-down for a hooded sweatshirt. She hadn't said a word since we'd started out, just plowed forward with her head down.

"You all right?"

She nodded, but didn't look at me. Her lips were pressed tight, like a hairline crack in a block of marble.

"You know what I was thinking? What do me and Greer know, right? I mean, seriously. Two guys with a stack of yearbooks and a test they made up one day when they were bored? It's not exactly scientific. Like, there were a few home-schooled kids in Black River. They wouldn't be in the year-books at all."

She glanced over at me, clearly unconvinced.

"Okay, fine, maybe it's a long shot, but your family is here somewhere. We'll find them. Did I ever tell you that me and Greer were world-famous private detectives before the out-break?"

The corners of her mouth lifted, faintly. "I just keep won-dering what it will be like when we find them," she said. "I mean, if I was standing in a room with my mom and dad, if they were right there in front of me . . ."

"They might seem familiar," I said. "Sometimes things from an infected person's old life feel that way. Certain peo-ple. Certain situations. Kind of like déjà vu, I guess."

"But when I see them will I *feel* anything? Will I still . . ."

She trailed off, but it didn't matter. I knew how the ques-tion was going to end. *Will I still love them?*

Warren Street hitched to the left. We followed it past the

empty playground outside Kinderbrook Elementary. Part of me wanted to tell her that love conquered all, even this, but then I saw Mom standing in that alleyway, sunlight streaming over her shoulders, and I couldn't do it. I shook my head. The girl didn't so much as break her stride, but I could see in the way she went back to studying the cracks in the pavement that it was a blow.

"But they'll love *you*," I said, dipping down to try to catch her eye. "And, you know, with enough time together, you'll love them again too."

Our eyes met and she smiled. A real one this time. It sent a wave of heat through my chest. Her hand was swinging beside her as she walked. It took everything in me not to reach out and take it.

Greer shouted from behind us. "Yo! Guys! Heads up!"

A truck was rolling into the intersection down the street. It was one of the big Marvin ones like we'd seen earlier, but with a dark canvas top covering the back. We ducked off the road and around the side of a nearby house as the vehicle slowed to a stop on the other side of the intersection. I heard voices beneath the engine's rumble, and then a flap opened in the back. A bundle the size of a large trash bag spilled out onto the roadway, and then the truck belched a cloud of exhaust and was gone.

Greer just shook his head. "Here one day, and they're already littering. No respect."

"It's not trash," the girl said.

"What?"

The bundle shifted and began to unfold. It was a man — gray-haired, wearing a long, dark coat. He moaned as he sat up, clutching the shoulder they'd dropped him on.

"Is that Freeman?"

Greer was right. Freeman Wayne — the town librarian. The same man I'd seen taken away by the Marvins at the ration drop.

"Come on," I said. "We better keep mov —"

Before I could finish, Greer darted out from behind the house and into the street.

"Looks like you got yourself into a bit of trouble there," he said to Freeman. "What'd you do? Refuse to renew somebody's copy of *Encyclopedia Brown*?"

The girl looked back at me, and then she joined Greer. The two of them helped Freeman onto the curb, and Greer handed him a bottle of water from his pack. The spire of St. Stephen's rose just beyond the houses across from us. We were five minutes from the sculpture garden, maybe less. *Damn it.* I looked both ways for more Marvins, then crossed the road.

Freeman Wayne was well over six feet tall and scrawny, with a beaklike nose and a rat's nest of white hair. Gray stubble ran from his jawline to the edge of his cheekbones. Despite the heat, he wore a dingy white button-down shirt and black pants, the knees shiny from wear, under the coat. I'd have bet anything that if Black River had any homeless people before the outbreak, Freeman was one of them.

He finished the bottle of water Greer had given him, then wiped his lips with his sleeve.

"Kept talking to me about papers," he said. "I told them this was America and I wouldn't show them my papers even if I had them. Then they asked my name. I told them it was Freeman Wayne, but they kept asking, so I said it was Josef K."

He made a spasmodic kind of gulp that I guessed was a laugh, then reached inside his coat and started hunting around for something. He exhausted nearly every pocket before he pulled out a piece of construction paper cut to the size of a business card. "Black River Municipal Library" was scrawled at the top of it. Freeman held it out to Greer.

"Letter of transit," he said. "Whatever you need, you come see me. I have the entire universe and all of time trapped within four walls."

"I already have a library card. Remember? Greer Larson?"

Freeman squinted up at him and then bowed with a flourish as he turned to the girl.

"For you then, Penthesilea."

She blushed a little and took the card. "Uh . . . thanks."

Greer clapped his hands together. "Well then! This has been great, but if you're feeling better, we'll just get —"

"You're the man in the iron mask."

Freeman was staring right at me. He had these intense eyes, small and ocean blue, beneath snowy eyebrows.

"You look after the children on the mountain," he said. "You and that other one. Layton. Belson."

"Larson," Greer said, raising his hand. "I'm *right* here, Free."

"My name's Cardinal."

Freeman's eyes narrowed to slits, looking at me, through me. "You must be very careful."

"I'm sorry?"

"To not have become one of us. All this time. Surrounded by the children of Lethe. You must be very careful."

"I keep my distance."

He looked at my mask and my gloves; then his eyes slipped down to my waist, where my hand gripped the knife. I snatched it away. He smiled.

"Yes," he said. "I suppose you must."

Greer stepped down off the curb. "So! Like I was saying, we have to —"

"Do any of you know how new planets are discovered?"

Freeman waited for an answer. Greer looked from me to the girl. We both shrugged.

"We, uh, don't know. Some kind of telescope maybe?"

The librarian let out a grunt of disgust, then he reached into his coat again and whipped out a nub of chalk.

"Planets that are too distant to be viewed directly are

sometimes detected by looking at the way light bends around them."

He leaned over the asphalt and drew a stick figure with a slash of a line growing out of its chest.

"It's the same with us. We, like light, attempt to move through life in a straight line, unchanged, but we encounter massive objects along the way."

He drew several lumpy masses in front of the stick figure and labeled them: SICKNESS. DEATH. LOVE. The line growing from the figure's chest was forced to zigzag around them.

"Each event bends our life into a new trajectory. It bends who we *are*. So if you look closely, you can perceive distant events in a person's life by observing the ways in which they've bent themselves around them. The ways in which they've been deformed. It's like looking back in time. But it's also like looking into the future."

He finished, and the three of us just stood there slack-jawed. What did you say to that? Did you applaud? Was it brilliant or was it insane? Freeman saved us the trouble of deciding. He whipped another library card out of his pocket and held it out to me.

"Letter of transit."

I took the card. Greer and the girl helped Freeman up, and he strolled away without another word.

Greer watched him go, then turned back to us. "Who the hell are the children of Lethe?"

The girl laughed. "Who the hell is Penthesilea?"

I wondered — *Who the hell is Freeman Wayne?*

The backpack was right where she said it would be, sitting beside a pink crocodile in the middle of the sculpture garden. The park's iron gate squeaked as Greer opened it. I expected the girl to run to the bag and start tearing through it, but she hung back near the fence, staring at it, her arms crossed tight over her chest.

"You want me to . . ."

She nodded. Greer knelt by the bag and unzipped it. I watched from the other side of the fence as he tossed out a pair of socks, a pair of jeans, a plain gray T-shirt. Next came an empty bottle of water and a couple energy bar wrappers. He looked discouraged until he saw another pocket on the front of the bag and opened it.

"Well, well, well. Lookee here, boys and girls!"

I let myself into the garden. "What is it?"

"We've got ourselves a driver's license!"

The girl jumped away from the fence. "Seriously?"

Greer pulled an orange wallet out of her backpack, then, with a grand, Freeman-like bow, turned to her and produced a plastic card. "Please allow me to reunite you with you. *Marianne.*"

The girl snatched the ID out of Greer's hand. He turned to me, grinning.

"Damn, Card, are we good or what? We'll have her back to her folks by the end of the day."

I nodded, but the truth was, I didn't feel like celebrating. It was stupid. This had been the plan. We figure out who she is and get her off the mountain; then things go back to normal. I should have been relieved — I *wanted* to be relieved — but when I thought of her being gone, I don't know, it was like all the air had rushed out of me.

"Hey! You okay? What's wrong?"

I thought Greer was talking to me, but when I looked up, I saw that the girl was at the fence, head down, with her back to us. The ID was clamped in her hands. When she moved to return it to Greer, I saw that she was crying.

"What?" he said as he scanned the license again. "You don't like the name? I think Marianne is nice. We could call you Mari if you want."

No response. Greer looked at me, helpless, and handed the card over. It was a New York driver's license all right and it was definitely her in the picture, green hair and all, but there was something about it, something I couldn't put my finger on. And then it hit me all at once.

"It's fake," I said.

Greer plucked the card out of my hand. "What? No way. How do you know?"

I started to answer, but the girl interrupted me.

"Marianne Dashwood."

Her back was pressed up against the fence, and she was clutching at the key around her neck. Her eyes were puffy and red. Greer looked to me, confused.

"She's a character in a book called *Sense and Sensibility*," I said.

"Well, maybe her parents just—"

"The address isn't real either," I explained. "Eighteen eleven Austen Street? Jane Austen wrote *Sense and Sensibility*."

"But it doesn't make any sense," Greer said. "Why would she have been carrying a fake ID? Where would she have even gotten one?"

I knelt down and opened the backpack again. There *had* to be something else there. I turned the thing inside out, but there were no pictures, no bank cards, no phone, no other ID. I went through the wallet, but all Greer had missed when he found the license was some cash in small bills. As I counted through them, a scrap of paper fell to the ground. It was rumpled and torn, but as soon as I unfolded it, I could see what it was. A Greyhound bus ticket stub.

It was for a route that ran from some town in Indiana to one that was barely an hour from Black River. But why would someone keep a bus ticket in her wallet for over six months? Just as that thought went through my head, I saw it. A few numbers printed at the bottom. The wallet dropped out of my hands.

"What's up, Card? You got something?"

I handed Greer the ticket. It took him only a second to see the same thing I did. "But that's not —"

"What is it?" the girl asked.

When Greer didn't answer, she snatched the ticket out of his hand. "So what?" she said. "You said some people were just passing through when —"

I took a step toward her. "Look at the departure date on the bottom."

The girl did and then looked up at me, uncomprehending.

"That was three days ago."

None of us moved. When the girl spoke again, her voice was hard and small.

"But . . . you said the town's been quarantined for months."

I turned to Greer. "Was there a charity group at the supply drop yesterday?"

"Yeah, some church was helping out, I think. Oh! That's it! I heard they came in the day before to get ready. She must have gotten permission to cross into the QZ to do some charity work and then ended up getting infected."

It made sense, but something about it didn't feel right. I turned it all over in my head. A bus ticket and a fake ID sitting in a mostly empty backpack. No phone. No ATM card. Her hair had been dyed recently. Each piece clicked together like the sides of a frame. When the picture inside emerged, I felt something cold in the pit of my stomach.

"I don't think that's it."

"Then what?" Greer asked.

I studied the girl as she stood there holding the ticket in her trembling hand. She looked exactly as she had the first time I'd seen her. Hunted. Frightened. Lost. But strong too. I took a breath to steady myself and looked her in the eye.

"You did it on purpose," I said. "You came here because you *wanted* to get infected."

"What?" Greer exclaimed. "No way, man."

"People have tried before. Gonzalez said —"

"That every now and then some mental case throws himself against the fence. You think that's who she is? No. Uh-uh."

The girl had started backing away toward the gate. Greer went after her.

"Listen, Card thinks he knows everything, but trust me, he's not as smart as he —"

Greer tried to grab her arm to keep her from leaving, but she drove both hands into his chest and knocked him to the ground. She threw herself through the gate and into the street. I called out to her, but she ran past City Hall and St. Stephen's and then down Elm Street. Greer groaned as he rolled over.

"You all right?" I asked.

"Fine," Greer said. "See? Told you. Former Navy SEAL. Come on, we better go after her."

I went back for her bag. As I stuffed her things inside, I saw a splash of yellow tangled up in the thorns of a rosebush near the fence. A thin jacket, like a Windbreaker. I remembered her saying she'd been hot as the virus took hold. I yanked it off the thorns and immediately felt something in the pocket. I reached inside and pulled it out. It was a small sealed envelope. On the front, in neat block letters, it said:

READ ME.

"So," Greer said. "You gonna take a look?"

We'd been winding through the streets for hours, searching for the girl without any luck.

"Take a look at what?"

Greer nodded toward the note I had clutched in my hand.

"No," I said. "And you're not either. Whatever she wrote, it's none of our business."

"Yeah, but you can't tell me it isn't killing you, right? It's killing me. Oh! Maybe she was like a bank robber or something and she came here to get away from the police."

"Then she'd want them to forget *her*," I said. "Not the other way around."

"Right. So maybe . . ."

Greer laid out a dozen more theories as we checked the park and the high school, but I could barely hear him anymore. My heartbeat was pounding in my ears. It seemed to grow louder every minute we stayed in town. I'd become hyper alert too, flinching at every sound and constantly seeing movement in the shadows only to turn and find nothing there. I could feel our house lurking out in the maze of neighborhoods, pulling at me, trying to draw me back. All I wanted was to find the girl and go.

Greer led us down to the alleys and the boarded-up shops on Main Street. Infected emerged from their homes, standing in the gloom of their doorways to watch us. Greer stopped and asked each one if they'd seen her while I waited on the street. The answer was always no. Nothing. Not a trace. The sun was just starting to fall.

"Come on," I said. "Maybe she headed back to camp."

Greer agreed and we left Main and rejoined Route 9 heading out of town. Lucy's Promise rose ahead of us. The pounding in my chest slowly eased.

"Hey, at least we know she's from Indiana," Greer said. "That's something, right?"

"We know she got on a bus in Indiana," I said. "She could have been anywhere before that."

"Yeah. Right. Good point. I still don't get it, though."

"What's to get?" I said. "She gives some charity group a fake name, then ditches them once she gets inside."

"I get *that*," Greer said. "I just don't get why. I mean, what could happen to a person that'd be so bad they'd throw their whole life away over it?"

Greer waited for an answer, but I didn't say anything. I kept my head down, watching the asphalt beneath my feet. I saw Mom in that alleyway. I saw the house. I saw you and Dad. Glassy chimes jangled in my head.

"Card."

We'd come to the bridge that spanned Black River Falls. The girl was standing out in the middle of it, leaning against the stone guardrail. She'd taken off the baseball cap, and her hair rippled in the spray-filled breeze. She didn't move as we came onto the bridge, didn't acknowledge us. I handed Greer the note. He took it over to her and then rejoined me. The girl stood looking down at the falls for a long time before she tore open the envelope with one swift motion. Inside was a plain white card, square, folded in the middle, like an invitation. It whipped back and forth in the wind as she read.

"Or maybe she's some kind of international spy and her bosses sent her here to —"

"*Shhhh.*"

It was a small card, but the girl took a long time reading it. She would come to the end, look up, start again. When she was done, she refolded it and placed it back in the envelope. Greer started to walk toward her, but I held up my hand to stop him.

She leaned against the guardrail and carefully ripped the envelope in two. She placed one piece on top of the other and tore them again. There was a whistle in the trees, and then a starling flew across the water. The girl held the scraps over the guardrail and let them drop into the falls.

12

S SOON AS Greer and I got back to camp, there was a shriek and Astrid came running toward us.

"Greer! Cardinal! Hi!"

Behind her, everyone else had congregated in the space between the four cabins. They were scrubbed clean and wearing their going-to-town finest. Even the boys. Strips of colored paper had been strung into chains that hung from trees and rooftops like a Christmas garland.

"We, uh, we didn't think you-all would be back so soon!"

"Well, here we are," Greer said. "What's going on, Astrid?"

"Where's the girl?"

"She's trailing along behind us," I said. "She'll be here in a minute."

"Oh, okay. Well, we all thought that since Cash and Shan and the green-haired girl—"

"Wait," Greer said. "Cash and Shan?"

"Oh!" Astrid said. "They're the kids from this morning. We gave them names till you find their real ones."

Astrid gestured behind her, and the Joseph's Point kids—Cash and Shan now—stood between Ren's and Makela's groups. They still looked a little shell-shocked, but they were clean and in fresh clothes.

"Anyway," Astrid continued, "since the two of them and that girl with green hair all joined us at the same time, we thought we should have a welcome party! Eliot was supposed to ask if we could this morning. He said he couldn't find you, but I think he chickened out and was lying about it."

"I did not chicken out!"

"You did too, Eliot!"

"Guys," Greer said. "I don't know if—"

"Wait! Before you say anything, we got our chores done early. And there's going to be a cake! Well, kind of. And presents! Kind of. We're going to have a dance party! Is it okay? Say it's okay!"

Greer and I exchanged a look.

"Listen," I said, lowering my voice. "This is all really great, but I don't think she's going to be in the mood for a dance party right now. Maybe we should —"

"Why wouldn't I be in the mood for a dance party?"

We all turned. The girl was standing at the top of the trail, hands in her pockets, the late-day sunlight washing over her. The tension that had hardened her shoulders and made her hands into fists had dropped away all at once. She barely even resembled the person we'd seen on the bridge just minutes before.

"Well, I just thought, you know, since —"

She marched right past Greer and me. "Don't listen to them, Astrid. I'd love a party!"

"Oh — yay!" Astrid grabbed her hand and pulled her toward the rest of the kids. "I'll introduce you to everybody! Oh! Wait! Did you find out your name?"

"We didn't. Not yet."

"No problem!" Astrid chirped. "Pick a letter!"

"Pick a letter?" The girl looked back at us. Greer nodded encouragingly. "Uh . . . *H?*"

"Perfect! Wait right here!"

Astrid sprinted back to the others. "Guys! She picked *H!*"

The kids held a conference, and then Astrid came racing back.

"We have options!" she said. "Hester, Helen, Hailee, or Hermione."

"Wow. Those are some really good choices. Um . . ."

Benny appeared by Astrid's side and tugged at her skirt. She bent down, and he whispered something in her ear.

"Oh. Okay. Sure. I'll tell her." Astrid stood back up. "Benny says he also likes Hannah."

The green-haired girl smiled at Benny. "You know what? I think I do too."

Astrid grabbed the newly minted Hannah by the hand and swept her away to join the rest of the kids. "Guys! Her name is Hannah!"

Isaac emerged from the boys' cabin with our radio. The

kids screamed as a thump and crash reverberated through the camp.

"Uh-oh!" Greer exclaimed as he ran off to join them. "This is it! This is my jam! Isaac's playing my jam!"

He dove into the crowd, and the dancing spread out from him in waves. Hannah kept to the sidelines with Benny and the younger kids until Ren pulled them all into the swirl of bodies. It was chaos at first, but then the kids linked arms and turned as one. Someone always seemed to be a half step off, though, so they were perpetually falling into huge, giggling pileups and then climbing out of them to start again.

I watched from the growing shadows by the boys' cabin. Over the next couple of hours, dozens of camp dramas, most of which I'd only heard about, emerged from the confusion. Carrie's tomboyish jostling of a noticeably uncomfortable Greer. Eliot dancing with Astrid and then dancing with Makela and then collapsing in a heap with Ren and Cash, where they whispered to one another and laughed. Isaac and Tomiko off by the supply shed, their arms wrapped around each other, their lips pressed together.

The longer I watched, the more it seemed like the space between us expanded. Even though I never moved, the twenty feet between the cabin and the dance soon felt like thirty feet, then forty. By the time the sun started slipping behind the trees, it was a hundred.

Then Hannah burst from the jumble, out of breath and laughing. Greer and Ren called for her to come back, but she waved them off, then wiped the sweat from her forehead with a lazy stroke of her arm. She'd tied her sweatshirt around her waist and a flush of pink had spread across her chest. The falling sun laid a streak of gold across her cheek.

When she saw me standing by the boys' cabin, she smiled and waved me toward her. The music fell away, and everyone behind her blurred into a wall of spinning bodies. I imagined myself stripping off my mask and gloves and crossing the space between us. I'd take her hand and sweep her back into the dance, where we'd turn with all the rest of them, laughing, falling into each other again and again, skin on skin, our breath mingling.

She took a step toward me, and just like that, reality snapped into place. I backed away, moving into the shadows. She called out my name, and Greer did too, I think, but I kept going toward the trail that led to my camp. I hurried through the woods until the music and the lights faded away.

The three of us soared across the Brooklyn Bridge and into Manhattan. Me and you and Dad, awkward in our rented tuxes. When the cab pulled up in front of the theater, you and I tumbled out of the car into a crowd of gowned and tuxedoed Manhattanites. Every man was Bruce Wayne. Every woman was Selina Kyle. Dad took us by our shoulders and guided us toward the entrance. The last thing I saw before we swept into the lobby were the words ALVIN AILEY AMERICAN DANCE THEATER spelled out in steel above the door.

Then we were in our seats, surrounded by that pre-performance murmur until the houselights flashed and everyone found their places and quieted. Dad was sitting between us. He took your hand and then mine and squeezed. Three links in a chain. The houselights went out, and the empty stage slowly filled with a canary yellow light, like a gradual dawn. The woman behind me leaned forward. I could smell the spice of her perfume and feel the warmth of her breath on the back of my neck.

Mom emerged from the wings, alone, barefoot, wearing a dress of green and yellow tatters, each one so light and so pale it was as if a ribbon had been cut out of the air and tinted. When she reached the edge of the stage, her whole body drew upward, as if she were being lifted by a string anchored in the center of her chest. We all watched her, breathless, waiting. And then the music started, violins and cellos, and she exploded into movement. Do you remember? Leaping. Spinning. Falling to the floor only to rise up again. Other dancers joined her then, their bodies like twists of wrought iron. You fell back in your chair, eyes wide and mouth slack. Dad was crying quietly and making no attempt to hide it.

When Mom came out the stage door, we all rushed her at once, crashing into this tight little circle, the flowers Dad brought in the center. Mom's hand and your hand curled around either side of my back while Dad's long arms reached all the way around us. We leaned into the circle and our breath swirled together, mingling with the scent of Mom's stage makeup and her sweat and a dozen yellow roses.

"Hey. You okay?"

I snapped out of the memory to find Hannah standing at the edge of my campsite, a flashlight in her hand.

I shook the past out of my head and jumped up. "Is everything all right? Are the kids—"

"They're fine," she said, waving me back down. "Greer's trying to move everybody toward bed, and I needed a breather. He figured you might be up here."

She settled onto a fallen log. My mask and gloves were in the tent behind me, but she was five feet away, maybe six, so I left them where they were. She pulled two cans of soda out of a plastic bag and held one up to me.

"Ren made a special trip into town and talked a guardsman out of two six-packs of soda. Said he did it just for me."

I waved the can away. No way to know how many infected had touched it. "He's lying. He talks Eliot into doing things like that and then he takes credit for it."

"No way! He said the only reason he did it was so I'd give him a kiss on the cheek."

"Guess you should kiss Eliot, then," I said. "Just watch out for Astrid and Makela if you do."

Hannah stretched her legs in front of her. "Ah, but you've been away too long," she said. "The girls decided that they're too mature and desirable to waste their time on a boy who clearly doesn't appreciate them. Besides, they really need to spend more time on *themselves,* you know?"

"And how do they plan on doing that?"

"Well, Astrid is going to rededicate herself to the art of sculpture. Makela wants to take up hunting."

"Hunting?"

"Yeah, and you'd better be prepared because tomorrow she plans on asking you and Greer how she can get hold of a shotgun."

"No way," I said. "I will not live in any camp that includes an armed Makela Whitman. She's scary enough already."

Hannah laughed. I didn't think there could be anything better than her smiling, but there was.

"You looked like you were having fun with them," I said.

"They're good kids," she said. "Exhausting, but good."

She upended the soda, her neck gracefully long and pale in the glow of the flashlight. When she lowered the can, our eyes met, and it was as if an electric circuit snapped into place. I quickly looked away and pointed to the key around her neck.

"Any feelings about what that might open?"

Hannah took it in her fingertips and turned it over. She shook her head. "Every time I touch it, I see the color blue, like sky blue, and then I feel happy for a second, but then . . ." Her face darkened. She shook her head. "I don't know. It's just gone."

She let the key drop. I pulled at the blades of grass by my feet while we listened to the night sounds of the woods.

"I didn't actually come up here to bring you a soda, you know."

She was leaning forward, her eyes on me, mussed hair framing her face. I felt a nervous trill in my gut.

"I never really thanked you," she said. "For yesterday. With those men."

"Oh." I shrugged it away. "Anyone would have done it."

"Not me, apparently. The second they grabbed you, I ran away."

"But you came back."

Hannah nodded, but I got the feeling it was an excuse she didn't really buy. "Anyway, I just wanted to say thanks. Whatever this — however this turns out, I'm really glad it was you who found me."

She smiled and my face went hot, as if every drop of blood had raced there at once.

"I'm glad it was me too."

"Also glad I got to see you without that mask," she said, then lightly touched her cheeks. "Otherwise I wouldn't have known about those dimples."

"Hannah! Card! *Guys!* Where the hell are you?"

There was a crash out in the woods and then a second later Greer exploded out of the trees, his clothes askew, his eyes wild.

I grabbed my mask and gloves. "What is it? Is it Raney?"

"No time to talk! We have to run! Now!"

"But why? What's going —"

Right on cue, the singsongy voice of Carrie Baldwin rang through the trees.

"*Gre-er!* I know you're *hi-ding!*"

Greer let out a yelp and took off into the woods. "Let's go! Now! Before she finds me!"

"*GRE-ER!*"

Hannah looked to me. I rolled my eyes and cinched on my mask. "Come on. We'd better get him before he breaks his damn neck."

Hannah and I tracked Greer's flashlight beam as it bounced through the forest. Carrie's voice faded as the woods closed around us and the trail narrowed. We didn't stop until we found him collapsed on the shore of the reservoir, doubled over and trying to catch his breath.

"Oh, man"—*gasp*—"that was close. That was really"—*gasp*—"close."

"So *that's* what all the whispering was about!" Hannah said, then turned to me. "The whole time Greer and I were talking, Carrie was on the other side of the camp whispering with Makela and Jenna."

I laughed. "Carrie Baldwin does not like it when someone messes with her man."

Greer wailed. "Dude! Shut up. Seriously. That is *so* wrong."

Hannah climbed onto an outcropping of rock by the water. "What's the big deal? She's one of the older ones, right?"

"Turned fourteen last week," I teased.

"Then I don't see what the problem is," Hannah said. "You're all alone on this mountain. It's the middle of a national emergency. And you're what? Sixteen?"

"Seventeen," Greer said. "And that's not the problem. The problem is that I'm in a position of authority here."

"Ha!"

"Shut up, Card! I'm like their big brother! Their wise and noble big brother."

"Who makes them dance the mambo between halves of fake football games."

"Exactly!" Greer said. "Even when I'm making them do ridiculous things for my own amusement, they trust me. I can't abuse that!"

"Even though you want to," Hannah teased.

"Oh God," he moaned. "I want to so bad, it haunts my dreams. That's it. I'm burning up. I need a swim." He ripped off his shoes and socks.

"Now?"

He yanked his shirt off over his head. "It's an emergency, Hannah!"

"What's that?" she asked, shining her flashlight on his back. Up near his shoulder blade was a tattoo in heavy black ink. Two numbers separated by a slash.

"Fourteen eighty-eight?" she read.

Greer twisted around to try and get a look at it. "Oh, yeah, that. Weird, huh?"

"What does it mean?"

"We don't know," I said. "I tried to look it up once, but it doesn't seem to mean anything."

"Just another part of the mystery that is me," Greer said. "Okay! Let's do this!"

He pulled off his shorts and underwear in one swipe.

"Greer!" Hannah squealed.

"What?" he said, wiggling his pasty butt in the moonlight. "We're all alone on a mountain. It's a national emergency. Anything goes."

"Not that! Anything goes but that!"

"You're just afraid of your own desires. That's all it is."

He took a running leap and threw himself into the water, popping up dozens of feet away doing a strong backstroke.

"Hey! Did I ever tell you guys I think I might have been an Olympic swimmer?"

Greer laughed, then turned over, chopping at the water freestyle. A white *V* spread out from the tips of his fingers and trailed behind him. I thought he'd turn back, but he kept on going until he was beyond the reach of our flashlights. Soon the splash of his strokes faded, replaced by the sound of crickets.

Hannah laughed. "Poor guy has no idea what he's in for."

"What do you mean?"

"I mean Carrie's not the only one. Judging from the way the younger girls look at him, she's gonna have some serious competition a few years from now."

Hannah took a pebble from the shore and playfully tossed it at my shoulder. "So which one of them's in love with you?"

I shook my head, feeling the blood rise to my cheeks again.

"Ah, come on," she said. "I bet there's one or two."

"Nah. I've always had to kinda keep my distance from them, you know?"

"Ah, so you were a ladies' man *before* the outbreak."

"Yeah, right." I laughed. "No. My brother, maybe. He had a new girlfriend every week since he was like thirteen. Not me."

"I don't know. I bet you could —" Hannah sprang to her feet. "Whoa! What the hell was that? Card! Did you see that?"

She was pointing out over the water. At first I didn't see anything, but then a few pinpricks of greenish-yellow light appeared over the surface of the reservoir.

"What?" I said. "The fireflies?"

"Fireflies? Oh! Look! There's more! They're so pretty!"

All across the reservoir, lights flared and then winked out, like match heads. I watched Hannah watch them, her eyes bright, her mouth agape. A few minutes passed, and then they were gone.

"Fireflies," she whispered, as if she were carving the word into her memory. "Hey, I guess that's another clue, right? I didn't know what they were, so that must mean I come from a place that doesn't have fireflies."

"Maybe that's why you left."

Hannah laughed. She pulled off her boots and let her feet dangle in the wavelets at the reservoir's edge. "Can I ask you a weird question? It's something I've been wondering."

"Sure."

"Is Cardinal your real name? I mean, that's a kind of bird, right? Your parents named you after a bird?"

"No. My dad — he, uh, he wrote comic books. Cardinal was a character of his."

"Seriously? That's so cool! What are the comics about?"

"This group of superheroes in a place called Liberty City," I said. "The Brotherhood of Wings. There's Black Eagle. Sally Sparrow. Blue Jay. Kestrel Kain. Rex Raven. Goldfinch. Lord Starling."

"And Cardinal," Hannah said.

The first few pages of issue one came flooding into my head. Mild-mannered Cameron Conner sweeping up the lab while he pines for Sally Sparrow, his true love, who barely knows he exists.

"He was a nobody at first," I said. "Just a technician and a part-time inventor who worked in the lab. And then one day the Brotherhood was defeated by a bad guy named Kirzon Sloat, and Conner threw on this experimental suit of armor he'd built from scratch and saved the day."

I flipped through the pages in my head until I came to one of my all-time favorite sequences — Cardinal being unmasked by Rex Raven. Sally Sparrow gasps in shock when she sees that their savior is some anonymous lab tech. Conner is heartbroken, convinced that she's going to make him give up the Cardinal armor and return to his lab, but in the very last panel Sally leaps into his arms and kisses him.

Holy heartthrob! Blue Jay exclaims. *Looks like there's only one bird for Sally Sparrow now!*

"That sounds amazing!" Hannah said. "Tell me more."

"About the comics?"

Hannah crossed her legs and leaned over them. "No. About you."

"About me? Why?"

"I've decided I like knowing things about people. And since you're the only person up here who actually knows anything about himself, I've got nowhere else to turn."

It was hard logic to argue against. "What do you want to know?"

"Umm. Let's see. You said you have a brother. What's his name?"

A picture flashed into my head — you standing on the sidewalk, hands jammed into your jacket pockets. I scooped up a handful of rocks and skipped one across the water.

"Tennant. His name's Tennant."

"Is that a strange name too?"

I couldn't help but laugh a little. "Kind of. Yeah. My mom was really into *Dr. Who*. It's this science-fiction TV show? Anyway, the tenth doctor was her favorite, so they named my brother after the actor who played him. If he'd been a girl, Mom was going to name him Vastra, so I guess he kinda lucked out."

"What's your mom do?"

I saw Mom onstage, mid-pirouette. My nose filled with the scent of roses.

"Card?"

"She, uh, she was a dancer. But she hurt her ankle a few years back and had to stop. She was going to start teaching when we moved here from the city, but it never really worked out."

"Wow. You have such a cool family. Are they all —" Hannah cut herself off. "Sorry. I was going ask if they were all . . . it's none of my business. I shouldn't have —"

"Tennant was away at college when Lassiter's hit."

There was a rustle as Hannah shifted position. Water lapped against the shore.

"Oh. Well, that's good," she said. "Lucky."

I nodded and pushed the rocks around in my hand. They made a click like bones knocking together. There was a splash out on the reservoir. I looked up and saw another white *V* streaming across the surface toward us.

Hannah stood up on her rock. "How was it?" she called.

"Cold!"

Greer pulled himself to the shallows and strode toward us, naked and shivering.

"You know, I take it back. I wasn't a professional swimmer.

But I'm pretty sure I might have been a nudist. Seriously, this is the way to go. Hannah, give it a try."

She laughed, untied the hoodie from around her waist, and threw it at him.

"Dry yourself off. You're indecent."

Not long after that, we were on our way back to camp, barefoot, our shoes hanging over our shoulders by the laces, as if we'd just come from a long day at the beach. I felt unbelievably light, like each step I took was covering miles. The talk flowed effortlessly, rising and falling, punctuated by laughter. At some point Snow Cone and Hershey Bar came running out of the woods and trotted alongside us. It was one of those times when you felt like there was some sort of current running through the world and you had stepped into it and been carried away.

Firelight from the camp appeared as a glow in the trees ahead, along with the faint sounds of the kids' voices. Hershey Bar and Snow Cone ran off down the trail. No one said anything, but I felt the three of us slow down until we were just barely drifting along, trying to delay the inevitable. Still, the end came. We hit the junction where the trail branched off to Hannah's and my campsites. Greer pressed on ahead, raising his hand in farewell.

"Maybe Carrie's still up!" Hannah called out. "You should go say hi."

Greer flipped her off over his shoulders with both hands. She laughed as his footsteps faded away. I looked down the branch of the trail that led to my campsite. Suddenly everything there — my tent, my books, my clothes — seemed stale and flat, an eddy off the current, circling endlessly.

"Walk me home?"

Hannah was standing across from me on the trail. Her skin glowed a ghostly silver in the moonlight. When we got to her camp, she passed the tent and went out to the edge of the mountain. The borders of the QZ were never so obvious as they were late at night. Since it was long past the time the state turned off the electricity, inside the fence was nothing but inky blackness. Outside was a map of light and movement. The highway that ran along the western edge was like a glowing artery, red blood cells streaming one way, white the other. The neon billboards for gas stations and fast-food chains were so bright you could almost read them from where we stood. Beyond, a constellation of small towns stretched into the darkness.

"Weird, huh?" I said. "There's a whole other world out there."

Hannah's hair whipped in the breeze. She tucked it behind her ears. "What's it like?"

I came up beside her, watching the lights move out into the dark. "A mess mostly."

"So we're not missing anything."

"Maybe not."

She was quiet a moment, watching the lights. "Greer thinks your friend Gonzalez can find out who I am."

"Is that what you want?"

Hannah turned her back on the valley and settled onto the rocks. "He said sometimes, even when he's happy, it's like there's this hole that runs right through him. All because he doesn't know."

"Greer said that?"

She stared down at her hands, almost as if she hadn't heard me. "When I found out that I did it, that I came here to — it was kind of a relief. You know? Like something must have happened that made me want to, made me *need* to do it. But then I thought, I had to have a family, right? And friends? What could have happened that was so awful I'd just leave?"

"The note you wrote didn't . . ."

Hannah shook her head. "It said I should decide who I am instead of worrying about who I *was*."

"That's not bad advice."

"Maybe. But the whole time I was reading it, even though I knew it was my handwriting, I kept thinking, *I don't know this person. Why should I trust her?*"

Hannah took hold of the key and drew it back and forth across the leather band.

"I don't know. Maybe nothing happened to me at all."

I found a place a little farther down the ledge and sat. "What do you mean?"

"I mean sometimes when I think about, you know, *before*, I get this feeling like maybe *I* was the one who did something. Something awful."

"No," I said. "No way."

"You don't even know me, Card."

I wanted to tell her she was wrong, that I did, but I knew it wasn't true. She was as much a stranger to me as she was to herself. I sat there staring at the ground, feeling stupid, wondering what to do or say. If things were normal, I could have put my arm around her, hugged her, told her it was going to be all right, but of course I couldn't do any of those things. Not then. Part of me wondered if I ever could have.

"What was her promise anyway?" she asked.

"What?"

Hannah was looking out to where the trees rose over the mountain's highest peak.

"Lucy must have promised somebody something pretty big for them to name a whole mountain after it. What was it?"

How strange was it that in all that time, I'd never asked the same question? There must've been a town legend about it, something they would have taught us in school, but as hard as I tried, I couldn't remember what it was.

"I don't know," I said.

Hannah thought for a moment, and then she turned to face me. "So I guess it can be anything we want."

We were sitting so close, closer than we should have been. Her eyes were dark and huge, twin universes. For what felt like a very long time, neither of us moved or said anything or looked away. The cabins in the camp below felt very distant. Black River was another world.

Hannah laid her hand on the rock between us. In the moonlight it was this pale, beautifully curving thing, like a dove. I moved closer. My hand shook as I reached out and placed it on top of hers, covering it. I thought I could feel a little bit of her warmth through my glove, and the gentle tapping of the pulse in her wrist. My breath grew hot under my mask as something rushed into the space between us. I didn't know what it was or where it came from, but it was there, warm and alive, connecting us both.

And then, just like that, it was gone. She drew her hand back, and time spun forward again. The air was just the air.

"I should probably get some sleep."

"Yeah," I said, my voice as thin as a slip of paper. "Me too."

I started to go but stopped at the trail and turned back. Hannah was standing at her tent, holding the flap open.

"My dad used to read me and Tennant all these Greek myths," I said. "Gods and heroes and monsters and all that stuff. Penthesilea was the queen of the Amazons. She was a great warrior and one of the most beautiful women in the world."

The treetops whispered in the high wind. Hannah smiled.

As I walked back to my tent I expected the world to come crashing back over me — my worries about the Guard leaving and the Marvins taking their place, my confusion over seeing Mom again. But some remnant of that moment with Hannah clung to my skin and kept it all at bay. I stopped at the bluff that overlooked the kids' cabins. They were silver and black in the moonlight. I could feel Greer and the others inside them, asleep on their cots, breathing as one.

Before I went into my tent, I looked down the path that led to Hannah's. There was another light out there in the trees. She'd gone inside with her flashlight, making the skin of the tent glow a greenish yellow. I watched the dance of shadows inside as she got ready for bed. And then the light winked out and everything was dark.

I lay down on my sleeping bag and closed my eyes. I could feel the in-and-out pulse of the camp's breath. Hannah's too. I fell into rhythm with it, imagining the air in their lungs flowing into mine and mine into theirs. We'd built an entire world out of ourselves and all the cast-off things around us. Right then it felt as if it would go on forever.

It felt unbreakable.

13

THE NEXT THING I knew, I was standing in my bedroom back home. It was late. I was still wearing the shorts and Captain America T-shirt I'd gone to sleep in. I thought I must have been dreaming, but I looked down at my feet and saw that they were caked in mud from my walk down the mountain. My hand went to my face and I felt a little thrill of fear when I realized I'd walked all the way through town without my mask or gloves.

The room was dark, but the little bit of moonlight coming in through the window revealed that it was just how I'd left it the night of the sixteenth. A pile of comic books lay at the foot of my unmade bed. The laundry Mom had done earlier that afternoon sat in the basket beside my desk—pants and shirts folded into neat squares, socks rolled into balls the size of fists. The air tasted like dust.

Downstairs, the front door opened and closed. Heavy footsteps moved from the entryway to the living room. I left my bedroom and started down to see who it was. When I came to the landing and made the turn for the final run of steps, I saw that it was Cardinal. He was standing at the end of the couch, perfectly still. This was Dad's Cardinal, not

Gonzalez's. He was a winged tank, nine feet tall, his armor the color of blood that had become glossy as it hardened into steel.

The living room windows filled with an orange light that sent shadows writhing across the walls and the floor. I smelled smoke and heard the ring of wind chimes. Cardinal turned and walked toward the front door. I followed him out onto the porch, but the porch wasn't the porch anymore. It was a shelf of rock at the peak of Lucy's Promise.

Cardinal sat down at the edge of the cliff and motioned for me to join him. When I did, he broke the seal on his helmet and set it in his lap. It wasn't Cameron Conner. It was Dad. He swept his hand across the landscape.

"Behold, the Gardens of Null."

As the words left his mouth, the sun rose over our backs and spread across a world that had been consumed by an immense fire. From where we sat, all the way to the horizon, there was only silence and great dunes of oily gray ash. No buildings. No streets. The Black River had boiled away and the forests had become groves of limbless pillars, charred to cinder. Lucy's Promise sat at the center of it all. The flames had burned it down to bedrock, leaving its slopes a glossy black. Here and there, fissures showed the deep orange flames that seethed in the heart of the mountain.

I turned back to Cardinal, but instead of Dad's face he had yours. I asked how the fire had started, and you leaned in close and whispered to me the great secret of the world.

"It *wants* to burn," you said.

The sun passed over our heads. The sky became a deep black nothing.

"What do we do now?" I asked.

A knife appeared in your hand. It was black-handled with a chrome blade. A kitchen knife. You placed it in my palm and closed my fingers around it.

"Forget."

You took my hand and gently guided it until the tip of the blade hovered just over my right eye. The next second you were gone and I was alone. A hot wind moaned around the top of the mountain. I turned to my right. Even though the sun was gone, I could see tendrils of shadow falling down the face of the rocks beside me. I thought about the great secret of the world, and then I gripped the knife in both hands and drove it through.

14

ND THEN I was standing in the middle of the woods. It was morning. I was barefoot. My T-shirt and shorts were damp with sweat. I looked for a landmark to get my bearings, but all I saw was that I was on a trail. I thought maybe if I kept going, everything would become clear.

The trail opened up to a small field. It was perfectly empty and quiet except for a low, moaning wind, but I wasn't sure if that was real or if it was in my head. I moved from the dirt trail to the grass. At the far end of the clearing were two gray boulders perched at the edge of the mountain. As soon as I saw them, everything snapped into focus. This was Hannah's campsite. But her tent was gone and so were all her things.

A wormy chill raced up my spine. Had I dreamed her? Dreamed everything that happened to us? And if I had, how far back did the dream go? Maybe there had never been any virus. Maybe you and Mom and Dad were still —

"Cardinal?"

Hannah was standing behind me, but I almost didn't recognize her. She was in shorts and a blue T-shirt with a picture of a rabbit on it. Her hair was pinned behind her ears, turning her face into a pale moon.

"You all right?"

"I . . ." I turned to look around at the barren campsite. "Where is everything?"

"I was just — I'm moving my things down into Astrid's cabin."

There was an ache in my throat as I said, "You're leaving?"

"No, I'm just —"

"When did you decide to do that?"

"This morning. I asked her and —"

"You asked *her?*"

Hannah's jaw tensed. "They have a spare cot, and I thought . . ." Her voice was like a steel wire that had been stretched too tight. "I thought it made more sense that way. For me to be down there with everyone else. I just came back for my —"

She pointed behind me. Her backpack was leaning against some bushes. I hadn't noticed it earlier. I picked it up, then returned to Hannah and held it out to her.

"Card, you're not . . ." She trailed off. She was looking at me strangely, but I didn't know why. "You're not wearing your mask."

I lifted one hand, and my bare fingers brushed against my lips. I hadn't even realized. I set the pack down and backed away from it until I felt stone against my legs. I sat down and found myself wedged between the two boulders. Something in me eased from being surrounded by them. I drew my knees up to my chest and held them close.

Hannah collected the bag, but didn't leave. She stood by the trail, fidgeting with the strap, twisting it back and forth. Our moment standing in the moonlight the night before came rushing back to me, but it was all mixed up with looking down at that burned earth and learning about the great secret of the world.

She asked again if I was okay, but I couldn't speak, couldn't even move my lips, so I nodded instead.

"It's just . . . you look pale, and your eyes are — did you sleep last night?"

"Yo! Hannah! Time to get moving! The natives are getting rest —"

Greer came up the trail at a run and stopped behind Hannah. The palm of his hand hovered over her lower back. "Oh! Hey there, buddy! Damn, you look like crap."

"Greer," Hannah said.

"What? Have you *seen* him?"

"He says he's fine."

Greer left Hannah and headed for me. "Okay, well, I'm glad you're here! That Raney guy came up this morning to bring us those clothes he promised, and he said the Marvins are throwing this big picnic thing down in the park today. The word is that there'll be barbecue! Now, Hannah thinks . . ."

Greer kept talking, but I dropped my head, curling my hands around the back of my skull. An ache had begun behind my right eye, and my nostrils were full of the stink of charred wood. Greer's voice turned into a knifelike buzz, and then Hannah joined in too. Monument Park. Games. A party. It was the same thing over and over again. Time had folded into a loop, tied itself into a knot, and still they talked.

"You can't go!"

Shouting like that made my head pound, but it was worth it. Silence. Finally. Greer looked at me and then at Hannah, a half smile on his face, as if maybe there was a joke he just wasn't getting.

"Oh!" he said. "Don't worry, me and Hannah figured out a whole new disguise for her. *Way* better than the last one. And besides, even if those creeps recognize her, there'll be so many people around, they won't dare do anything, right? I mean it's not every day that the kids get to go to a party. A *real* party with —"

"What did I just say? You're *not* going."

"Excuse me?"

I sprang off the rocks and stabbed my finger at Hannah. "What do you think's going to happen if Raney sees her?"

"You said Gonzalez could cover for us!"

"As long as we're not *stupid.*"

Hannah said, "We're not going to be stupid. We're going be careful."

"Careful? You'll be *careful*? A party? You think this is a joke?"

"I don't think it's a joke. I think —"

"Guys!" Greer shouted from the sidelines. "Come on. Let's —"

"What?" I said. "You think the Marvins are doing this out of the kindness of their hearts? Throwing you a party? Giving you presents? This is for *them*. They want something, and they're using this to get it. How can you not see that? How can *neither* of you see that?"

"Using it to get *what*?" Hannah asked. "What could they possibly want from *us*?"

I steamrolled past them toward the trail. "It doesn't matter. You're not going, and that's it."

"Come on, buddy, wait —"

Greer's hand grazed my shoulder. I jumped away from him. The muscles in my arms and my back tensed, like a steel spring twisted down tight. I thought of Dale and Tommasulo and remembered how good it felt to let go completely. My hand became a fist.

"Card!"

Hannah was standing just behind Greer, presenting a united front. The two of them against me. The world shifted on its axis. I stepped back slowly, putting more distance between us.

"We're here for *them*," I said. "For those kids. To make sure nothing ever happens to *them*."

"We will," Hannah insisted. "Nothing's going to happen."

"You were right," I spat. "It *was* your fault. You had people who loved you — friends, family — and you threw them away and ran because you didn't give a damn about anybody but yourself."

She went perfectly still. She barely breathed. I could have walked away, but it was as if she were standing on a ledge and some part of me couldn't resist pushing.

"Some things don't change when you get infected," I said. "I never should have brought you here."

Hannah said nothing, and neither did Greer. I continued down the trail.

The latch sprang open when I dropped the tackle box, sending weights and lures spilling out onto the shore of the reservoir. I'd stopped by my tent for my mask and gloves and my fishing things. All I could do was get as far away from them as possible and focus on something else.

As I gathered the tackle, that ache reignited behind my eyes. It moved to encircle my head like a belt, tightening a little at a time. I dropped the lures and filled my hands with water, then splashed it against my face and over my greasy hair, hoping it could wipe away the morning, the last couple of days, the last year. I sat back, eyes shut tight, waiting for the thrum inside my head to ease.

"Anything biting?"

Greer's reflection appeared in the water. He was leaning

against a tree behind me, his hands slipped casually into his pockets. I gathered up a handful of lures and threw them into the box. Greer chuckled to himself in that annoying way of his and then took my fishing rod. He found a place farther down the shore and fiddled with the reel.

"Did I ever tell you that I'm pretty sure I used to be an expert fisherman?" he asked. "And I don't mean this pond fishing, I mean the real thing, deep-sea fishing, for like sharks and whales and stuff."

"We live a hundred miles from the nearest ocean," I said. "You've probably never even been."

"Details," he said. "I've got the salt water in my veins, Cassidy. No doubt about it."

Greer whipped the rod back and made a perfect cast that flew nearly out to the center of the reservoir. The lure hit with a plop and vanished, leaving the red and white floater bobbing on the surface.

"See?"

I tore up a root beside me and threw it into the water.

"So if you're so great at it, why don't you do it once in a while?" I asked. "Maybe cancel one of your Super Bowl dance-a-thons and pitch in. I could use the help."

Greer laughed. "Oh, no argument there. You need help, buddy. *A lot* of help. You're not sleeping. You barely eat."

This again. "I've told you a hundred times, Greer. I *eat*."

"No you don't," he said. "I asked Tomiko."

"You're having Tomiko spy on me?"

"Oh, not just her," Greer said. "The whole camp does it in shifts. There is literally not a second in your day when you aren't secretly being watched by a twelve-year-old."

"I don't need to be watched."

"Dude, the things you said to Hannah—"

"Greer."

"—the words 'titanic jackass' keep coming to mind, and I *know* you, you are not a titanic jackass. Buddy. Seriously. I remember like two percent of my entire life, and I'm still pretty sure you are like the *least* fine human being I've ever met."

Greer set down the rod and turned to me.

"Look, man, I don't know what all happened to you on the sixteenth—"

"Nothing happened."

"Card—"

"Nothing happened that didn't happen to a thousand other people."

"Yeah, but you remember," Greer said. "Whatever it was, you *remember* it. And, hey, if you don't want to talk to me about it, that's fine. As your friend, it hurts me deeply, but fine. But you should talk to somebody."

"I don't need to."

"Ha!"

"You and Hannah—" I clenched my jaw to bite off the rest.

"What?" Greer said. "Say it."

"You two think this is a game."

Back when Greer was his old self, he almost never had to use his fists. Remember? He would fix his eyes on any of us, either at the bus stop or in the schoolyard, and we would wither. There was something in the way he looked at you that said he saw right through whatever sad little defense you were trying to mount, whatever bluff. It also said that what was inside of him was no bluff at all. Greer looked at me like that as we sat by the reservoir.

"You really think you know what's going to happen because you know what *did* happen?" he said. "You think you know who people are because you know who they *were?* Trust me here, man. You don't know a damn thing."

I turned away. I could feel his eyes on my back as I watched ripples of water strike the shore. He got up and headed back down the hill.

"You know what?" he said. "Forget it. I'm going to go find a nice green-haired girl and try to convince her that, no matter what stupid thing you said to her, we all want her here and she shouldn't take her things and go live in some Guard rooming house full of rapists and pedophiles. And then, if I can manage *that*, I'm going to take her and all the kids down to the park to eat some barbecue. Because if I don't, if I spend all my time on this stupid mountain worrying that it's all going to come crashing down around me any minute, I honestly think I'll just go ahead and blow my brains out. Okay? If that means I think all this is a game — which, by the way, is an incredibly freaking insulting thing to say to your best friend — then so be it. Now, you wanna come or you wanna sit here moping and pretending to fish?"

"I'm not —"

He held up one finger to silence me. "No. Come or mope. Those are your choices."

I got up and grabbed the fishing rod. The line hissed as I reeled it in and then recast it.

"We *are* friends," Greer said from behind me. "Right, Card?"

I watched as the floater bobbed on the water. Greer turned away and headed back to camp. I dropped the fishing rod. Soon the ripples faded and the reservoir spread out in front of me, as flat and bright as a razor.

THE GARDENS

OF NULL

15

THAT AFTERNOON, I did what I should have done the minute Greer and the others showed up on Lucy's Promise. I packed my things and moved as far away as possible.

I found a spot on the opposite side of the reservoir. It was in the deep forest, far from any trail, a tangle of brush and vines and deadfall. It took me a full day to hack a path through it and then another to carve out a spot big enough for my tent. It was worth the effort. The woods around me were so thick that I couldn't hear a sound except for my own breathing and the occasional rustle of a bird's wings up in the branches. Even at noon on a cloudless day, it might as well have been dusk.

I spent my days fishing and foraging for mushrooms, crabapples, and blackberries. I even started gathering firewood in preparation for my first winter alone on the mountain. It was tough with just my knife, but there were enough dead trees and branches around that I got a decent pile going. The best part was that, for the first time in almost a year, I didn't have to wear my mask or my gloves. The air tasted like earth and wood instead of hot plastic. It was so strange to touch things without gloves that I compulsively ran my fingers over tree bark and flower petals and my own skin, just for the thrill of it.

Time had a strange way of expanding and contracting. A morning would seem to last a year, and then all of a sudden it would be past midnight. Sometimes I pretended I was living millions of years in the future and was the only human left alive. I imagined walking a thousand miles in any direction — up into Canada or down into Virginia and the Carolinas — and seeing nothing but empty houses and crumbling highways. It was strange how comforting the idea was.

In the beginning I thought about Hannah and Greer and the kids all the time, but as the days went by, they emptied out of my mind one by one. Pretty soon I figured there'd be nothing left in my head but *find food, find water, build a fire.* I couldn't wait for that moment to come, but it didn't turn out that way. Once they were gone, someone else appeared and took their place. Dad.

It wasn't even like I was thinking about him at first. Not exactly. It was more like he was this presence that hovered around me all the time. There, but not there. I'd walk into a stand of trees, certain that I was going to find him on the other side, waiting for me. Or I'd think I'd heard his voice, but it would turn out to be a flock of birds or a tumble of dead branches blown by the wind. During the few hours a night I managed to sleep, he moved in and out of my dreams.

It didn't stay that way, though. Soon it was as if there was this filmstrip of memories unspooling in my head all the time. Dad taking us to the sideshow at Coney Island or to those art movies at the Angelika. Dad leading us on a forced march to the Strand bookstore, where he'd press his favorites into our hands: *Harry Potter. The Dark Is Rising. The Left Hand of Darkness. The Autobiography of Malcolm X.* Every day there were more images, and they came faster and faster until I felt as if I were on a treadmill that I couldn't keep up with and couldn't get off of either.

The only time I could escape it was when I was running, so each night after sundown I'd leave my tent and sprint the mountain trails. The batteries in my flashlight had died — I lost count of how many times I fell in the dark. How many skinned knees and bruised elbows. It didn't matter. If I stumbled, I got up and pushed harder, ran faster. I'd run until the sun came up and then I'd pass out. Sometimes I'd get a few hours of sleep before Dad was there again, just outside my tent, calling me for breakfast or to get ready for school.

One night I finished my run at the reservoir and collapsed on the shore, my legs sore and my lungs feeling like they had sprouted thorns. When I caught my breath, I sat up and looked out at the water. It was a patch of blackness, just a little darker than the woods around it. There was a rhythmic splash as little waves fell against the beach and retreated. Owls hooted and frogs croaked. For a second the world was caught in this easy balance. I breathed in and out, calm, centered, but then there was a flash in my head and the reservoir on Lucy's Promise became the reservoir in Central Park. It was a bright summer day, and we were on our way to see the polar bears at the zoo. Dad had me on his shoulders and you were walking by his side. It was all so clear. I could hear Dad's voice. I could smell his aftershave.

I stripped off my clothes and dove in. I was still aching from my run, but I leaned into the pain instead of ignoring it, digging my arms through the water. As I swam, it hit me how all of my memories of Dad were from when we lived in Brooklyn, as if the minute we moved to Black River, he began to fade. Instead of doing his work in a corner of the living room—blasting his music while we played video games on the couch—he was in his office, usually with the door shut. Six hours of work a day became eight, then ten, then twelve. Weekends evaporated. Then it was missed dinners, missed performances, missed track meets. We told ourselves it was nothing. A temporary thing. He'd just won the Hugo, and everybody was saying the Eisner was right around the corner. People were talking movies. TV shows. Even Mom laughed that night when you said we weren't living with Derrick Cassidy anymore, we were living with Derrick Cassidy, Award-Winning Creator of *Cardinal and the Brotherhood of Wings.*

But then he forgot that doctor's appointment—yours or mine, I don't remember—and Mom decided she'd had enough. The second she walked in the house, it was doors slamming and the two of them screaming at each other, and me thinking, *Is this really Mom and Dad?* They were like strangers with our parents' faces. You tried to get between them, but it was no use. I remember hiding out in your room, wondering what world we had stumbled into and if it would ever be possible to get back to our own.

Once I got out to the center of the reservoir, I flipped onto my back and let myself float with my arms stretched out. Tiny waves lapped at my ears, alternating the sounds of the surface, crickets and frogs and night birds, with the silence below. I'd heard that the reservoir was nearly fifty feet deep at its center. Every inch of that darkness pulled at me.

Sometimes late at night I'd leave my room and walk toward the slip of light coming from beneath Dad's office door. This was a few months before the outbreak, after he'd started sleeping in there instead of in bed with Mom. Only it never seemed like he was sleeping. I could hear his chair squeaking and his pencil scratching. Sometimes, standing there in the dark hallway, I'd lay my palm on the door, the way they taught us to do in school if you thought there was a fire in the house. But it didn't feel like a fire. It felt like we had a black hole trapped within our walls, like Dad had collapsed into this infinitely dense, infinitely cold thing.

Other times I'd lie in your room, staring at the ceiling while you talked. *Dad's overwhelmed. Mom's frustrated. Things will go back to normal soon enough. Don't worry, Cardinal. Everything will be fine, Cardinal.* You'd say it with a smile and a laugh, and then you'd flop into bed next to me and we'd read issues of Love and Rockets or Ms. Marvel. And I believed you. Of course I believed you. You were my big brother. You were right about everything.

I flipped over and kicked my feet against the surface of the reservoir, diving until I was surrounded by an echoey hush. With every stroke the darkness thickened and the world above seemed farther away. I decided I had to touch the bottom, had to feel it with my own hands.

It wasn't long before the last glimmer of moonlight from the surface disappeared. The temperature dropped in bands the deeper I went. The cold seeped through my skin and into my muscles and bones. Worse, though, was the pressure. It felt like a hand had wrapped itself around my chest and was squeezing tighter and tighter. I thought it would be like when I was running, that I'd push through the pain and come out the other side, but this pain grew until it felt bigger than I was, bigger than anything. I started to turn back, but that's when I heard Dad's voice whispering in my ear, as real as if he were swimming along beside me. He said the only mistake he ever made was that he didn't go far enough. He said that if I made it to the bottom, if I touched it and didn't let go no matter what, then I'd have what he'd always wanted, what *I'd* wanted ever since the night of the sixteenth.

I tumbled end over end and pulled for the surface, clawing at water that seemed to have become as thick as wet concrete. Time stretched. My lungs burned. I felt as if I'd been swimming for hours and hadn't moved an inch. Was it too late? Had I gone too far? All I could see was darkness in every direction. What strength I had left was draining away, but then, above me, there was a faint splash and a flicker of light. I thrust my arms through the water and heaved toward the surface, but there was still so far to go. My lungs were screaming. Cramps knotted every muscle. Dad's voice was telling me that the only thing that would stop the pain would be to let go, to let myself sink. I could feel how hungry the dark below was for me to do it, how hungry I was to give in.

But then I heard another voice — a woman's voice, faint but glassy. Mom's. I couldn't make out what she was saying, but I felt a pair of hands clasp me under my arms and draw me up. The water raced by until the moon appeared above me, then individual stars, then the peaks of the trees as I crashed through the surface and gasped for air. My lungs spasmed as they filled.

It took every ounce of strength I had to swim back to shore. I collapsed on the rocks, shivering, gulping air. The last thing I wanted to do was move, but I knew I had to get dressed, had to get warm. I managed to find my clothes, and then I stumbled through the woods to my tent. I should have made a fire, but I didn't have the energy, so I curled into a ball, pulling every blanket and every scrap of clothing I had over top of me, burying myself in them.

I lay there shaking, but then a slow warmth grew in my

chest and spread out through my arms and legs and the tips of my fingers. I heard Mom's voice again. Soft. Musical. As bright as a pin. The last thing I remembered before I tumbled into a dreamless sleep was the feel of her hands brushing across my forehead and down my cheek.

16

EVERY **NIGHT** for the next week I left Lucy's Promise and walked into Black River.

I wandered empty streets, from the shops and apartments near Main Street to the mansions at the north end of town. I tried the doorknob of every house I came to. If it turned, I'd go inside and drift from room to room, imagining myself as one of Benny's ghosts. I'd lie on unmade beds and sit at dusty dining room tables and on rumpled couches. I went through closets and explored attics and basements, digging out photo albums and children's toys and stacks of old letters. When I left, I'd put everything back just the way I found it so that it would be like no one had ever been there.

I never wore my mask or gloves, so I avoided any infected I saw, until the fifth night when I came upon a crowd gathered in Monument Park. The bulbs in the streetlights had burned out and never been replaced, so the infected had built a bonfire in the middle of the soccer field. A few dozen people gathered around it, drinking black-market booze and cooking hot dogs over the flames. I found a spot twenty or thirty feet away and crouched in the shadows to watch.

I recognized most of them, but they stood in odd

combinations, as if everyone in town had been tossed into a bag, shaken up, and spilled out again. Mrs. Stewart, my sophomore year English teacher, was standing with her arm around the waist of our old mailman, beaming. Mr. and Mrs. Ellery, who'd always been inseparable, were on opposite sides of the group. Mrs. Ellery had been absorbed into an entirely new family, and Mr. Ellery stood alone near the border of the park, looking lost and confused. A few pre-outbreak families had managed to stay together, but they were few and far between. I couldn't help but wonder where I would have ended up if I'd gotten infected that first night. Would I have a new family? A new name?

A familiar voice called out over the crowd. "Okay, I'll see you tomorrow, then. No! I have to go! I do! I have to!"

Mom was standing at the edge of a small circle of women. She laughed at something one of them said and then waved and headed toward the park exit. I left my spot and followed from a distance, losing her briefly when she slipped out of the circle of firelight. A second later I saw her climbing the rise that led to the street, and I settled in behind her.

The noise from the park faded as she turned onto Maitland and then Belvedere, where she stopped by a tall white fence. On the other side of it was a grassy slope that was covered with rosebushes. They were overgrown, spilling thorny runners and flowers out over Mom's head. She reached up for one of the blossoms, but her fingers barely touched the lowest petal. She tried again, and this time it seemed like there was a helium balloon trapped inside her chest. As it ascended, it drew the rest of her body along with it. Her chin lifted, and so did her shoulders and her hips. As she rose up onto the balls of her feet, one leg floated off the ground behind her, forming a straight line that stretched from the tips of her toes to the tips of her outstretched fingers. The phantom sound of violins started up in my head as she stood there perfectly poised. I felt Dad beside me, and you too. I could smell the perfume of the flowers as if I were standing right beside them.

And then, all at once, it was over. Mom plucked a flower off the branch and continued on her way.

We came to the end of a cul-de-sac and Mom climbed the front steps of a small two-story house. She pushed open the front door, calling out to someone as she went inside. The lights were on, but the curtains were drawn, so all I saw was her shadow moving toward the rear of the house. I circled around to the backyard and found a spot behind an oak tree.

Two windows looked into a living room. The shades were open, so I could see Mom as she came in and leaned against the window frame, the flower in her hand, its petals against her chest. She looked distant, thoughtful, as if she were searching for something out in the dark.

A man I'd never seen before came down the stairs behind her. He was about her age and built like a wrestler, with deep olive skin, and bald except for a fringe of black hair above his ears. Mom turned to him as he came into the room. He smiled wide and threw his arms around her, squeezing her close before leaning back to look into her eyes. He said something, and Mom nodded. And then he leaned in and kissed her.

Mom didn't flinch. She didn't resist. The man moved one hand to the small of her back while the other cupped her face. When he was done and they parted, he brushed his fingertips down her cheek and then stepped back and held out his hand. Mom took it, and they climbed the stairs together.

A few seconds later the lights went out and the house was dark.

My head buzzed as I walked back to Lucy's Promise. My arms and legs felt thick and numb. Sitting in front of my tent later that night, I replayed every second of what I'd seen. Mom turning toward that man as he came down the stairs. Mom lowering her head to his shoulder, then lifting her chin so he could kiss her. I watched it all over and over, hundreds of times, and as I did, the strangeness of it started to come into focus. The way she moved — it was as if she were under a spell. Or as if she were afraid. And hadn't she seemed that way the day I saw her in the alley too? Hadn't she been anxious as she looked over her shoulder?

An idea settled inside of me until it seemed so obvious, there couldn't have been any other explanation.

Since the first days of the outbreak, men like Tommasulo had targeted the newly infected. They were so trusting, they could be made to believe almost anything, made to *do* almost anything. What if this man was like that? All he would've had to do was get to Mom early and then hide her from the Guard until he convinced her that she was his wife. She'd never have any reason to suspect the truth, would never go to the Guard to find out who she was before the sixteenth — because she already knew. Mom hadn't abandoned us; she hadn't abandoned herself. She'd been stolen.

Everything in me wanted to run down the mountain and kick in their door, but I had to be smarter than that. The wait through the next day was excruciating. As soon as the sun was down I took everything I needed and went back to the house.

I hid in the yard until all the lights went out and a deep nighttime stillness settled over the neighborhood. I checked my mask and gloves and then zipped up my black sweatshirt, bringing the hood down low over my forehead. As I made my way around the side of the house, I slipped my knife from its sheath.

The doors were locked, but I found a basement window with a rotted-out frame. I popped it open, then climbed inside and crept through the dark until I came to a set of stairs that led up to the moonlit living room. There was an antique-looking couch draped with knitted blankets and lace doilies, lamps with gobs of crystal hanging from cut-glass shades. Ranks of pictures in silver frames sat on the mantel above the fireplace. It looked like something that would've belonged to an old lady, not a middle-aged man. He must have stolen the house too.

I crept up another set of stairs, carefully testing each one for creaks before committing my weight to it. The top floor was tiny, nothing but a short hallway of deeply worn wooden slats with two doors in the middle and one at the far end. They were all open. Moonlight filled the room at the end of the hall. I could see two figures lying beneath a white sheet.

My pulse beat in my throat. I closed my eyes and pictured Cardinal. I felt armor slapping down over my skin and wings growing from my back.

A floorboard groaned as I came into the bedroom. The man didn't stir, but Mom's eyes popped open and she shot upright against the headboard. I got to her before she could make a sound, clamping one gloved hand over her mouth and motioning for her to stay still with the other. She started to struggle when she saw the knife.

"I'm not going to hurt you," I whispered, letting her see me put it back in its sheath. "I need you to get up and come with me. Do you understand?"

There was a pause, and then she nodded slowly. I lifted my hand away from her mouth.

"Good. Let's move. Downstairs."

I motioned toward the door. She pushed aside the sheets and stood up, moving with that same dreamy obedience I'd seen the night before. Of course, I knew what it was now. She was terrified. I hated scaring her, but if it kept her quiet and doing what I said, I'd have to live with it. Once I got her up to Lucy's Promise, I'd explain everything, just like I'd done with Hannah.

I kept an eye on the man in the bed as she headed for the door. He was on his side, the sheets rising to mounds at his shoulders and his belly. My hand went to the hilt of the knife, and I felt some part of myself drain down into the blade. The steel edge hummed.

Mom's voice broke through her shock. It was small and trembling. "Don't hurt him. Please. I'll do whatever you want, just don't hurt him."

I felt a sliver of rage. She'd been taken in by him so completely that she wanted to *defend* him. I told myself she didn't know any better, *couldn't* have known any better. I nodded toward the door.

"Go. Now."

Mom took a last look at the man in the bed, then started down the hall toward the stairs. When we got to the first floor, she stopped in the living room, as if she were waiting for instructions. The front door was to my left, just beyond a small kitchen. We'd be home free in no time.

"Come on," I said, hurrying past her to the door. "We'll go out this way, and then —"

Something plowed into my back and sent me sprawling out in the entryway. When I turned over, I saw Mom standing by the kitchen table with a metal chair in her hands.

"Fred!" she screamed. "There's someone here! There's someone in the house!"

"No! Wait! You don't understand. That man, he isn't —"

The room exploded with light. The man came running

down the stairs with a baseball bat. I didn't hesitate. I pulled my knife and charged him, swinging as soon as he was within reach. The blade bit into the back of his hand, and I dragged it across his knuckles. He dropped the bat and fell into a heap at the foot of the stairs, bent in half over his injury, pressing it into his stomach. When he sat up again, his white T-shirt was soaked with blood. The red of it was electric in the bright lights. Throbbing.

"You have to listen to me," I said as Mom ran to him. "You're not who you think you are. This man isn't . . . he isn't . . ."

Darkness came flooding in from the corners of the room and closed in around the point where the man's hand was pressed to his belly. A stream of blood filled his lap and spilled out onto the floor. My stomach turned. The stench was so strong that I could smell it through my mask, like copper and lightning. Metallic chimes rang in my head. I stumbled backward toward the front door. My vision blurred. I was going to be sick.

I fumbled with the doorknob, my fingers slipping uselessly against the metal. Finally, I managed to turn it and fresh air flooded the room. I fell out onto the porch and down the stairs. The last thing I heard was Mom crying as I ran into the night.

I tried to make it back to Lucy's Promise but got only as far as Monument Park before I fell to my knees in the grass. I clawed off my mask and gulped at the air but couldn't seem to clear the stink of blood. It had seeped into my clothes and my skin and my hair. It filled my mouth. When I closed my eyes and saw that blaze of crimson splashed across the man's middle, I vomited into the grass until my throat burned. I wanted to pass out, but I forced myself up onto my feet and strapped on my mask. I had to get back to Lucy's Promise. Back to my camp.

"Quite a little tour you're taking."

A flashlight beam pierced the dark. A man's voice came from behind it.

"Six nights running now," he said. "Everybody's talking about some kid treating our town like his own private museum."

The voice was familiar, but I couldn't place it. I started backing away, but then another beam hit me and then another one after that, until I was frozen in a cage of light. Dark shapes loomed on the other side of the flashlights. And there were more behind them. I counted six men. Then seven. Then ten.

"Imagine my surprise when the descriptions of this kid started to sound a wee bit familiar."

I turned back to the voice. Light from behind me glanced off his shoulders, illuminating the pale, bald head and gleaming off the gold frames of his glasses. When he lowered his flashlight, I saw bruises on his face and around his neck. I looked over his shoulder toward Lucy's Promise, but it was lost in the darkness, too far to reach even if I ran.

I pulled my knife from its sheath. "I just want to leave."

A wave of laughter circled me.

"Well, son, I'd like to take a trip to Rio de Janeiro, but I think we're both gonna be disappointed."

"Please," I said. "All I want to do is —"

There was a rush of movement behind me, and then I was face-down in the dirt at Tommasulo's feet. More laughter. I got up and lunged at my attacker, but a boot hooked under my foot and I went down again. Another boot found my ribs and dug in. After that, they were all on me at once. Callused knuckles and boot heels. Blows landed on my arms, my back, my chest. Eventually the pain crested and started to fade, seeming more and more distant, like someone knocking on a faraway door. I wasn't afraid anymore. I wasn't in pain. I wasn't angry. I wasn't thinking about Mom or Dad or Hannah or Greer. Or you.

The last thing I remember is Tommasulo leaning over me and reaching for my mask. Before he could get a hold of it, a harsh light splashed across his face, followed by the wail of sirens. Someone grabbed me by the shoulders and pulled. After that, everything went black.

17

I WOKE UP in the Gardens of Null.

Cardinal was on his knees, with his back to me, watching a pack of dogs sniff through a mountain of garbage that had been left to rot. His armor was charred and dented, ripped in places and held together by wire and bandages that had gone a rusty brown from dried blood. On his back there were two ragged stumps where his wings had been.

The land around us was a sea of rubble — ruined streets, collapsed skyscrapers, piles of scorched concrete with rebar sticking out of them like cracked rib cages. The sky was a seething red, brushed with black smoke coming from the incinerators that ran night and day out near Abaddon.

When he spoke, the dying electronics in his mask made his voice sputter and wheeze.

"I tried to save them, but I failed. Black Eagle. Blue Jay. Kestrel Kain. Rex Raven. Goldfinch. Lord Starling. Sally. My Sally."

I put my hand on his shoulder. A fever ran through the broken steel.

I said, "There's only one thing to do."

Cardinal turned toward me. One of his electronic eyes had been put out, so I could see all the way down to the real one. It was bloodshot and glassy. The chrome blade of a butcher knife shimmered in my hand. I held it out to him.

"Forget."

I sat up with a gasp. I was on a couch in a small dark room. My mask was still on and so were my gloves. Even my knife was where it was supposed to be. Every inch of my body ached.

There was a window just above my head. I strained to look out, but it was too dark to see what lay beyond it. I could hear footsteps, though, and an odd whispering sound. Someone was out there.

I slowly got to my feet. The pain made my head swim, but I managed to hobble out of the room and into a narrow hallway. At the end, there was a soft, amber-colored light. I made my way to it, one hand against the wall to hold myself up. When I came to the end of the hall, I turned a corner and found a large open space. Candles sat on every available surface, their warm glow illuminating a maze of floor-to-ceiling shelves. I was in the library.

I wound through the stacks, surprised to find entire rows of shelves sitting empty. It looked like nearly half of the library's books were gone. Most of what remained lay in messy heaps in the aisles. I stepped over a mountain of Stephen King paperbacks and a crumbling pyramid of Tennessee Williams and Eugene O'Neill. Some had pages torn out of them; some had been ripped in two.

I found Freeman not far from the circulation desk, taking books from the floor and methodically re-shelving them. His coat was draped over a chair, leaving him in his dingy black pants and a sweat-stained shirt with the sleeves rolled up to his elbows. He glanced up when I came in, but he didn't say anything, just nodded toward one of the empty shelves. Sitting on it was a bottle of water and a bottle of aspirin. I shook four into my palm and chased them with a gulp of water.

"Thanks."

Freeman slid another book onto the shelf. I figured I should start heading back to Lucy's Promise, but I was too tired, too sore. The bruises along my chest and sides screamed as I lowered myself onto the floor beside the collected works of Charles Dickens. The spine of *Great Expectations* was broken. The cover of *A Tale of Two Cities* had been torn off and tossed aside.

"What happened?"

Freeman knelt by another pile of books and started turning each one over in his hands, lovingly checking it for damage.

"The latest skirmish in an old war," he said.

"What war?"

"The library versus the powers that be."

The powers that be? There's no way the Guard would have done something like this, which left only one possibility. "Martinson Vine did this? Why?"

He selected a handful of volumes and took them to an empty shelf.

"Since the beginning of time, rulers have held on to power by making the masses believe the order they impose is permanent and inevitable. That resisting it would be like resisting gravity." He nestled a book into place. "What could be a greater threat to that than the contemplation of alternate realities?"

Freeman stepped back and brushed his fingertips along the spines of the books he'd just arranged. He seemed so different from the last time I saw him. He stood straighter. His eyes were sharper. He was calm. Was it because he was here in the library? Or was it something else?

There was the sound of a distant siren and then a flash of red lights as a Guard vehicle passed by and continued on down the street. I was thrown back to earlier that night — my back in the mud, Tommasulo leaning over me, and then someone's hands on my shoulders, dragging me away.

"You were the one who called the Guard," I said. "The one who pulled me out when those men were —"

Freeman nodded.

"Why?"

He returned to his pile of books and held one up so I could see the cover. *To Kill a Mockingbird.*

"I don't understand."

Freeman set the book down again and went back to his work, moving between the shelves and the stacks on the floor. "I came here the night of the sixteenth," he said. "By then I understood what was about to happen to me, so I wrote down everything I knew about myself. Things I'd done. Things I'd seen and thought and believed. I decided that once the virus had finished its work, all I'd have to do was read what I'd written and I'd be able to recreate the man I was."

Freeman finished the shelf he was working on, but instead of returning for more books, he took one of the candles and sat on the carpet across from me, careful to keep a gulf of distance between us. Yellow light flickered over the creases of his face.

"But the next day, when I read what I'd written, it became clear to me that I had no desire to be the man I once was."

Freeman looked out across the mountain range of books scattered across the room.

"That's when I realized what this place actually is," he said. "It's not a repository of paper and ink. It's the memory of the world, the memory of a thousand worlds, from the Big Bang to the darkness that lies in wait at the end of time. For weeks, I didn't sleep. I barely ate. I did nothing but read, constructing Freeman Wayne sentence by sentence from this place's memory instead of my own. One book became my heart. One my mind. One my soul."

He took the copy of *To Kill a Mockingbird* in both hands,

as if he was afraid it might crumble to dust and blow away. He opened it, and for a while the library hush was filled with the dry sweep of pages turning. When he looked up at me again over that book's spine, there was a clarity in his eyes I'd never seen before.

"Tell me," he said. "What raw materials did you use to build Cardinal Cassidy?"

"I'm not—"

"I know you're not infected."

Freeman waited, his sea blue eyes never wavering.

"I thought you said that you could just look at someone and see their past and their future."

He studied me a second longer, and then a slow grin softened the lines of his face. He closed the book and set it in his lap.

"What were you doing at Mr. Addad's house?"

"Who's Mr. —" Then it hit me. The man in the house. The man who had taken Mom. "How did you know I was there? Were you following me?"

Freeman said nothing. I shrugged and picked at a stray bit of carpet. "I thought I knew the woman there."

"Sara?"

The word hit me with a jolt. So that was her name now. Sara. I nodded.

"She's been good for him."

I made myself look up. "What do you mean?"

"Sara found Fred wandering in the woods two weeks after

the outbreak. He was alone. Nearly starving. She got him to the Guard. It turned out his mother had died a week before the outbreak and he was in town for her funeral. That's her house they're staying in. He and Sara have been together ever since."

"So he didn't . . ."

"What?"

I swallowed back an ache in my throat. "He didn't . . . take her?"

An even greater intensity flooded Freeman's eyes. "So *that's* why you came," he said. "You wanted to rescue her."

Freeman assured me that Fred wasn't that kind of man. That he was gentle and seemed to love Mom. Every bit of the exhaustion and pain I'd felt over the last few days came surging back at once. Maybe I should have been happy to know that Mom wasn't with some monster, but all I could think about was how she had gone to the Guard to get some stranger his name back, and had left her own behind.

When Freeman was done, I forced myself up and started toward the front door.

"Did you know her?"

I turned back. Freeman was still sitting on the floor, surrounded by his books.

"Sara," he said. "Did you know her?"

From where I was standing I could see down a line of shelves to the front desk and the windows behind it. While we'd been talking, the sun had begun to rise, filling the library with a blueish early-morning light. Near the desk was a small round table surrounded by four plastic chairs. I saw the four of us sitting there that first week in Black River when we came with Mom and Dad to get our library cards.

"No," I said. "I didn't know her. Thanks for the help, Freeman."

My legs shook as I made my way through the stacks. But I didn't go straight to the front door. I veered off into the dimmer sections of the library, wandering aimlessly until I decided to stop lying to myself. I knew where I was going.

I found all four volumes of *Cardinal and the Brotherhood of Wings* on a shelf toward the back. Their scarlet spines seemed to glow in the low light, standing out against all the others. I ran my finger down the length of them. A bell tolled in my chest as I read each title:

VOLUME 1. THE RADIANT CITY AND THE EMERALD HORDE

VOLUME 2. SALLY SPARROW DANCES AMONG THE STARS

VOLUME 3. BEHOLD, ABADDON

VOLUME 4. EXILE IN THE GARDENS OF NULL

I picked up the first volume and became lost in it immediately. The pain of my injuries faded as I breezed through the Brotherhood's battles with Madame Night, Slim John, and Professor Hurricane. I was right there when Blue Jay learned what being a leader meant on the day the Brotherhood was trapped in the Gray Waste. When Black Eagle and Rex Raven survived the three trials of the King of the Molemen. When Sally Sparrow danced among the stars.

Before I knew it, I was at the end of the second volume and staring at *that* page, you know the one, the panel everybody said won Dad his Hugo. The one that made him famous.

The Rose Prison.

I'd seen it a thousand times, but it still stopped me cold. It was so simple. Cardinal and Sally Sparrow imprisoned at the heart of an immense rose of coral-colored steel. I'd looked at the panel a thousand times and still couldn't understand how Dad had managed to make something that was so beautiful and so horrifying at the same time.

The sun was fully up by then and the room was bright and warm. The green curve of Lucy's Promise showed in one of the south-facing windows, but I knew I couldn't go back there, not yet. There was somewhere I needed to go first.

I took the Brotherhood comics off the shelf and tucked them under my arm as I walked out of the library.

Sun-bleached trash blew across the parking lot of the Seeger Museum. Trees that had once been trimmed into lollipop rounds like something out of *Willy Wonka* were overgrown and leaning.

I pushed aside the Guard's yellow NO TRESPASSING tape and ducked through a gap in the chainlink fence that surrounded the property. The building's glass front doors and the steel roll-down barrier had been smashed, maybe the night of the outbreak, maybe by people looking for shelter later on. I found an opening big enough and squeezed inside.

Sunlight filtered down through the skylights. Most of the artwork had been evacuated by the Guard long ago, so the walls were empty. Just ghostly rectangles where the paintings used to hang. I felt my way through the darker hallways until I came to a door set in a concrete wall. The metal sign riveted beside it read RICHARD SERRA: *TORQUED ELLIPSES*.

I stepped through the doorway into that immense room.

The first time I'd seen the sculptures, that day we came to Black River on a house-hunting trip, I didn't even understand what I was looking at. Twenty-foot-high walls of rust-colored steel all lined up in a concrete room. So what? It wasn't until we got closer to the first one that I saw that its walls were curved. The wall was actually a ring with an opening on one side that led into an empty space that was easily as big as our apartment in Brooklyn.

I ran to the second ellipse — two rings, one inside the other. I got to the third one before any of you and discovered a maze of rings within rings, three or four of them, the openings staggered around their circumference, making a kind of spiral. It was bright inside when I first entered, but the way the walls leaned into or away from each other as they curved sent me from day to twilight and back to day again. I staggered along like I was on the deck of a sailing ship. When I was finally let out into the heart of the ellipse, I was so dizzy

I fell right on my butt. The walls soared over my head, bending up and away toward the skylights. The sun made their brown steel seem warm and alive. I felt sure that if I laid my hand against one, I'd feel a pulse moving just beneath the metal.

And then the three of you came in, you and Mom a little giddy, Dad quiet. I remember how we all ended up on our backs in the middle of the floor, taking turns describing the ellipse. You said it was a carnival funhouse. I said it was the hull of a ship we were sailing through a storm. Mom said the walls were like the petals of an immense rose. When Dad's turn came, he was quiet for a long time before he said that it wasn't a rose, it was a prison, and we were all trapped inside.

Now I made my way through the dusty room, passing the other ellipses and going straight to the third. I found the rift and walked inside, curving around the spiraling walls, the palm of my hand skimming along the rough steel. When I reached the center of it, I dropped the Brotherhood comics in a pile and sat on the scuffed concrete floor. The skylights overhead were frosted with dust and bird droppings, turning the light into a spoiled-milk haze.

I pulled off my mask and lay flat on my back. The walls towered above me. I heard Freeman's voice in my ear. *What raw materials did you use to build Cardinal Cassidy?*

The trip to Lake George was supposed to fix everything. I know it probably seemed out of nowhere when I first mentioned it that morning at breakfast, but the truth was I'd been planning it for weeks. Six full days in a two-bedroom cabin a hundred and fifty miles from Black River. All of us packed in together just like it was when we were back in Brooklyn. At first I was pretty sure Dad was going to flat-out refuse, but I guess the nudging from Mom helped.

I got more and more excited as the weeks stretched by. It was kind of like when you buy someone the perfect Christmas present and it feels like you'll jump out of your skin if the day doesn't hurry up and get there so you can give it to them. I think I drove you a little crazy, didn't I? Admit it, in the weeks leading up to Lake George, the decision to save money by living at home instead of in the dorm your first year in college was seeming like a truly terrible one.

Anyway, the day finally came, and there we were, you and me and Mom. We'd loaded our bags into the car and were standing at the end of the driveway, waiting for Dad. Autumn had turned the slopes of Lucy's Promise and the rest of the Highlands scarlet and gold. The air was crisp and smelled like dry leaves and fireplace smoke. I felt like there were fireworks going off inside my chest. I couldn't stop talking.

"Did I tell you guys about the boats? You can rent them at the place and then take them all the way across the lake. They have rowboats and motorboats and those ones that have the pedals, like bicycles. Oh! And there are horses."

Mom put her hand on my shoulder, as if she were trying

to keep me from leaping into the air. "Yes, you told us about the horses."

You rolled your eyes as you tapped away on your phone, probably texting that girl from your art class. "*And* all the great antiquing opportunities. Seriously, Card," you said, "what sixteen-year-old kid gets pumped about looking at antiques?"

You were messing with me, but I didn't care. Right then, I was invulnerable to it.

"You'll see. You and me, bro. We've got us a date with some reasonably priced mid-century modern home furnishings!"

"You are such a freak."

"I can see you're a tough sell, kid. That's why I saved the best for last. Did I mention the twelve miles of hiking trails? Or the generous daily breakfast prepared to order by a genuine French chef?"

Mom pulled out her phone, checked the time, and then put it back. It was the third time she'd done it in the last twenty minutes.

"Dad just has a few things to finish up," I said. "And then he'll be ready."

Mom tried to smile, but it was a poor effort. She kept her eyes locked on the front door. I pulled out my brochures and put the finishing touches on the plan. We'd probably all want a little rest after the drive, so I thought naps first and then we could cook out on the charcoal grill the place provided. I'd already talked to the manager about the best grocery store to go to in town for steaks and things. After that I figured you and I could go over to the main house and grab a whole bunch of board games. Day Two was definitely horseback riding and then maybe a trip into town. Day Three was —

Footsteps on the sidewalk. My heart jumped into my throat. When I looked up, though, it wasn't Dad coming out of the house, it was Mom going in.

"Mom, no, wait! He just needs more time! He'll be here in —"

Mom slammed the door behind her, and the fight started almost immediately. Mom yelled. Dad yelled back. I could hear every word, almost as if there were no walls between us at all. It was a familiar enough sound by then, but standing there with those brochures clenched in my fists, I felt like there was this iron bar running down the middle of me and someone had taken it in both hands and shaken it.

I turned to you, but you had your head down and your fists jammed in your jacket pockets so hard I could make out the peaks and valleys of your knuckles through the black corduroy.

"We can still get there before dark," I said. "We can take one of the boats out on the lake. Or maybe Mom and Dad can. I brought the Xbox. Me and you could hook it up and —"

You looked up from the sidewalk. Your eyes were angry slits, rimmed in red, and your jaw was clenched. I found myself stepping back, moving away from you.

"It's going to be fine," I said. "We'll be away six whole days. By the time we get back, everything will be the way it —"

"You're just like them."

"Tennant —"

You turned your back and walked away, your body framed by Lucy's Promise, which autumn had turned into a wall of flames. I wanted to say something. I wanted to call out to you, to stop you, to tell you that everything was going to be okay, but I couldn't talk and I couldn't move because that iron bar was still rattling inside of me. You turned a corner and were gone, leaving me alone on the sidewalk as the house and the street and the world shook with Mom's and Dad's voices. I didn't see you again until late the next night.

October sixteenth.

I rolled up off the floor and knelt before the ellipse. You were all there, pressing in closer, surrounding me until I could hardly breathe. I pulled my arm back and drove my fist into the wall as hard as I could. It was like punching a downed power line. I hit the floor and curled around my throbbing hand, waiting for the pain to burn you all out of my head, knowing that it never could.

18

AT SOME POINT I must have fallen asleep. When I woke up, Hannah was across from me.

It was late, either that same night or the next. She was alone, sitting next to the rift in the wall with a backpack in her lap. A lantern sat in the middle of the ellipse beside my mask and the pile of comics. It filled the chamber with an amber glow.

"Greer ran out to get some supplies. He'll be back in a minute."

Hannah didn't look at me as she spoke. She kept her eyes on the concrete floor, twisting at the backpack's strap.

"How'd you find me?"

She shrugged. "We asked around. Some people saw you heading this way."

I started to get up, wincing as I did. "Is everybody —"

"Everybody's fine," she snapped. "Benny has mostly stopped asking why you just up and left, which is good, since Greer and I ran out of excuses a few days ago."

The rough steel of the ellipse raked across my back as I fell against it. Freeman's aspirin had long since worn off, leaving my body feeling like a bag of splintered bones. Bruises snaked around my knuckles like vines. My hand was swollen. I flexed my fingers to make sure nothing was broken.

"You okay?"

I drew my hand back into the shadows and said I was fine. Hannah turned to stare into the darkness on the other side of the rift in the wall. I looked up at the skylight, hoping I might see a few stars through the dirty glass haze, but the sky was blank, like something that had been hollowed out.

"These are your dad's."

She had pulled the stack of comics closer to her. I nodded.

"I read the first two while you were sleeping," she said. "They're good. I like Blue Jay."

"Dad based him on this kid he knew growing up."

She picked *Behold, Abaddon* out of the stack and paused at the cover, struck by it the way people always were. She turned it over, but of course there was nothing on the back. No explanation at all. Dad had been so proud of that.

"It's an origin story," I said. "Well, the first half is, anyway."

Hannah glanced up at me. Her eyes were a deep liquid brown in the lantern light. I held out my hand, and she slid the book across the floor. The cover of *Behold, Abaddon* had always been one of my favorites. That clawed hand exploding out of the sidewalk. The Brotherhood reeling back in horror. I slipped on my gloves and opened it to the two-page splash that began and ended the book. A city of crumbling black towers that stood against a blood red sky streaked with smoke.

"A hundred years before the Brotherhood, there was a nuclear war," I said, tracing the lines of the drawing with one finger. "Liberty City was one of the last cities left, only it wasn't called Liberty City then. It was called Abaddon."

I moved from the city to the desert plain that enclosed it.

"It was surrounded by this wasteland called the Gardens of Null."

I turned the page. A gleaming alien ship breaking through the atmosphere above the ruined city.

"Then one day the Volanti appeared. They said they were the last survivors of a war that almost destroyed their own planet, and they wanted to make sure something like that never happened to anyone else. They remade Abaddon into Liberty City and created the Brotherhood of Wings to watch over it. Then they disappeared."

"Why?"

Hannah was leaning deep into the glow of the lantern.

"Nobody knew," I said. "After a few decades with no sign of them, most people thought they were some kind of fairy tale and went on with their lives. But then, a hundred years after they first arrived, the Volanti reappeared."

"Where had they gone?"

I turned to the middle of the volume. Abaddon was Liberty

City again. The skies were clear and blue. The Brotherhood's Aerie sparkled in the sun.

"They never really left," I said. "They just went into hiding. Only a few Volanti had made it to Earth so they decided to wait until their numbers grew and the world became something worth conquering."

"So it was a trap," Hannah said. "They were never trying to save anybody."

I nodded.

"But the Brotherhood stopped them."

I wanted to say yes, the Brotherhood saved the day. But I couldn't even open my mouth. I paged through the last half of the story, but stopped before I got to those three pages toward the end.

"Card? Come on, you're killing me."

Part of me wanted to rip that volume in half and toss it away, but who was I to keep it from her? I sent it skidding back across the floor and into her hands.

Hannah leaned against the wall and opened it to the middle. She tucked her hair behind her ears and pored over the pages, moving from panel to panel, eagerly at first, but then more and more slowly as she got toward the end. I knew those panels so well I felt like I was reading them right along with her, or like I was sitting beside Dad as he drew every line and wrote every word.

I could tell when Hannah got to those three pages. Her

whole body stiffened. She read them once, then again, and then she was still for a very long time before shutting the book and pushing it away from her. All the air had gone out of the room and the light from the lantern felt small and feeble.

Footsteps echoed upstairs. Greer. I grabbed my mask and headed for the door.

"Card, wait."

I stumbled through the spiral. Greer was there when I came out on the other side.

"Buddy! Good to see —"

He dodged out of the way as I ran past, strapping on my mask as I went. He called my name, but I kept going, up the stairs and into the lobby. Those three pages unfurled through the dark. Sally Sparrow. Cardinal. Blue Jay. Then you were there too. And Mom and Dad. And me.

I ducked through the opening in the door and suddenly realized that I'd left Dad's comics behind. Part of me wanted to just go, but I knew I couldn't. I slipped into the shadows of a nearby hallway and waited. Surely Hannah and Greer would head back to Lucy's Promise soon. Minutes ticked by. An hour, maybe. Finally I couldn't wait any longer. Who cared if they were there or not.

I made my way back down the stairs and into the Serra room. It was quiet. Maybe they'd gone out another way. I passed the first two sculptures and started into the spiral of the third. There were voices up ahead.

". . . turn up anybody who saw what happened last night?"

It was Hannah. I eased myself into the dark a few feet away from the opening that led to the center of the ellipse. The lantern light threw two sketchy shadows against an inside wall.

"I talked to a guy who lives near the park," Greer replied. "He said there was some kind of fight the Guard broke up. Somebody on the ground. A bunch of people around him."

"He see who they were?"

"Couldn't make out the face of the guy on the ground, but it sounds like it was Card. Said it was too dark to really see any of the people wailing on him, except for one. Older white dude. Bald, with glasses. That sound like the one who tried to grab you?"

There was a pause, and then the shadow Hannah nodded.

Greer got up, appeared and disappeared as he stalked through the ellipse. "What the hell was he even *doing* down here?"

"Looking for a fight?"

"What? No way. Card?"

"You didn't see him that day he found me."

"You mean the day he saved your *life?*"

"You weren't there," Hannah said. "You didn't see it. The way he went after those guys. And what about the morning he left? The way he looked? He was one second from hitting *you.* You had to have seen that."

"So — what? You're saying Card's *dangerous?* That's insane."

"How do you know he's not?"

"Because I know Card."

"All you know is what he's told you," Hannah said. "You don't know anything about him from before."

"Before doesn't matter."

"Of course it matters!" Hannah said. "How do you even know for sure that he doesn't remember you? I mean, how likely is that? It's a small town. You guys went to the same school. He says he doesn't remember you, but—"

"I know he remembers me."

I moved closer to the opening. Greer was sitting up against one of the walls, his arms crossed over his chest, his head down.

Hannah leaned in toward him. "What? How do you know?"

Greer shrugged. "Things he says. The way he looks at me sometimes."

"But you've never asked him to—"

He shook his head.

"Why not? You said you think about it all the time. You said—"

"If Card thinks I'm better off not knowing, then maybe I am."

"You trust him that much?"

Greer laid his head against the steel wall, looking up at the skylight. He shrugged helplessly.

"He's my best friend."

Not long after that, they decided it was too late to hike back up the mountain. They pulled sleeping bags from their packs and blew out the lantern, dropping us into darkness. Once they were asleep, it would have been the perfect time to get my things and go, but I didn't move. I sat there in the spiral with my back against the wall, my eyes closed, hearing Greer's words over and over in my head.

Greer came up to Lucy's Promise for the first time just before Thanksgiving. I was leaving the supply shed when I heard someone walking up the trail. Not knowing what to expect, I ducked back inside and watched through a crack in the door. As soon as I saw who it was, I dropped what I was carrying and reached for my knife.

"Hello?" he called. "Anybody here?"

There was something off about his voice. It wasn't the growl I remembered. It was lighter, softer, less certain. For a second I thought maybe it wasn't Greer Larson at all, just someone who looked liked him, but then he came closer, and there was no question. Before I could decide what to do, the first two kids appeared behind him. Ren and Makela. They were a mess. Blank-eyed, in dirty clothes. Carrie came next. Then Isaac and Tomiko. They all huddled around Greer. He made a joke I didn't hear, and they laughed nervously. I came out of the shed slowly and stood between the cabins, my hand resting on the hilt of the knife.

"Hi there!" Greer chirped when he saw me. "Few quick questions."

"Uh . . . okay."

He waved his arms around the campsite and the surrounding woods. "All this — it's not a mirage, right?"

"No. It's real."

"Perfect!" Greer clapped his hands in front of him and looked back at the kids. "It's cool, guys. It's *not* a mirage." Back to me. "And are these cabins yours or are they for, you know, whoever?"

"No, they're not mine."

"Great. Awesome. Last question. You ready?"

I nodded.

"You don't by any chance know who the hell I am, do you?"

He gave me that grin of his, the one that would soon become a daily part of my life, but that I'd never seen the slightest hint of up until that point. I hadn't even been sure he *could* smile. And all at once, I understood. Greer Larson was gone. This person had his face and his voice but he was someone else entirely. My hand fell away from the knife.

"No," I said. "Never seen you before in my life."

I don't know how many times I'd told myself what a good thing I'd done for him in that moment, what a friend I'd been. I'd never considered until right then, sitting there against that steel wall in the dark, that maybe I had it backwards. Maybe I hadn't been a friend to him at all.

The next morning, Hannah and Greer found me lying

against the wall of the ellipse and said they were heading back to camp. I nodded and let them pass, listening to their footsteps as they left the Serra room and climbed to the lobby. Once they were gone, I went inside and began gathering up the comics, but stopped the second my hand touched *Behold, Abaddon*. I stared at that cover for a long time before opening it and slowly turning to those pages.

I thought maybe seeing them again after all that time would feel different. Maybe the horror wouldn't be as sharp, maybe that sick feeling in my gut would be gone. But I was wrong. It was as if no time had passed at all. I felt exactly the same as I did the very first time I saw them.

Sally Sparrow on her knees, beaten bloody, her armor torn, the barrel of a gun pressed to the back of her head as she cried.

Cardinal, wings flailing as he screams across the Liberty City skyline, desperate to warn the others about his discovery of secret protocols the Volanti buried deep in the Brotherhood armor that, when activated, would render them utterly helpless.

An explosion of glass as Cardinal smashes through the window, and then —

Sally Sparrow lying crumpled on her side, her hands tied behind her back, her lifeless body framed in the same pool of blood that surrounds the rest of the Brotherhood. Black Eagle. Kestrel Kain. Rex Raven. Goldfinch. Lord Starling. Blue Jay.

Cardinal sees that he's too late. They're all gone. He's the only one left.

I dropped my face into my hands and cried until my throat burned. When I was done, I closed the book and looked up at the walls of the ellipse. What was it, really? A carousel? A ship? A rose? A prison? Right then it didn't feel like any of those things. It felt like an empty room in a house where no one had lived in a long time.

I stepped outside the museum. The rising sun was painting the sky above Lucy's Promise pink and gold. I tightened the straps on my mask and started the long walk back. I left Dad's comics behind.

19

A COUPLE OF DAYS later I was sitting by my tent when Gonzalez emerged from the woods.

"Love the new digs, Cassidy! Very Yoda in Dagobah. Luckily, Mr. Larson's quite the spymaster, or I never would have found you."

For the first time since I'd known him, Gonzalez wasn't wearing his Guard uniform, just camo shorts and a Green Lantern T-shirt. I was about to ask him if it was casual Friday, but then I saw the backpack he had over his shoulder and it hit me how much time had passed.

This is it. He's leaving.

He dug a slip of paper out of his pocket and dropped it in front of me as he sat on a nearby tree stump.

"What's this?" I picked it up and turned it over. A picture of Mr. Tommasulo. Two of them, actually — a front and a side view.

"That the guy who went after Hannah?" Gonzalez asked, then pointed to the bruises on my face. "Guy who gave you that beating?"

"How'd you —"

"Chitchatting with the guys who answered the call that night," he said. "I thought the kid sounded like you, but then I thought that would be impossible because A, Card said he was keeping his ass up on the mountain where it belonged, and B, if something like that happened, Card *definitely* would have told me."

"Listen, Gonzalez—"

"Damn it, Card! This animal messes with you again, and this is how I hear about it?"

"Well, it's over now, right? They got him."

"That's not the point!" he shouted.

I started to argue, but then I dropped my head into my hands. "Yeah. I know. Sorry, Hec. Look, things have been kind of..."

What? Things have been kind of what? I didn't even know how to start.

"You all right?"

I looked up. Gonzalez has that type of face that always looks like he's smiling even when he isn't. I nodded. "So, they going to put him away?"

"Oh, *hell* yes. They found a ton of seriously creepy stuff in the dude's house when they went to talk to him. He and a few of his buddies are going to be spending the rest of their natural lives in a detention center. Thank God for Freeman Wayne, right?"

"What? Why Freeman?"

"He's the guy that tipped them off," Gonzalez said. "Waltzed right into their HQ and ratted the guy out for what he did to you and for an attempted robbery and assault one of his buddies committed earlier that same night. Crazy, huh?"

I picked up the mug shot of Tommasulo again. First Freeman saved me in the park, and then this. Why would a guy spend a year playing hermit in that library and then out of nowhere decide to become my own personal Superman? It didn't make any sense.

"Hey," Gonzalez said, "did I tell you? Word is they're going to be screening footage from that new *Cloak and Dagger* movie at the Con. Supposed to be hot."

I dropped the picture, then looked from Gonzalez to the backpack next to him. "So you're really heading out, huh?"

He snapped a twig in half and tossed it into the woods. "Day after tomorrow. Rest of the Guard will be pulling out pretty soon after that."

"Hear anything new about the Marvins' plans for us?"

He shook his head. "They're buttoned up tight. All I know about is that carnival Raney is throwing next week."

"Carnival?"

"Yeah, turns out he wasn't kidding about doing something fun for you guys. It's going to be down in the park. Rides and food and stuff. Hear they're even carting in a Ferris wheel. Jerks are waiting until after we pull out. Guess they don't feel like springing for a little cotton candy for their brothers in the

Guard. Greer and Hannah are taking the kids to it. You didn't know?"

"Guess I've been a little out of touch lately."

"Yeah, look, about that —"

Before he could finish, I turned and grabbed his portfolio out of my tent. "I got a chance to look at your stuff," I said. "The drawings are solid. Really good. Like I said, I'm not an expert or anything, but if I were you, I might ditch the Wolverine and do another woman or two. Batgirl maybe? Or Ms. Marvel. Supergirl could be good. Maybe even —"

He snatched the portfolio out of my hands and threw it on the ground.

"Gonzalez, what are you —"

"Come with me."

"*What?*"

He leaned forward on the stump. "I can get you out of here *today*, man. They'll put you in isolation for twenty-four hours to confirm you're not infected, and then we're out of here."

"But everything's fine now," I said. "Tommasulo's in —"

"This isn't about him," Gonzalez interrupted. "And everything's *not* fine. Listen, me and you, we go to Comic Con, and then after that . . . you don't want to go stay with whatever family you've got on the outside, that's fine, my folks are in the Bronx. I've already talked to them. You can stay with them while you finish high school, and then you start looking at colleges. You can —"

"No."

"Why not? What the hell are you doing here, man? There's a whole world out there!"

"There's a whole world here, too."

Gonzalez looked around at the sagging trees and the vines and the twilight gloom. He shook his head.

"Yeah," he said. "Hell of a world you got yourself here."

He kept his eyes locked on me, but I didn't waver. Didn't look away. Finally he shook his head and pulled something out of his pocket. It hit the ground in front of me. A cell phone.

"My number's programmed in," he said. "It's got a full battery, and there's a tower just over on the next mountain, so you'll always have a good signal. If you change your mind — shut up, let me talk — if you change your mind, call me. Even if I'm already gone. You want out of here, you call me and I'll make it happen double quick. Got it?"

I picked up the phone and turned it over in my hand. I nodded.

"Now get up," Gonzalez said.

"What?"

"Dude, just do it. Stand up."

As soon as I did, his hands clasped my back and he pulled me into a hug. I could hear his heart beating alongside my ear. How long had it been since someone hugged me? As hard as I tried to remember, I couldn't.

"You take care of yourself," he said in a choked-up whisper. "You need anything, you send up the bat signal."

I said I would. Gonzalez pulled me in tighter, then let me go. His eyes were shining. He wiped them with the back of his hand and then tucked his portfolio under his arm.

"So I guess . . . I guess I'll see ya around."

My throat ached, like I hadn't had a drink of water in days. I flashed back to that first time he'd come up the mountain. It seemed like the second someone walked in the door, they were on their way out again.

"Yeah," I said. "See ya around, Hec."

He took his backpack and started off through the brush. After a few steps, he turned back.

"How about Storm?" he said. "For the portfolio."

I thought for a second. "Yeah, but it's gotta be mohawk-and-leather-jacket Storm," I said. "That's the only good Storm."

He grinned. "Yeah. Definitely. Take it easy, kid."

Gonzalez turned away again. Leaves and branches crunched under his feet as he walked away. The sounds grew fainter and fainter, as if the silence was rushing back in to cover his tracks. Just before he disappeared from view, he turned back one more time and waved. I waved too. A few seconds later he was a smudge in the trees, and then it was like he'd never been there at all.

Greer's camp looked deserted when I came down the trail.

Were they at the supply drop? I tried to count back to the day I went to town with him and the kids, but it felt like that was a million years ago. I tightened the straps of my mask, then walked through the cabins, gathering up a few of the things that were scattered around — our football, the croquet set, some board games. I put everything back in the supply shed and was about to leave when I had an idea. I pushed some old camping gear out of the way and rummaged through the dusty shelves. When I found what I was looking for, I filled my arms and went back outside.

A door slammed shut. Hannah came out of the dining hall with Snow Cone and Hershey Bar trotting along behind. She didn't see me. They went inside Astrid's cabin and closed the door. Nerves twisted my stomach in knots.

I checked my mask and gloves again and then, since my hands were full, I kicked at the base of the cabin door. It opened a crack and Snow Cone shot out, bowling me over onto my butt. She forced herself into my lap, tongue lolling, her stubby tail wagging a hundred times a minute. I rubbed at her side, shying away from her rash until I saw that it was nearly gone.

"Looks like somebody's been taking her medicine, huh, girl?"

"Kids take turns giving it to her."

Hannah was standing just inside the door, her hand resting on the knob.

"You looking for Greer?"

I shook my head. She gazed out over the empty camp. I thought she was going to tell me to leave, but she backed into the dimness of the cabin, leaving the door open. I gathered the things I'd taken from the supply shed and followed her inside.

She was set up in the back corner. She didn't have much, just a cot and a few stacks of clothes. Some of the kids' drawings were pinned to the wall around her bed. A psychedelic landscape that was clearly Astrid's hung next to a blueprint-like sketch of the bridge over Black River Falls that could only have been done by Makela.

Hannah sat on the edge of her cot and patted the space beside her. Hershey Bar jumped up and lay his head in her lap. I found a spot on a bunk across the room and tried to figure out what to say.

"Oh, hey. I talked to Gonzalez. The Guard arrested those guys who tried to grab you when you were first infected. So no need to go around in disguise anymore, I guess."

"Good," she said without really looking at me. "That's good."

Everything went quiet again. I could feel the seconds ticking by.

"So how's the life of a camp counselor?"

She tried to smile, but it looked forced, tense. She pinched the key around her neck with two fingers and slid it back and forth on its band.

"They need a lot," I said. "Don't they?"

Hannah nodded. "Did you know Crystal wets her bed sometimes?"

I shook my head.

"She didn't want anybody to know. Not even the other girls. I caught her cleaning up one night, and now it's our little secret. And then Astrid and Makela are fighting half the time and Tomiko has nightmares. Oh, and Greer found out who Cash and Shan are. Ricky and Margo Westlake."

"They're brother and sister."

Hannah nodded. "Their folks are here, but infected. We tried to get them together but it didn't really work. So we've been dealing with that."

We were quiet a moment. Snow Cone came in panting and lay down at my feet.

Hannah nodded toward the stack in my arms. "What've you got there?"

Oh. Right. "The camp has a few shelves of books in the back of the supply shed. It's not much, mostly kids' stuff, but I thought . . . well, I thought maybe one of the good things about losing your memory is that you get to read all your favorite books again for the first time. Bits and pieces might seem familiar but, you know. I made some guesses about what you'd like."

I handed over the stack, and she went through them. "*Pride and Prejudice. Great Expectations. The Dark is Rising. Harry Potter. Bridge to Terabithia.*"

"I liked that last one a lot when I was a kid," I said. "It's kind of sad, but good."

She thanked me, then set them on the nightstand next to her cot. Snow Cone nudged my calf with her nose. I reached down and scratched her ears.

"Gonzalez said you guys were going to some kind of carnival."

"Next week," Hannah said. "Whole town will be there. They're trucking in rides and games and stuff for the kids."

"I heard a Ferris wheel."

"Yeah, can you believe that? Raney said there's going to be some kind of big announcement too."

"About what?"

She rolled her eyes. "Greer says he thinks it has something to do with the multimillion-dollar skate park and arcade they're building us." She paused and shifted gears. "Card, we've already decided that we're going to go, so —"

"I'm not here to stop you."

"Then why are you here?"

I couldn't seem to look at her. It felt like the walls of the cabin had lurched closer, shutting us up in this airless little box.

"Card?"

"I wasn't down there looking for a fight," I said.

There was a flicker of recognition that I'd been listening to her and Greer talking that night in the museum, but she let it pass. "So why were you?"

The bruises along my ribs ached as I took a deep breath.

"My mom was infected on the sixteenth. She lives in town,

and I thought she might have been . . . I thought somebody like Tommasulo might have gotten to her."

"Did they?"

I shook my head.

"Is she all right?"

A pressure was building behind my eyes. I closed them to block it off and found myself standing in the dark outside that window, looking up at Mom as she embraced Mr. Addad.

"She's living with someone now, and she seems . . . I don't know. She seems happy."

Neither of us said anything for some time after that. I felt hollowed out, as if I'd just run a dozen miles.

"Anyway. I just wanted you to know that. And to tell you that all those things I said to you the morning I left—about things being your fault — I was just . . . I didn't mean it."

"For all we know, you were right."

"No," I said. "I wasn't."

Snow Cone stirred at a flurry of voices outside and ran for the door. Greer appeared at the top of the trail with Cash and Shan and Isaac dancing around him, vying for his attention.

"Guys, I don't care how many times you ask me, I'm not going to let you bring a goat up here."

"But *Gre-er!*"

"No goats!"

There was a peel of laughter and then a shriek as DeShaun

chased Cash and Shan — Ricky and Margo now — toward the dining hall in the main lodge. I got up from the bunk and headed for the door.

"Card, wait."

Hannah was standing by her cot with Hershey Bar at her side.

"I was thinking maybe you could come down and eat with us tomorrow. It's hot dog night. For some reason the kids have decided that's something they're really, really excited about. We end up playing games and stuff after. I'm sure we can find a way to make it safe for you."

I thought back to the music and the swirl of bodies the night of the dance and how strongly I felt pulled toward it. I shook my head.

"Then maybe the three of us can go look at fireflies again sometime."

The way Hannah was smiling made her whole face brighten. The whole room. All the knots inside me loosened and fell away.

"Yeah," I said. "I'd like that."

I hung out at the edge of the camp and waited until Greer got the kids corralled into the dining hall for lunch.

"Hey, save your old buddy Greer a little something, okay, guys? A morsel. A crumb. I beg you."

He came to the doorway, wiping his hands with a dish-towel. When he saw me, he stopped cold.

"So," he said. "How'd the mission go?"

"Mission?"

He stepped out of the doorway and onto the grass. "Yeah, you were gone so long, I figured it must have been because you were a secret agent who'd been activated to deal with issues of national security. Either that, or you were just a titanic jackass."

He balled up the towel he was carrying and lobbed it at my chest. I caught it and kicked at the patch of ground in front of me.

"Titanic jackass," I said. "Definitely."

Greer laughed. "Damn. I was really hoping for the secret agent thing."

Benny came to the doorway and yanked at Greer's sleeve. "We got any more lemonade?"

"Yeah, in the kitchen. I'll grab some in a second."

"Hey, Ben."

Benny didn't even look at me. He turned around and went inside without a word. My stomach sank as I remembered what Hannah had said about all the excuses she and Greer had made for me. I'm sure they'd done their best, but Benny was smart. He had to have known what they were doing.

Back in the dining hall, there was a crash of glass breaking and then Astrid called out for Greer. He rolled his eyes wearily.

"Duty calls." He started into the hall, then turned back. "Hey! You still working on that garden?"

"I don't know. I guess so. Why?"

He smiled that big, goofy smile of his. "Feeling the urge to return to my roots as a subsistence farmer. Let me get these demons squared away, and I'll meet you there."

He put up his hands, and I tossed the towel back to him.

"All right, monsters!" he bellowed as he went inside. "What's going on in here? Who's up for more lemonade?"

The kids responded with a shouted chorus. All except Benny. He dropped his fork, then left the table and stomped out the back door. I started to follow him, but thought better of it. Greer and Hannah had given him excuses. Did I have anything better?

I stopped at the supply shed on the way out of camp and grabbed the packets of seeds, a rake, and a shovel. Hershey Bar came out of Hannah's cabin and trotted along beside me as I set out for the garden, hoping there were enough summer days left for anything I planted to grow.

20

Y OU KNOW WHAT our problem is, man?"

"No. What's our problem, Greer?"

"We never had any *fun* with this whole thing."

It was a few days later. The day of the Marvins' carnival.
Greer wanted to escape the insanity of the kids getting ready,
so we were walking from one side of Lucy's Promise to the
other. It was past time to start heading back, but Greer kept
taking these random little turnoffs that stretched the trip out
longer and longer. Also, he wouldn't shut up.

"We had a golden opportunity. Kids came up here with,
like, zero knowledge about the world. We could have told
them anything!"

"Like what?"

"Nothing bad! Just like, I don't know, the virus was caused
by aliens. Or unicorns!"

"And we would have done this for fun?"

"Sure," Greer said. "But also for science. We could have
seen what believing things like that could do to people, like,
psychologically."

"So you're saying we should have spent the last year

performing psychological experiments on a group of deeply traumatized children."

"Well, when you put it like that . . . No, it'd be like we were giving them a more exciting world. They'd probably thank us! If they ever found out about it."

"It's almost hard to believe we never put this plan into action."

A turn that would have led us right to camp appeared up ahead, but Greer dodged at the last minute and we looped back around onto another trail.

"Uh, Greer?"

"Yeah."

"Where are we going?"

"What do you mean?"

"I mean we've spent the last hour taking a twenty-minute walk."

"So what?" he said. "The birds are singing. The sun's out. Oh! You know what we should do? Go for a swim."

"You have to leave for that carnival in like an hour."

"A short one! Come on!"

He tore off down the trail, but I didn't move. When he finally realized I wasn't following, he turned around.

"What?"

"Dude," I said. "What's going on?"

"Nothing. Why?"

I just glared at him.

"Hey! Look at this!"

He dashed over to a stand of trees just off the trail. I stood there and watched as he poured every ounce of his attention onto what was clearly an entirely ordinary leaf. Turning it over. Bending it in half. Holding it up to the light. I came up behind him.

"Seriously," I said. "What's going on, man?"

"Nothing. I was just — I was thinking. That's all."

"About what?"

Greer held up the leaf. "Check out the veins on this bad boy. Is that insane or what? Did I ever tell you that I'm pretty sure I used to be a botanist?"

"Greer."

"It's nothing," he said. "For real. I was just thinking about how you brought Hannah up here, and at first that seemed like it might have been a really bad idea, but then it turned out to be a pretty good one, right? It's been good for the kids, I think."

"That's great."

"Yeah, it is. It totally is." He went back to fiddling with his spectacular leaf. "And I was thinking about how in general she's, uh — she's pretty cool, right? Like, as a person."

He glanced up at me for half a second, then away again.

"Uh . . . yeah," I said. "She is."

"Yeah," Greer repeated. "She's like a really solid person, right? Nice, but not goody-goody nice — *genuinely* nice, but with a little bit of an edge still. Like how she'll laugh at your jokes and all, but you're pretty sure she could also kick your ass if she had to. Which — I don't know why that seems so cool to me, but it totally does. Anyway, that's what I thought, that she was pretty cool. And that's what I thought you'd think too, so that's why I wanted to"— he swallowed hard — "you know, check with you."

"Check with me?"

"Before I said anything. To her. About, uh . . ." He looked away, grimaced, started again. "About her being cool."

"Greer —"

"It's totally okay if you, you know, think she's cool too. I can back off. I will back off. I'm happy to back off. I mean, if you feel that way—"

"I don't."

He cocked his head, clearly skeptical.

"I *don't*. And even if I did, it wouldn't matter."

"It *would* matter," he said. "It'd matter to me."

"No, I mean . . ." I looked down at my gloved hands. "Greer, we can barely be in the same room with each other."

"Well, yeah, but sooner or later that Lassiter guy is going to get his act together and come up with a cure, and then you could —"

"Things are the way they are," I said. "You should talk to Hannah. Today."

Greer thought for a second, then tossed the leaf aside and started marching toward camp.

"No! No way," he said. "Forget it. I changed my mind."

"What? Why?" I chased after him. "Greer, I want you to!"

He threw his hands in the air. "No, it's stupid. I don't know what I was thinking. I wouldn't even know what to say. And there's no way she'd ever—I mean, I'm sure I had all kinds of slick moves before I was infected, but—"

"You didn't."

Greer stopped short, with his back to me. I hadn't meant to say it—didn't even know I was going to until the words came out of my mouth. But I guess it had been building up since that night in the museum, and there was no taking it back now.

I eased up behind him, the crunch of my feet on the trail overloud in my ears.

"You want to know anything else?"

He slowly turned. When our eyes met, there was a second of acknowledgment—that I'd known and said nothing—and then he looked off into the woods.

"My family," he said. "Are they here?"

I shook my head.

"What happened to them?"

"You're sure you—"

"Just tell me."

I wanted to hand Greer a prettier world than the one he'd grown up in, but I couldn't bring myself to do it. His past belonged to him. If he wanted it back, I had to give it to him.

"You lived on this compound out in the woods near where

the quarantine fence is now. You and your mom and dad, and your brother. I think your folks stayed, hoping they could wait out the virus, but then you got infected."

"And they just . . ."

"Yeah," I said. "They left."

Greer scuffed the toe of his shoe in the dust, then looked up at me. "So we knew each other. Back then."

"Yeah."

"Were we friends?"

"No."

"Did I *have* friends?"

My throat clamped shut, but I forced the words through. "No. You didn't."

He was quiet for a moment. A small wind ruffled our clothes.

"It's weird," he said. "But I think I knew that."

"How?"

He shrugged. "All this — you and Hannah, the kids — it feels new. You know?"

Greer turned and started back along the trail. I joined him, and we walked in silence awhile.

"So is there anything else I should know?" he asked a little hesitantly. "I didn't go around kicking puppies or anything, did I?"

I didn't want to lie to him, but I couldn't bring myself to tell him the whole truth either. I went back over everything I knew about him, everything I'd ever seen or heard. There had to be something he'd want to hear. A bridge between the old and the new. Something good.

"You were never afraid of anything," I said.

Greer's eyes brightened. "Seriously?"

"Not anything or anybody," I said. "Certainly not girls with green hair."

He smiled to himself. "Cool."

We came around a bend in the trail and started to hear the kids' voices from down in the camp.

"And you're *sure* I didn't have any slick moves."

"Oh, no," I said. "You definitely didn't."

"So . . ."

"So, what?"

"So what do I do now?"

There couldn't have been a worse person to ask, but I was the only one there, so I tried to come up with something. I remembered our first year in Black River, when Mom and Dad took us to the county fair and you met that girl at the shooting gallery.

"There's going to be a Ferris wheel at this thing, right?"

"I think so."

"Wait for it to get dark," I said. "And then take her up in that."

"Then what?"

"Just . . . be you."

"Old me or new me?"

"New you," I said. "*Definitely* new you."

By the time we got back to camp, it was utter pandemonium. Music was pumping from the radio as kids ran from cabin to cabin and in and out of the dining hall. Hershey Bar and Snow Cone were exhausting themselves, barking and jumping as if they wanted someone to simply stop and explain what the hell was going on. To add insult to injury, one of the kids had tied a pink party hat to Snow Cone's head with a length of green string.

"That dog's going to snap one day," I said.

"No kidding."

Makela ran by, and Greer shouted to her. "Yo! Makela! Where's Hannah?"

"Haven't seen her since breakfast," she said as she disappeared into her cabin.

Greer ran a shaky hand through his hair. "All right, I better go find her so we can get this train moving."

"Why don't you let me?" I suggested. "You go get ready."

"You sure?"

I looked him up and down. He was sweating like a madman and his clothes were rumpled and stained with dirt.

"Yeah. A lack of moves is fine, but looking and smelling like a homeless guy is not going to work in your favor."

"Right. Good point. See ya later."

He took off. After a little searching I found Hannah at her old campsite, sitting at the edge of the mountain with her back to me.

"I think you've got the right idea," I said, taking a spot down the ledge from her. "It's crazy back there. Greer's going to have to —"

I turned toward her as she hurriedly wiped at her cheeks with the back of her hand. Her eyes were red and puffy.

"You all right?"

She nodded briskly, then wrapped her arms around her middle and looked out at the valley below. Her hair blew in the wind.

"What happened?"

"Nothing. It's stupid."

"Hannah."

She glanced at me, then took hold of the key and squeezed it until her fingertips went red.

"I yelled at Crystal this morning."

"What? Why?"

"I don't know," she said. "We've gotten kind of friendly over the last few weeks. More than with the other girls, I guess. And it's been nice, but . . . she's got this huge crush on Ren and she found out this morning that he doesn't feel the same way. She showed up wanting to talk about it, *needing* to talk about it, and I just —"

Hannah's eyes narrowed on the stone between us, as if she were searching for something in its crags.

"What?"

"I told her I didn't have time for her and her stupid crush." Her eyes flashed up at me. "I actually said that. I didn't even know why. It was like I was watching myself do it."

"It's just — it's stress or something."

Hannah shook her head. She let go of the key and hugged her knees to her chest.

"You remember the night we saw the fireflies? How after Greer left, it was just me and you up here and we . . ."

I nodded, feeling the pinch of that memory.

"After you left, I had this feeling like I couldn't breathe," she said. "Like the tent was collapsing around me. The second the sun came up, I was down in camp, talking to Astrid about moving in with them."

Hannah made a fist and laid it over her chest.

"It's like there's this second heart in my chest, right next to mine, and whenever I get close to somebody, it starts to beat harder and harder. And I know there's only one thing I can do to make it stop."

"What?"

"Run," she said. Her voice was hollow, frightened. "As fast and as far away as I can."

Her eyes glistened but she wiped at them before any tears could fall. More than anything I wanted to put my hand on her shoulder, or draw her to me—but I knew I couldn't.

"And it's not new," she said. "I'm sure of that. Every time I feel it, I can tell." She turned to me again. "Why would Lassiter's wipe everything else away — my name, my life, my family — and leave that behind?"

"Hannah . . ."

There was a rustle in the trees behind us.

"Guys? Hannah? Card?"

DeShaun and Ricky were standing in the clearing, just off the trail.

"Greer says it's time to go," Ricky said.

"Actually," DeShaun corrected, "he said if you guys make him deal with 'those pint-sized demon spawn' on his own, you're both dead to him forever."

"Okay," Hannah said. "We'll be right there."

"You all right, Hannah?"

She managed a brave smile. "Yeah, D. I'm good. You guys go ahead."

Once they left, Hannah dabbed at her eyes and tried to fix her hair.

"So. Any carnival-going tips for me?"

Her face was red and her hair was a tangle of vines. She was so beautiful I didn't think I could stand it.

"If someone asks you to ride the Ferris wheel with them, say yes."

By the time I got back to camp, the kids had disappeared into their cabins to finish getting ready. Greer wasn't in his, so I decided to check the dining hall. I went into the kitchen and found it empty. At first I thought the dining room was empty too, but then I saw Benny.

He was sitting alone at one of the tables, with a can of soda in front of him. As soon as he saw me, he got up to leave.

"Ben. Wait."

"I have to get ready. It's almost time to go."

"Just a second. Please."

He stopped where he was, his little body framed in the sunlight coming through the open front door.

"I shouldn't have left like that."

He was still for a moment, then slowly looked over his shoulder. "So why did you?"

I sat down at the table. He'd had enough excuses. "Ever since that night, since the sixteenth, I . . . it's like I get caught up in this current I can't even see. And before I can stop it, I'm a hundred miles away from where I started. You know?"

There was a long stretch of silence, and then he nodded. Outside, the rest of the kids were emerging from their cabins and gathering at the head of the trail.

"Anyway. I just wanted to say I was sorry. Looks like you better get moving."

He started to leave, then paused at the door. "You going to be here when we get back?"

"Are you kidding? Can't miss hot dog night."

Benny grinned, and then Greer hollered out in the camp, "Listen up, everybody! We are leaving in five . . . four . . . three . . ."

I gave Benny a nod, and he ran out into the sunshine. I tossed his soda can into the trash and followed.

Greer managed to get the kids into some semblance of order, then did a final head count. His face was scrubbed, and he'd changed into a cleanish pair of jeans and a button-down shirt that was only a little too big for him. He looked good, despite the fact that on closer inspection he was clearly more than a little jumpy. Whether it was because he was about to lead his charges into the largest gathering of infected since the outbreak or because of his impending date with a Ferris wheel and a green-haired girl was hard to say.

"Maybe you should dip into some of Makela's happy pills before you go," I said. "Might take the edge off."

He chuckled nervously. The door to the girls' cabin slammed open behind us, and then came Hannah's voice.

"I'm coming! Sorry I'm late!"

"No problem," Greer said. "We were just —"

He shut up the second he saw her. I didn't blame him. She'd changed into a white dress that was speckled all over with small blue flowers. Her arms and shoulders were bare, and she'd put her hair up with a few clips Astrid had made out of twigs and sparkling bits of stone. She stopped dead a few feet from us, likely because our slack-jawed staring was freaking her out.

"What? Do I look stupid? I look stupid, don't I?"

"No!"

"It's the boots, isn't it?" She looked down at her feet, which were still clad in her old black combat boots. "Can you believe that? We find *this* dress, but no shoes that fit me. Forget it, this was a dumb idea. I'm going to change."

Greer almost jumped out of his skin to stop her. "No! Don't. You look great. Seriously. Awesome. You look like a *completely* different person."

Hannah gave him a look. Good lord, Tennant, he really didn't have any moves whatsoever.

"You guys should probably get going," I said, hoping to save him from any further embarrassment.

"Yes!" Greer said. "Let's go! Good times ahead!"

He trotted off, but Hannah didn't move. She stood there fiddling with the hem of her dress, looking nervous and worried.

"It's going to be fun," I said.

"Yeah. I know."

"Dude!" Greer called out. "Come on!"

Hannah rolled her eyes, smiling at the same time. "Better go."

She started toward the others, green hair bouncing, dress swishing at her knees. In no time at all she'd be around the corner, down the mountain, and gone.

"I feel it too."

She stopped and turned around, suspended halfway between me and the kids. My mouth felt as if it were coated in sand.

"That heartbeat," I heard myself say. "I feel it too. All the time."

Greer called out again, but Hannah made a motion for him to wait. She came back up the trail.

"What do we do?" she asked.

There were all sorts of things I could say, some of them even sounded pretty good in my head, but in the end I told her the truth.

"I don't know."

For a moment it was like we were back on that trail under the moonlight. Hannah reached out and took my gloved hand. She started to come closer but stopped herself midstride.

"I wish we could—"

"I know," I said. "Me too."

Greer called again.

"Go on," I said, barely able to speak around the catch in my throat. "I'll see you later. We've got a date with some fireflies, right?"

Hannah smiled, then hurried toward Greer and Benny and Margo. She took Benny's hand, Greer scooped up Margo in his arms, and they all continued down the trail. There was a bark behind me as Snow Cone and Hershey Bar raced out of a cabin to see them off. I stood there listening to their fading voices. Once they were gone, the dogs came trotting back. They followed me as I returned to the garden.

BEHOLD,
ABADDON

21

WAS IN MY tent reading when I heard the helicopter.

It was a distant buzz at first, but it grew steadily louder until it shot by, right overhead. The dogs jumped up and ran down the trail. I'd moved back to my old camp by then, so I made it to the cabins in no time. Just as I did, helicopters screamed by, skimming the treetops on their way to town. I picked out Marvin logos on their bellies as they slipped past. The Guard had flown helicopters over the QZ plenty of times when they were in charge, but never so many at once and never so low. Did it have something to do with the carnival? Some kind of air show? The dogs stayed close as I headed farther down the trail for a better view.

The Marvins' carnival had transformed Monument Park into a pool of light in the middle of the dark valley. The helicopters swept across town and took up positions high above it. I grabbed my knife's hilt as Hershey Bar and Snow Cone whined. Something was wrong. They could feel it too.

"Come on, guys."

The dogs ran ahead as I sprinted back to camp and found our radio in the boys' cabin. Nothing but static on every channel. There was a shout coming from up the mountain. I dropped the radio and went to the back window. Flashlights lit up the trees. Jen and Marty, the couple who'd told Greer about Ricky and Margo, came stumbling down the trail, pushed along by a pair of Marvins. As they passed out of view, another couple appeared behind them, then a family of four, then more Marvins. They were herding the infected through camp toward the trailhead that led off Lucy's Promise.

"You can't do this!" Marty screamed as they dipped down into the trees. "This is our home!"

"Don't worry." One of the Marvins laughed. "I hear Arizona is great this time of year!"

Arizona? I ran back to my tent and pulled the phone Gonzalez had given me out of my backpack, thinking maybe he'd know what was going on. But when I powered it up, there was no signal. Not a weak signal. *No* signal. It didn't make sense. Gonzalez said there was a cell tower on the next mountain.

I pulled on my mask and gloves, then tossed the phone into my pack and threw it over my shoulder. The dogs tried to join me as I came back through the camp, but I warned them off and started down the mountain.

By the time I got to the foot of Lucy's Promise, Jen, Marty, and a dozen other infected were being loaded into the back of one of the Marvins' big cargo trucks. I searched for someone in charge and spotted a familiar face right away.

"Raney! What's going on? Where are you taking them?"

As soon as he saw me, Raney barked an order to his men,

then headed for a Humvee that was parked on the side of the road.

I ran to catch up with him. "What the hell are you doing? You said nothing was going to change. You said everything was going to stay just like it was."

"What did you think?" he barked. "The governor was going to wall off an entire town and play nanny to you and your friends for the rest of your lives? There are thousands of uninfected people out there who want their homes back. Who want their businesses back." He yanked open the Humvee door. "World's moving on, kid, starting tonight."

"Where are you taking them?"

Raney slid into his seat and signaled to the driver. The engine rumbled.

"Good places," he said. "Safe places. We've got facilities in Arizona, Oregon, The Dakotas. A few in Canada. Your friends will be perfectly safe until somebody figures out a cure for this thing. In the meantime, Black River, New York, will be back in business. Hell, a month from now it'll be like none of this ever happened."

"But it's not right! You can't just—"

I was interrupted by a deep boom coming from somewhere across town. The ground trembled, and then a ball of fire rose over the treetops. All around me radios screeched and Marvins scrambled to their vehicles.

"What was that? What's happening? Raney—"

But he was already moving. His Humvee sped away, and

so did all the others around me. There was another boom, smaller this time, followed by a crash. I spun around, trying to figure out where the sounds were coming from. A third explosion made it clear. They were coming from Monument Park.

I ran flat out, jumping fences and cutting through yards. Every street I passed was full of sirens and flashing lights and roaring engines. When I got to within a block of the park, I heard thousands of voices all yelling at once, so many that they merged into a storm of white noise. I hooked around the back side and climbed the hill, staying low, moving from shadow to shadow until I reached the crest. Once there, I found a thicket of trees and dropped to my belly.

There wasn't much left of the carnival. The Ferris wheel and a few wooden booths were about the only things still standing. Everything else had been trampled under the feet of nearly five thousand infected who stood shoulder to shoulder below me, fists raised and shouting. They were facing a stage that sat on the far side of the park. It was empty except for a podium and a couple of knocked-over mic stands. There was a knot of Marvin blue to one side of it. It looked like they'd been trying to make their escape, but had been blocked by a wall of infected. Three of their vehicles had been flipped over and were spewing flames and black smoke. Hannah had mentioned there was going to be an announcement at the carnival. I was pretty sure I knew what it was and about how well it had gone over.

Gonzalez had been right. Black River was nothing but a contract to the Marvins. Everything Raney had done had been to keep us quiet until the Guard was gone and no one was watching.

A horde of Marvin vehicles arrived with a screech of sirens. They began lining the road that circled the park, like bricks in a wall surrounding it. Once they were all in position, they'd have the infected trapped. They'd only have to load them onto trucks and drive them away. I scanned the crowd, becoming more and more anxious, until I caught a flash of green. Hannah. She was locked in the middle of the mob with Greer and the kids. They were bunched together, hand in hand, making a chain to fight the tides of people pushing against them. They were barely a hundred yards away, but a trio of Marvin trucks sat between us. I looked up and down the line but didn't see a single break.

A black bus pulled up near the stage. An amplified voice came from loudspeakers on top of it.

"By order of the governor, you are to disperse. Return to your homes and await further instruction. Anyone who does not comply is subject to immediate arrest."

A door opened in the side of the bus, and dozens of Marvins poured out. They were in riot gear — black body armor, helmets, gas masks. As they advanced toward the crowd, they beat truncheons against Plexiglas shields. The infected retreated at first, but then there was a rallying cry and they threw themselves forward. Another patrol car was flipped onto its side, with a crunch of broken glass. More carnival booths collapsed. Once the infected saw what they could do, they surged even harder. The riot cops were pushed back, but the reaction was immediate. Two of the three Humvees in front of me backed out of their spots and headed toward the center of the chaos. It was my opening. I bolted down the hill.

"Hannah! Greer! This way!"

Hannah turned, and when she saw me, she grabbed Greer's arm and he started shouting at the kids, turning them in my direction. There were screams on the other side of the park, single voices at first and then a chorus. Fire from one of the burning patrol cars spread to the stage, and flames shot out over the crowd. Silhouetted by the blaze, the infected looked like trees writhing in a forest fire. My stomach flipped and my vision started to collapse, but I couldn't give in to it. I waved the kids past me and up the hill, then followed behind. By the time we all made it to the top, the kids were nearly hysterical with fear. Not Hannah, though. She seemed almost eerily calm. Her eyes were filled with the same kind of hunted intensity as the first time I'd seen her.

"Did you hear what they're going to do?" she asked. "They must have been planning it the whole time."

Behind her, Eliot wailed. "They're going to split us up. They're going to send us away!"

"What do we do?" Astrid cried. "What are we going to do?"

Everyone was looking to me. I searched around us, trying to find some kind of out. Somewhere to go. Something to do.

All I saw was the dark outline of Lucy's Promise rising above the town.

"We go back up the mountain," I said. "It's our only choice."

"They'll come looking for us," Hannah argued. "Every infected person in Black River is getting cleared out. That's what they said."

"Then we'll go deeper into the woods," I countered. "Over the quarantine fence if we have to. We stick together and we stay out of sight until people find out what the Marvins are trying to do. There's no way they'll let them get away with it."

There was a roar as another helicopter streaked over the trees toward the park.

"Go!" I yelled. "Run! And don't look back."

Hannah took the lead and the kids ran after her. I started to follow until I realized that Greer wasn't behind me. He had moved to the edge of the hill, his head down, his hands curled into fists.

"Greer, we have to go. Now!"

I grabbed his shoulder and spun him around. His gray eyes locked on mine. It was as if time had slipped its gears and turned backwards. It was the old Greer. I stepped back without thinking, my hand falling to the hilt of the knife.

"They can't do this," he roared. "Black River is ours! It's our home."

Just then five trails of white arced over the heads of the infected. Tear gas. When the canisters landed, plumes of smoke billowed in every direction. The crowd screamed and reared back. People were clawing at their eyes and struggling to breathe. The Marvins waded into them, clubs raised over their heads.

"You want to go?" Greer cried. "Then go! Run!"

He turned away, but I managed to get a hold of his arm and yank him back. The glare he gave me was the same one he'd given a hundred kids on the schoolyard. It had always been enough to send us all running, but right then I refused to back off, refused to wither like I had so many times before.

"Hannah and I need you," I said. "We *have* to stay together!"

"Greer! Card!"

Hannah had stopped running. The kids were huddled behind her. Benny. DeShaun. Astrid. Makela. Eliot cradled Margo in his arms, her face buried in his shoulder. They were all streaked with soot and tears. I turned back to Greer, and it was as if a switch flipped inside him. His arm slipped out of my hand and he ran toward Hannah. He took Margo from Eliot and waved them all down the other side of the hill. I turned for a last look back at the park. The Ferris wheel had fallen over, and every last trace of the carnival was gone, crushed underfoot. A house on an adjacent street was burning. Smoke from the fires mixed with the tear gas, churning in the rotor wash from the helicopters. Deep inside the haze, faceless forms grappled hand to hand.

Behold, Abaddon.

I turned and fled. By the time we hit the roadway on the other side of the hill, the riot had spilled into the streets. Main was blocked by a barricade of vehicles, so we ended up twisting through Black River's neighborhoods, just barely avoiding the Marvins. I kept my eyes locked on the summit of Lucy's Promise with every turn we took, frustrated by how it drew closer and slipped away over and over again.

At Washington Street we stumbled into one of the clouds of tear gas and the kids started coughing violently. I could breathe because of my mask, but it was like a swarm of bees gouging at my eyes. Greer pushed everyone into a nearby yard, then stripped off his shirt and told Ren and Eliot to do the same. He handed the shirts to me and I used my knife to cut them into wide strips. Greer and Hannah moved through the group, tying the fabric tightly around mouths and noses. It wasn't much, but it was all we had, and it was enough to get everyone back on their feet and moving.

There was a full-on brawl underway at the end of Washington, so we jumped fences until we hit the next street over. I caught a flash of the bridge up ahead and called out to the others, but by the time we'd turned toward it, a Marvin patrol cut us off and we lost sight of it again. We tumbled from street to street, as if we'd fallen into the churn of Black River Falls. The world became flickers of light and darkness. There and then gone again. I saw riot clubs falling. Clouds of smoke. People running. All around us was the sound of broken glass and sirens and the *pop pop pop* of gunfire.

Astrid fell, and I helped her up and pushed her on. Blood poured from a cut on the side of her head and across her pale skin, but she didn't seem to notice. Hannah had DeShaun in her arms. Greer carried Margo. Makela snatched a rock off the street and hurled it at a passing car. Every few minutes another mass of infected crashed into us, overwhelming and scattering our group. We fought to pull ourselves together again and again, clasping hands, making a chain. *Stay together. Keep moving.* It was all I could think. All I could do.

"Card! Look!"

My head snapped left at Hannah's voice. Gray stone showed through the trees, and then there was a rush of sound that I took for the roar of voices until I realized what it really was — white water crashing over the falls.

By then we'd mixed in with at least three other groups of infected. We turned a corner, and suddenly there it was. The bridge. The roadway was clear. It was a straight shot to Lucy's Promise. Seeing it gave us a jolt, and we raced out onto it. Hannah and I looked around wildly as we ran, counting heads, making sure everyone was there. I panicked when I didn't see Tomiko, but then the crowd shifted and I caught sight of her.

We were halfway across when the truck appeared. It shot out of a side street and came to a stop at the far end of the bridge, blocking our way. Marvins in riot gear poured out, ten or fifteen of them, some with shields and clubs, some with tear gas launchers, some with sleek black rifles hanging from their shoulders and side arms strapped to their hips. The crowd didn't turn back, didn't even slow. We hit them as one body, determined to break through. Clubs fell. Gas billowed. An older man crumpled beside me, eyes shut, blood on his forehead. A woman went down next. I heard a scream and turned to see Jenna and Tomiko trapped by the flow of the crowd, their backs pressed against the stone guardrail. I tore through a clot of infected and pulled them away from the Marvins.

"Go! Run!"

By then the Marvins were advancing, pushing us back to the other side of the bridge, toward Black River and away from Lucy's Promise. There were still a few infected out in the middle of it though, some fighting, others who just couldn't escape.

I led Jenna and Tomiko to a spot on the grass, then started searching for everyone else as a stream of escaping infected raced by. I found them on the other side of the road, huddled around Hannah. They were trapped by the riot, but safe. Ren. Eliot. Makela. Astrid. Crystal. Isaac. Hannah. Greer. DeShaun. Carrie. Ricky. Margo.

Someone was missing. Benny.

I stood up and saw him among a group out in the middle of the bridge. The crowd was thinning, but he was caught in an eddy of people near the Marvin line and couldn't get away. I ran for him, but the retreating infected slammed into me, knocking me backward.

"Benny!" I called, throwing my elbows out to try to clear a path. "Let me through! Benny!"

Someone rammed into me from behind and hurtled past. I saw a flash of skin and a black tattoo. Greer. He punched a hole through the crowd and grabbed Benny by the shoulder, tossing him back out of danger. As he went to follow, a Marvin jumped out of the line and swung his club, connecting with Greer's side. I heard one of his ribs snap with a wet pop. He spun to face the man, teeth bared, his fist whipping out to the side as he turned. The Marvin flinched. There was something in Greer's hand. A flash of silver and black. My hand dropped to my hip. The sheath was empty. My knife was gone.

I threw myself against the tide, screaming Greer's name as the Marvin dropped his club and went for his side arm. Greer looked back at me, and for a split second our eyes met; then he turned to the Marvin, the knife still clenched in his fist. The Marvin's gun cleared his holster and the black barrel rose. Greer took a step forward.

"No!"

There was the crack of a gunshot and then a second of quiet so huge it was as if all the noise had fallen out of the world. It was followed by a single bright ping as the knife hit the concrete, and then the thump of a body falling to the ground. No one moved. No one made a sound. We all stood there, frozen, listening to the roar of the water as it crashed over the falls.

22

THE NEXT THING knew, I was lying on the floor, knees to chest, wedged into the corner of a dark room. It was noisy — raised voices, thumping steps, slamming doors — but it all seemed far away, echoey, as if I were listening from deep under water. Dark shapes swam all around me, appearing and disappearing as they moved past a line of bright rectangles along the wall. I tried to sit up, but every muscle in my body was cinched into a series of knots.

Someone pushed a plastic bottle into my hands. Water. My throat was burning. I pulled my mask aside and took a long drink, then poured the rest over my eyes to try to clear my vision. Everything shimmered, then came into focus.

I was in a square chamber, lit by flashlights and candles. There was a large wooden desk in front of me and, beyond that, rows of smaller desks and metal chairs. A classroom. In the high school. Strangers moved in and out, hauling away the furniture and replacing it with makeshift cots. Some of the people on the cots were crying, some were screaming, some weren't moving at all. The scent of smoke and sweat and blood was heavy, even through my mask.

Someone ran down the hall screaming. "We did it! We pushed them out. We pushed them right the hell out!"

Whoever it was laughed loudly and madly and then was gone. Why wasn't I with the others? I had to find them. I had to make sure everyone was all right. My backpack was beside me. I grabbed it, then reached for my knife, but the sheath was empty. I made it to my hands and knees, grasped for the edge of the teacher's desk, and climbed to my feet. My legs wobbled and my vision grayed out, but I managed to stay standing. My clothes were torn and filthy, and there was a strip of white cloth tied tight around my leg. Blood showed through it. I tried to remember how it had happened, but nothing came to me.

I threw myself from the desk to the wall by the door and staggered out of the room. There were more people lying in the hallway and still more in the classrooms beyond. I came to a staircase and started down, my hand clamped to the railing. A boy, eight or nine years old, ran up the steps, calling out to someone. His shoulder hit mine, spinning me around. There was a crack of thunder, and then I dropped my pack and fell against the railing. Darkness swirled. I hit the ground and the world went shooting away.

When I came to, I was in another classroom. Dusty sunlight streamed in through the windows. My backpack was on the floor by my feet.

"It's all right. We got separated."

Hannah was sitting in front of me, clutching the key

around her neck. Her blue-speckled dress was torn in places and filthy with ground-in dirt and sweat and blood. Her eyes were shadowed with exhaustion.

My body ached as I sat up. The others were huddled behind her. I looked from face to face, ticking off the names in my head. They were all there. All but one. I turned to Hannah.

"Where's Greer?" I asked, but as soon as I said it, I knew.

The days passed strangely after that. I didn't sleep. I wasn't hungry or thirsty. I never left the high school, just drifted from room to room. People talked endlessly. In the classrooms. In the halls and stairwells. In the lunchroom. They knew everything. They knew nothing. The Marvins had been pushed out for good and their leaders arrested. The Marvins were mounting an imminent counter-attack, this time backed up by the National Guard and Special Forces.

Hannah and the kids had claimed a small classroom in a remote corner of the school. I spent most of my time there, watching from the other side of the room in my mask and gloves as Hannah tended to the kids. Everyone was in a shell-shocked daze, but Benny and DeShaun and Carrie had it the worst. They barely moved or spoke. Hannah did what she could. She held them. Whispered to them. Fed them. She kept them all close, bound up into a warm knot of bodies. They held hands. They slept draped over one another at night, as if they were being stalked by some dark and prowling thing and if there were any stragglers, if anyone wandered from the fold, they'd be consumed. I wanted to help, wanted to add my body to theirs, but what could I do?

One day I left the school and walked through Black River.

There were signs of the riots everywhere. Broken windows. Torn-up lawns. Roads that were crisscrossed with black skid marks and littered with the casings of tear gas shells. There was a Marvin Humvee lying on its side at a corner, scorched black, its windshield shattered. The familiarity of it all, the feeling like I'd been in exactly this place before, was overwhelming.

At the end of one street I came to a pile of rubble made up of wrecked cars, scrap wood, and old furniture. It stretched out of sight in either direction. Teams of infected were using wheelbarrows to haul more debris up to the line and heap it on, so the barricade grew and grew. It was patrolled by men and women carrying hunting rifles or shotguns that had probably been stolen from fleeing Marvins. Still others carried axes, baseball bats, shovels, kitchen knives.

Beyond the barricade was a narrow no man's land and then a Marvin wall made of sandbags and a new quarantine fence of steel and razor wire. On the other side, a mix of Marvins and state police leaned against their vehicles, sipping coffee and chatting, high-powered rifles hanging from their shoulders. Behind them was a third line. The news vans. CNN. MSNBC. Fox. PBS. Satellite dishes reached up into the sky like sunflowers. Reporters primped and fussed in side-view mirrors.

I turned toward Lucy's Promise. The green of the mountain was dazzling. My eyes ached just looking at it. I could see the notch in the trees near the top, where our camp sat. I thought of the cabins and of Snow Cone and Hershey Bar trapped up there alone. I felt a tug deep inside me that grew until I had to turn my back to the mountain and walk away.

Eventually I found myself back on our front lawn. The house still seemed practically untouched. I climbed the stairs and stood on the porch. The door was unlocked, so I went inside, passing through the entryway without daring to glance at the wall by the door. I pulled off my mask. The air was dusty and stale, heavy with old humidity. There was a sour, rotten smell too, one that became sharper as I moved into the kitchen. The refrigerator was nearly empty, but what was there had slumped into piles of green-black mold. In the back corners of the cabinets by the fridge there were a few forgotten cans of tuna and beans. Unopened boxes of cereal.

A shattered wine glass lay on the floor by the stove, the gleam of the shards dulled by a layer of dust.

I went to the sink and turned the spigot. Water splashed against the stainless steel and swirled down the drain. I stared at it for a long time, lost in the staticky rush, and then I took a paring knife from the block by the stove and left the kitchen.

I paused at the edge of the living room, my hand resting on the cap of the banister. The stairs to the second floor were gray with dust. I started up, then heard something behind me and turned. That's when I saw Cardinal. I was surprised I hadn't noticed him before. He was standing between the coffee table and the TV. He looked smaller than he had last time. His armor was dented and scorched, broken at the joints, so that bits of red plate hung loose, the exposed wires sparking. In some places I could see down to his skin, the deep brown of it crisscrossed with wounds and slick with blood. His wings were gone, leaving only ragged stumps.

The couch groaned as Cardinal lowered himself onto it. He didn't look at me, and he didn't say anything, but when he held out his arm, I knew exactly what he wanted.

A few sections of his armor were held together by dirty rags and bits of wire. I cut those first. Once they were gone, I had to cut into the plate itself. It was like sawing through a lobster's shell. The armor fell away in sections. The arms. The legs. The breastplate. Each time I removed a piece, Cardinal pointed to me and I put it on my own body. It was strange because Cardinal was twice my size, but each section fit me perfectly, the components coming together with a satisfying click. Eventually he was down to his helmet and a torn blue jump suit. The Brotherhood's insignia — the Aerie tower with a pair of wings unfurled behind it — was sewn onto his left breast pocket in bright yellow thread.

Cardinal lifted the helmet from his shoulders. Beneath it wasn't Dad or me or you or Greer. It was Cameron Conner. He leaned forward to help me snap the helmet into place. Then I saw the world as he did, a video feed that made everything seem extra sharp, but far away and flat at the same time. I got up from the couch and left the living room. The stairs moaned under the weight of my armor. I made it to the first landing, stopped, rested, and continued on. The curtains on the stairwell windows were open, filling the upstairs with buttery sunlight.

My room was just the way I'd left it. The sheets a blue, rumpled mess. A pile of comic books at the foot of the bed. I went back into the hall. The other rooms sat in an arc in front of me. Mom and Dad's room. Your room. Dad's office. I could see the edge of Mom and Dad's bed through their open door and the corner of your bookshelf through yours.

Dad's office door was the only one that was closed. The walls shot up over my head, and the next thing I knew, I was sitting at the top of the stairs with my armor-clad legs out in front of me, warning lights in the helmet flashing red. Malfunctions. Fatal errors. I blinked in a proscribed pattern and they all went out. I blinked again and the video turned off too, leaving me in total darkness. The house was quiet, except for the water as it splashed against the sink in the kitchen below. It was incredibly loud, like a scream.

23

THE FRONT DOOR opened and Hannah walked in.

She was carrying a plastic bag in each hand. I was sitting on the couch in the living room. It was morning but I didn't know how long it'd been since I'd left the high school. One day? Two? The water was still running in the kitchen sink, so she turned it off, then went to the counter, which was covered in garbage I didn't remember being there before. Hannah cleared the trash away and began unloading the bags, never once looking up at me. It was like I was there but invisible.

I watched her as she worked, making neat stacks of cans and cardboard boxes in the cabinets. Her blue and white dress was gone, traded for jeans and a T-shirt. Her hair was pinned up behind her ears, and when she turned into the light, I could make out a band of brown in the part, pushing against the green. I saw Greer standing in a meadow, his hands cradling the back of her head as he tipped her face into the sun. *A light, honey brown.* My chest ached. I pushed myself against the arm of the couch and drew my knees up to my chest.

"How'd you find me?"

Hannah glanced up from her work. "Easy," she said. "Just checked every house in Black River."

"In one night?"

Hannah stopped emptying the bags.

"It's been eighteen days since the riot, Card."

I looked over her shoulder and into the kitchen. The cabinets were open and nearly empty except for what she'd just put in. The trash she'd pushed aside was empty cans of tuna and beans. Boxes of cereal. *Eighteen days.* I tried to remember any of them, but all I saw was the bridge and the school and then Hannah walking through the door.

"We're still living at the high school," she said. "A lot of people are."

She took one of the bags off the counter and came into the living room. I lifted my hand to my face and suddenly realized I wasn't wearing my mask or gloves. They were sitting on the coffee table. I grabbed them and quickly put them on.

"There are plenty of empty houses," she went on. "But I guess people just like being together. They've pretty much let Tomiko take over the kitchen. Oh, and Snow Cone showed up the other morning. She must have made it down the mountain before they moved the quarantine fence. No sign of Hershey Bar, though."

Hannah set the bag on the table in front of me, then retreated to the opposite side of the room. I peeked inside. Three small, golden biscuits. I saw a bundle of red set on a stone by the side of a trail. I saw Greer. I pushed the bag away from me and looked out the back window through a gap in the curtains. The lawn was overgrown and the flowers Mom had planted our first year were in bloom. The sky was bright and cloudless.

"You haven't missed much," she said. "They've turned the power back on for now and we're getting supplies again. Mail too. Astrid got a letter from some long-lost uncle. Don't think I've ever seen her so happy. Other than that, the Marvins sit on their side of the border and stare at us, and we sit on our side and stare at them."

"They're stalling," I said. "As soon as the reporters leave —"

"The adults say they can work something out."

I laughed. Hannah turned toward the wall. Her lips drew taut, and she took a hard breath. I stared at the floor in front of the couch.

"There's a cookout in the park tonight," she said. "I guess everybody's sick of eating out of the school cafeteria. I thought you might want to —"

"I'm not going to a party."

"It's not a — look, the kids want to see you. They want you to come back."

"I can't do that. You know I can't."

"No," she said. "I don't."

I looked up. A shaft of sunlight had cut across her face.

"It's like the flu," she said, that old intensity coming into her eyes. "Right? The way it's transmitted? These kids would do *anything* to make sure you never get sick. We can make it work. You just have to want to."

I lowered my head, twisted at a bit of fabric at the edge of the couch.

Hannah's voice softened. "They get why you're here," she said. "But they miss you. So do I. What do you think?"

"I think if none of you ever met me in the first place, then you wouldn't have anyone to miss."

Hannah started to reach out to me, but I got up from the couch and went upstairs to your room. It was as neat as ever. Clothes put away. Desk clean. Books arranged on the shelves alongside your trophies and ribbons from track. Your bed was rumpled, though, which was strange. I wondered if I'd been sleeping there all this time.

I sat on the floor with my back pressed up against the foot of your bed. In front of me were four large plastic bins with blue tops. They were the ones you kept in the attic, so I figured I must have pulled them down at some point. I popped off the lids. The comics inside were just as you left them, alphabetized, with the titles divided by hand-labeled sheets of white cardboard. *Alias. Alpha Flight. Avengers. Batman. Blue Devil. The Brotherhood of Wings.*

These were the single issues, before they'd been collected into volumes. Mint condition. I pulled them out in a stack and sat there with them in my lap, shuffling through the covers and then dividing them into four piles, one for each of the four volumes. I started at the beginning and worked through the series until I found myself back at *Behold, Abaddon.*

"So how does it end?"

Hannah was standing in the doorway. Some time must have passed because the light coming in from the window behind her had turned a twilight bluish gray. She nodded toward the comic in my hand.

"He didn't just end it with everybody dead, did he?"

I shook my head. Hannah sat down behind me, on the far side of the bed.

"So what happened?"

I turned through the pages until I came to Cardinal running through the Aerie as bombs exploded all around him.

"Cardinal had built this experimental time machine," I said. "He used it to go back a hundred years, to when Liberty City was still Abaddon. He thought that since he knew what was going to happen, he'd be able to stop everything before it started. He thought he could bring his friends back."

"Did he?"

I moved the last stack. Pulled an issue from the bottom. Cardinal surrounded by a crowd of men and women in rags. His armor shattered and burned, hanging off him in pieces. His wings gone.

"He tried," I said. "But everyone thought he was crazy. They drove him out of the city and exiled him to the Gardens of Null."

"And that's it?"

"There was supposed to be more, but . . ."

"But what?"

I didn't say anything. Hannah got up from the bed and moved through the room, her hands brushing over your trophies and your pictures and your books. She stopped at your closet and opened the door. Hangers rattled and pressed shirts swayed. Your running shoes were lined up neatly by the hamper. A scent I thought of as distinctly you—grass and sweat and just-washed clothes—drifted into the room.

"Your brother's not at college, is he?"

I turned and looked out the window by your bed. Lucy's Promise was a black swell against a gray sky. I thought of the waters of the reservoir and how it felt to dive into them, to feel the world recede as the cold seeped into my veins. More than ever before, I wished that I was Cardinal, the real Cardinal. I wished I could fly out over the Marvin lines and land by that shore. I told myself that if I could, I wouldn't be such a coward this time. I'd dive in and never come out.

"Cardinal?"

Hannah sat on the bed by the headboard, waiting, clutching one of your pillows to her belly. I felt like someone had taken an entire universe and stuffed it down inside my chest. It was straining against my ribs and pressing down on my heart.

"My mom and dad had been fighting." My voice sounded strange in my ears, as if it were coming from somewhere else in the room. "The night of the fifteenth. I guess Dad got sick of it 'cause the next morning he left early. I hadn't slept at all, so I heard the door slam when he walked out. I didn't see him again until that night. He must have gone to the park at some point, because by the time he got home, he was already infected."

I closed my eyes and saw him as he was when I ran downstairs behind Mom. He was standing in the kitchen with his back to the stove. His eyes were red and glassy and he was covered in sweat. When he saw us, he started raving in a voice I barely recognized as his.

"Mom tried to calm him down, but he didn't understand what was going on. He took the carving knife out of the block to keep her away from him. That's when Tennant got home. He grabbed me and we ran outside. Things were already happening by then. Sirens. People running in the streets. Fires. Tennant told me to stay where I was, and then he ran back inside to get Mom."

Hannah shifted on the bed behind me. I was there, with her, but at the same time I could feel that night on my skin. I could smell it. I could see you running toward the open front door and the way the light in the hall made the hardwood floor glow this molten brown.

"I heard them arguing, and then something glass broke and Mom screamed and Tennant kind of stumbled back into the doorway. He had one hand on the wall behind him and the other pressed into his stomach, like he'd just been laughing or something. And then he fell back against the wall and slid down, and his hand fell away and . . ."

There was so much blood. Throbbing red in the porch lights. There were streaks of it against the wall behind you and a growing pool on the floor.

"Dad still had the knife in his hand when he came out onto the porch. He and Tennant gave each other the weirdest look, like they were strangers, and then Dad ran off down the street. Mom and I got to Tennant at the same time. He was so pale. It got really quiet, and then there was this sound of wind chimes coming from one of our neighbors' yards. Tennant looked up at me and he whispered, *We weren't supposed to be here*, before he closed his eyes."

There was a long silence. My throat ached and my mouth was dry. I started restacking the Brotherhood comics.

"I don't really remember much else about that night. I guess Mom must have gone for help, and that's when she got infected. The next thing I knew, it was a day or two later. I was in Monument Park and they were gone."

The sheets rustled as Hannah moved to the foot of the bed and laid down on her stomach.

"That wasn't your dad," she said. "He didn't know what was happening to him. He was scared."

"Everybody was scared."

I lowered the comics into the bin and snapped the lid shut.

"What happened to him?"

"I heard the police caught up with him a few days later," I said. "He'd ended up with some other guys and they all . . . they're in prison somewhere outside Black River."

"You haven't tried to . . ."

I shook my head. Hannah touched my shoulder. It was gentle at first, tentative, but then her fingers tensed, pressing into my skin. The place where we touched bloomed with heat.

"Hannah . . ."

She wrapped her arms around me from behind and her forehead fell onto my shoulder. She was only there a second though before I felt her stiffen and start to move away. I reached up and grabbed her hand.

"Wait."

"Card, we can't be —"

"Don't go," I said. "Please."

"It's not safe. We —"

I pulled my mask down and kissed her. Hannah's lips parted with a gasp. I tore off my gloves and took her face in my hands. Her skin was warm and soft.

"Card," she breathed.

"It's all right," I said. "It's done."

I kissed her again, and this time she didn't back away, so I took her by her shoulders and slid her off the bed and into my lap. Her fingertips dug into my back, and mine tangled in her hair. Tremors moved between us, and soon it was hard to tell whether they had started in her chest or mine. Time slipped away. No past, no future, only that moment, right then, with her.

Sometime later we leaned back from each other to catch our breath. She brushed the back of her hand against my cheek.

"How long until . . ."

"Eight hours," I said. "Maybe ten. A little after dawn tomorrow, I guess."

"Where do you want to be?" she asked. "When it happens."

There was a framed picture on your desk. It was too dark to make it out, but I didn't need to. I knew which one it was. It was the photo Dad took of him and Mom standing side by side, drenched in sweat and grinning madly, giving the camera a goofy thumbs-up. Just behind them was the side of a white moving van. Looking closely, you could see my hands reaching up into the van while you handed me a cardboard box. It was the day we moved to Black River.

"Anywhere but here."

24

HANNAH AND I sat on the hill overlooking the park. Below us, hundreds of infected circled a bonfire. The hum of their conversation mixed with the smell of smoke and roasting meat.

"The Ferris wheel was your idea, wasn't it?"

I looked away from the fire and found Hannah watching me.

"It's okay," she said. "Greer told me. I was standing by one of the booths with Ren and Makela when he ran up and said, 'Card said we should take a ride on the Ferris wheel. Just me and you. Together.' He was all jumpy when we got on. Talking a mile a minute. But then we got to the top of the wheel, and our car stopped. It was so beautiful, with the lights and all the people, that it even shut *him* up. Before we got moving again, he leaned over and kissed me."

She drew her legs up to her chest, hugging them.

"It lasted about two seconds before we both started laughing. He said he didn't know if he had any cousins, but he was pretty sure that kissing me was like kissing one of them. I told him I'd rather be kissing Snow Cone."

She smiled a little at the memory.

"Every time I close my eyes, I want to be back there at the top of the Ferris wheel, but I end up on the bridge instead. Was it like that with you and . . ."

I nodded. She moved closer and laid her head on my shoulder.

"Does it get better?"

"Sometimes it goes away for a while," I said. "But it always comes back."

"Not for much longer, I guess," she said. "Not for you."

"Yeah. I guess."

A few guys managed to bring down a small tree at the edge of the park. The crowd cheered as they dragged it over and hauled it up onto the fire, branches and leaves and all.

"Who was he really?" Hannah asked. "Before."

"It doesn't matter."

"It *does*."

"Why?"

Hannah was quiet a moment. "Because I want to know all of him," she said. "And once you forget . . ."

Down below, the bonfire leaped higher as it consumed its new fuel. Leaves curled and turned to ash. What could I do? Tell her that when I met Greer, practically the first two words out of his mouth were "mongrel" and "trash"? Or that half a second after that, his big brother pinned my arms behind my back so Greer could give me a black eye? Or that they'd done the same thing to Luke Tran and Rashawn Walken and to a dozen other kids like us? Telling Hannah any of that felt like killing him all over again.

"That other Greer —" I said, "— that wasn't him."

We watched the fire until it died down and the crowd thinned, wandering off into the dark. Eliot waved up to us, and then the others fell in behind him and he led them back toward the high school.

"How much time is left?" Hannah asked.

I looked at the moon hanging just above the tree line. Pretty soon the sun would be coming up over Lucy's Promise. "Not long."

We started down the hill side by side. Hannah took my hand and held it tightly. The feel of her skin, warm and slightly rough against my own, was still so new. We passed the remains of the bonfire and crossed the park. In the days since the riots the rubble had been cleared away and the worst scars in the grass had been filled in. Softened by the moon-light, Monument Park looked almost like new.

"We moved into the school's auditorium after you left," Hannah said. "There's more room and we can get away from everybody else. One day Freeman came by and gave us a copy of *Hamlet*. He said no one could truly understand what it meant to be human until they'd read Shakespeare."

"Sounds like something he'd say."

"So we started reading it which, of course, led the kids to actually wanting to perform it. Maybe it's crazy, but I thought it'd be good for them. Take their minds off things. Turns out Makela was born to be on the stage."

We came up out of the park and started along Magnolia Street.

"Makela?"

"I know," Hannah said. "I thought it would be Astrid, but as soon as Makela got onstage, it was just obvious. She'll be playing Hamlet, of course. Tomiko is Ophelia. I'm playing the queen."

"So you're an actor now."

She laughed. "I was going to say no, but then I started reading it, and — have you ever read Shakespeare?"

"A little."

"I don't think I knew anything that beautiful existed. Most of the time I feel like I'm this jumble. You know? But when I'm up on that stage, saying those words, it's like I come into focus."

"I guess we missed it when we tested you," I said. "You weren't just a nerd, you were a theater nerd."

She shook her head. "That's what I thought at first too," she said. "But there's nothing familiar about it at all. I think maybe that's the reason I like it. It feels new."

The high school appeared at the end of the street. Its windows were all lit up, casting a warm glow on the brick walls and the lawn that surrounded it. I could see shadows moving around inside. Every room seemed to be filled.

"We've still got a few parts we haven't cast yet," Hannah

said as she crossed into the schoolyard. "I bet you'd make a pretty good Horatio. Oh! Or you could be King Claudius. I think we've even got a crown that'll fit you. We'll check it out tomorrow after breakfast, and then we'll—"

"I think I should be alone."

She turned around and saw me standing at the edge of the sidewalk. The wind whipped her hair over her cheeks.

"When it happens," I said. "I think I should be alone."

"Why?"

I thought about the bonfire, how the flames had burned the leaves and the branches off that tree and made the bark into a crust of ash. I imagined the core of it deep inside, pale and untouched. When Lassiter's was done with me, I wondered what would be consumed and what would be left behind. Would I come out the other side like Greer? Like Dad?

"Because I don't know who I'm going to be yet."

I thought Hannah was going to fight me, but instead she came and took both my hands.

"You want to come inside and get your things first? We've got your pack and—"

I shook my head. There was nothing I needed. Nothing I wanted.

"There's a stand of dogwoods on the other side of the park," I said. "Near the fence. I'll be there. Come find me in a few hours."

Hannah's lips touched my cheek, and then she whispered in my ear.

"Who do you want to be when it's done?"

Everything that had happened in the last year ran through my mind all at once. The outbreak. Mom and Dad. You. Greer. I felt like a handful of barbed wire had been tied in a knot and buried in my stomach.

"No one."

She kissed me again, then squeezed my hand and crossed the lawn to the school's front steps. The door squeaked on its hinges as she opened it. Hannah looked back one last time, and then she went inside. The door shut behind her with a click.

Black River was hushed and still. I left the school and moved along the empty streets until I came to the dogwoods on the other side of the park. I found a place beneath one of them. Wind rustled the leaves, filling the night air with the scent of it. I thought of you and Mom and Dad and Greer and Hannah, and then I turned toward Lucy's Promise and watched as the first traces of dawn stretched over the summit, turning the black sky a deep ocean blue.

25

THE SUN ROSE over the town and fell again. I stepped onto the bridge that spanned Black River Falls.

The Marvin barricade was a mile and a half up the road, shadowed in the blue-gray twilight. I didn't see anyone manning it, just a line of sandbags and razor-topped fence. I walked out to the middle of the bridge and knelt in the roadway. The roar of the falls was like a radio caught in between stations. I laid my hand against the concrete and closed my eyes, praying there'd be nothing there, just darkness.

But no. Greer ran past, bare-chested, a blade flashing in his hand. There was a crack of thunder and then the sound of the knife hitting the ground. The world stopped, rewound, unspooled again.

I left the road and went to the stone guardrail. Forty feet below, the Black River was a ribbon of slate turning to foam as it went over the rocks. The sound was tremendous. I saw myself standing beside you down on the bank. It was summer. A month after we'd moved. We were tossing rocks into the water and you were telling me that as soon as you learned how to kayak, you were going to be the first guy ever to go over the falls and live to tell the tale. You laughed, but then the river was gone and I wasn't on the bridge anymore. I was in the yard across the street from our house, watching as you came stumbling out of the kitchen and onto the porch. You looked like you'd been laughing, but then your hand dropped away from your side and you fell against the wall next to the open door. Dad appeared and was gone again. And then I was on the porch, taking your hand. It was cold, and you were pale. There was the sound of wind chimes. Someone struck me from behind. Greer. Running past. I was on the bridge. There was the flash of a knife and then a crack and the ping of steel on concrete. A door slammed. I was in my room. Mom was running down the stairs. I followed. Dad's eyes were red. His back was pressed up against the stove. He had a knife in his hand. He raised the knife. There was a scream, and then you came stumbling out of the kitchen and onto the porch, your hand pressed into your side like you'd been laughing. Wind chimes clattered and pinged. The world smelled like the burnt head of a match. Cardinal told me the great secret of the world, and then he slipped a knife into my hand. His armor was torn. His wings were gone. There was a crack and then a scream and then the clang of a knife hitting the ground. You came stumbling out of the kitchen and onto the porch.

I took hold of the light post at the end of the bridge and climbed onto the railing. It was narrow and peaked in the middle, so my toes hung over the edge and I tipped forward. All I could see was stone and white water. Gravity tugged at me. I closed my eyes again, but you were still there and so were Greer and Mom and Dad.

"Cardinal."

It was a man's voice. Quiet enough not to startle me. I saw gray hair and a black coat out of the corner of my eye.

"Leave me alone, Freeman."

"Just come down off the railing," he said. "We can talk."

"There's nothing to talk about." He came closer, trying to get within arm's reach. "I said leave me alone!"

I faltered. Righted myself. Freeman backed off and put up his hands.

"You're immune," he said. "Aren't you?"

The wind whipped at my clothes. I nodded.

He took a small step toward me. "I knew it. All that time with those kids. You had to be. Think about what this means, Cardinal. Whatever's in your blood might be able to keep people from getting this. Maybe cure the ones who do."

"I don't care about that."

"I know that's not true. Cardinal—"

I was sick of talking. My fingers uncurled from the lamp-post and came free. I shuffled down the railing, out toward the center of the bridge where it rose the highest over the falls. Freeman shouted, but I ignored him. I stopped halfway across. Jagged rocks reached up toward me. Water spun in eddies around them and then shot away. I shut my eyes and thought of Hannah and the kids, but it lasted only a second before I was back where I belonged — with you and Greer in the Gardens of Null. I took a deep breath. The muscles in my legs tensed.

"I can make you forget!"

I looked over my shoulder. Freeman was just behind me on the sidewalk, his white hair dancing in the wind.

"The virus can be changed," he said, his voice trembling. "Re-engineered. A version can be made that will infect you."

"How do you know that?"

Freeman took another step closer. He held out his hand.

"Because," he said. "I'm the one who created it."

THE HAUNTED
PLAIN

26

EVERYTHING STARTED with Henry Allan Forrest."

We had left the bridge and were moving fast up Main Street. Freeman had his head down and his hands stuffed in his coat pockets.

"Henry was a U.S. Marine from Indiana. The son of a barber and an elementary school teacher. Blue eyes. Freckles. Red hair. Twenty-five, but he looked nineteen. He served two tours in Iraq and one in Afghanistan before returning home to a hero's welcome. Two and a half weeks later, while his parents were out getting the car washed, he used the dog's leash to hang himself in their basement."

We passed St. Stephen's and City Hall and then started up the streets that wound through the northside mansions. Freeman produced a small flashlight from his pocket. Its beam slid over once well-manicured lawns that had become thatches of weeds and wildflowers.

"And Henry wasn't alone," he said. "There were thousands just like him. Young men and women who came home only to discover that the war they thought they'd left behind was still lodged inside them.

An address on the side of a mailbox glimmered when

the light hit it. Freeman left the street and led me across an overgrown yard. A house emerged from the dark. No, not a house, more like a castle. Freeman started down a fieldstone walk and stopped at the foot of the stairs. White columns, like palace guards, stood on either side of a nearly eight-foot-tall front door. Freeman moved the flashlight's beam over the door's brass fixtures and up to a chandelier hanging over the porch.

"A team of researchers decided that the solution was to reach inside their heads and pluck out their memories of the war. Without those memories, they believed, soldiers like Henry Allan Forrest would be transformed back into the people they were."

Freeman climbed the stairs to the porch slowly, delicately, stopping just shy of the front door. He lowered the flashlight.

"Freeman, what are we doing here?" I asked. "Who lived here?"

"Charles Ellis Dumay."

"Who was Charles Ellis Dumay?"

Freeman brushed the brass doorknob with his fingertips. "Me," he said.

Behind us, there was the distant beat of a helicopter's blades as it flew over Black River. I climbed the stairs, stopping a few steps short of Freeman.

"You were one of the researchers."

"No," he said. "I *was* a scientist, though. Once. A good

one. But then some people offered me a very large sum of money to do something else."

"What?"

Freeman sat down at the top of the stairs, facing me.

"Travel the country, identifying research that had the greatest potential for profit. I became aware of the work of a small group of researchers in a lab in Atlanta. I thought it was something that could be expanded on and sold, most likely to one military or another. I bought the company, moved them here to Black River in secret, and steered their research in a direction my employers thought would be most profitable."

"A virus."

There was a click as Freeman turned off the flashlight, dropping us into darkness.

"Think about it," he said. "A weapon that can erase the past. What government on earth wouldn't want that?"

"What happened?"

He looked into the dark beside the house. "Will you go somewhere else with me?"

"Freeman —"

"It's close," he said. "I promise. And I think things will make more sense this way. Please."

He left the front porch and I followed him around the back of the house and across an immense lawn that ended at a tract of woods. We pushed our way through the trees until we emerged at the edge of a paved road. On the other side of it there was a large, dark clearing. Freeman crossed the road and kept going, his flashlight picking out heaped piles of rubble that we had to maneuver around.

"Where are we?"

Freeman said nothing. He stopped and turned in a circle, playing the flashlight beam over the wreckage around us. We were surrounded by piles of charred wood, metal, and cinderblock. I saw the skeletons of tables and chairs. Two partially collapsed walls rested against each other in the distance. I was standing in the remains of a building that had burned to the ground. I suddenly realized it was a place I'd seen a thousand times before, but always from the top of Lucy's Promise, where it looked like nothing more than a black smudge north of town.

"The Greeks believed that when you died, you had to cross five rivers before you could enter paradise."

He was a few feet away from me, ankle-deep in ashes, moving his light over the black hills of debris.

"The first four were the rivers of hate, sorrow, lamentation, and fire. The last was Lethe. The river of forgetfulness. No one could enter paradise until they'd had their old lives wiped away."

"What happened here?"

Freeman glanced over his shoulder. "The scientists I brought to Black River were idealists, but they weren't stupid. They put together what we intended to do with their research and decided to expose it. My employers asked me what

I thought they should do to prevent this from happening. I told them it was obvious. Infect the scientists with the virus, then take their research and start over somewhere else."

A breeze stirred the ashes at our feet. Freeman's eyes were gray hollows.

"Two of them escaped the lab after I infected them," he said. "I don't know if they made it to Monument Park that morning or if someone they infected did, but the outcome was the same."

His light slid over the remains of a wooden desk and blackened steel cabinets. Bits of broken glass glittered in the ashes.

"When I realized what was happening, I started a fire in the lab to erase the evidence. My employers said they'd get me out, but they were lying, of course. I was a loose end. I tried to escape before a quarantine was put in place, but I was infected."

Freeman jerked aside as I came at him through the ashes, but he wasn't fast enough. I planted both hands square on his chest and knocked him onto his back. He tried to scramble away, but I fell on him, straddling his chest and pinning him in place. I dug in the debris beside us and lifted out a charred plank the size of a baseball bat.

"Wait. Cardinal, please."

"You did this. You did *all* of it."

I lifted the club over my head, aiming for his skull.

"I wasn't lying when I said I could make you forget!"

My arm froze where it was. I tightened my grip on the end of the plank.

"Your friend," Freeman said. "In the National Guard. Can he still get you out of Black River?"

I nodded. He pointed awkwardly to his right coat pocket.

"Take them," he said. "Please."

I kept one eye on him as I reached inside and pulled out four small black notebooks.

"What are they?"

"My memory," he said. "Everything I wrote before and after I became infected. Names. Dates. Enough to make sure everyone who needs to be held accountable for what happened here will be. There are details about the virus too, how we engineered it, how it works. With that and whatever's in your blood that's made you immune, I think Dr. Lassiter will be able to make a cure. A vaccine at least."

I got up slowly, holding the plank in one hand and the notebooks in the other. Freeman scurried away and retrieved his flashlight.

"You've had these all this time? You could have sent them to the police. The newspapers."

"They've been watching me," he said. "They're always watching me."

"Who?"

Freeman nodded toward the notebook on the top of the stack. I opened it, and he shined his flashlight across the pages. They were filled with names and dates and formulas that meant nothing to me. But one thing stood out. A name was referenced on nearly every single page. As soon as I saw, it was so obvious that I wondered how I hadn't realized it before.

"Martinson Vine," I said. "They were your employer. That's why they pushed to take over the quarantine from the Guard. Why they arrested you that first day."

"And why they ransacked my library," Freeman said. "They wanted to see if I was still a loose end. Luckily, there's no better place to hide a few books than a library. My antic disposition was enough to convince them that I wasn't a threat."

I weighed the notebooks in my hand. "What about . . ."

Freeman produced a thin white envelope from another pocket deep in his coat.

"Like I said, I was a scientist once too. Dr. Lassiter will be able to use what's inside this envelope to engineer a version of the virus that will infect you."

"Why would he do that?" I asked. "Infect some kid he doesn't even know."

"Because, unlike Charles Ellis Dumay," he said, "Evan Lassiter is a good man. He'll understand that the reason those scientists started their research in the first place was to help people like you."

"What do you mean people like me?"

"People who are trapped somewhere they don't want to be."

I took the envelope and turned it over in my hands. It

contained nothing but a few sheets of paper. Was it really possible? A new world. A new me. I slipped it into one of the notebooks.

"You trust me with all of this?"

Freeman allowed himself a thin smile. "I told you, one glance and I knew your past and your future."

"If all this gets out, the Marvins won't be the only ones in trouble."

"I'm responsible for the deaths of hundreds of people," he said. "Including your friends and family. Even after I testify against my employers, I expect to be in jail for a very long time."

"And you're okay with that?"

Freeman looked over the ruins, back toward Black River.

"I've stood on that bridge too, Cardinal. Many times. Whatever the powers that be decide to do with me will be better than I deserve."

He held out the flashlight and I took it.

"You're not coming?"

Freeman didn't answer, he simply turned his back on me and walked out into the wreckage, until the darkness swallowed him up.

27

WAITED UNTIL I was sure everyone would be asleep before I went to the high school. The front door creaked as I pushed it open. I snapped the flashlight on and followed its beam down halls lined with stacked chairs and tables. The walls were covered in construction-paper posters from before the outbreak. I felt like I was walking through a haunted house.

I found Hannah and the others sleeping on cots in the auditorium. Safety lights by the doors cast a cool glow through the cavernous room. I crept down the aisle and onto the stage. Hannah was on her back, her eyes closed. In the flashlight's beam the white sheet that covered her looked like a mantle of snow. My backpack sat on the floor beside her.

I turned off the flashlight and knelt by her cot. Hannah moved onto her side, her lips slightly parted, her breath ruffling the thin sheet that draped her shoulder. I forced myself to look away from her face and reach for the backpack. I unzipped it and felt around inside. My notebook. A pen. At the very bottom was the cell phone Gonzalez had given me. I dropped Freeman's notebooks inside and zipped the pack closed.

When I stood up, a hand snapped around my wrist.

"Card?"

I tore myself away and sprinted out of the room. I was nearly to the exit when I hit one of the stacks of chairs that had been left in the hallway and went sprawling across the floor in a rattle of collapsing steel. I tried to get up again, but Hannah was on me before I could move, her hands on my shoulders, pinning me down.

"It's still you, isn't it? You're still Card."

"I don't —"

"We tried to find you, but you were gone. We looked everywhere. What happened? How did you —"

I knocked her hands off me and rolled away, scrambling for the backpack amid the fallen chairs. There was another crash of metal as I yanked it out of the pile.

"You're immune."

I pulled the backpack close and wrapped my arms around it. Outside, moonlight struck the sidewalk and lawn. They were only a few feet away, on the other side of the glass doors, but I suddenly felt so tired I stayed where I was, kneeling on the tile floor, my back to her. I nodded.

"So, you're leaving?"

She was sitting cross-legged behind me in a pool of moonlight coming through the windows in one of the open classrooms along the hall. Her hair was mussed. She was barefoot, in plaid pajamas.

"Yeah."

"I could go get the kids if you —"

I shook my head. If I saw them, if I talked to them, I knew I'd never be able to do what I had to do. "I think I should just go."

Hannah stared at me. Footsteps sounded on the floor above us. Someone was coming to check on all the noise. I lifted my backpack and started for the door.

"Hey."

Hannah was standing in the hallway.

"Let me change," she said. "I'll walk out with you."

It was a clear summer night. The streets were empty. I told Hannah everything that had happened with Freeman. Who he was. What he'd done. The notebooks, his hope for a cure, and his certainty that Dr. Lassiter would be able to infect me. She nodded through it all, saying little. When we passed a neighborhood playground, she left the sidewalk and sat on one of the swings. I took the one beside her, and we drifted back and forth.

"Do you think they'll send you back here?" she asked. "Once you're infected."

"Guess they'll have to send me somewhere."

"Well, if it's here, you don't have to worry. We won't bother you."

"Hannah —"

"Not *bother* you," she said. "You know what I mean. We'll let you be no one, like you want."

We were quiet for a while, and then Hannah jumped off

the swing and crossed the playground to a set of monkey bars. She climbed the ladder and crawled out to the middle, where she sat with her legs folded beneath her. I climbed up behind her and found a spot of my own, four or five feet away. Old habits.

"Do you really think he'll be able to make a cure?" Hannah asked.

"Freeman seems to think so."

"You don't?"

I shrugged. Miracle cures and villains brought to justice. They seemed like things that happened in the pages of one of Dad's comics.

"If there's a cure, do you think they'll *make* us take it?"

She was leaning over the edge of the monkey bars with her arms wrapped around her middle, staring at the ground.

"You don't want to find out who you are?" I asked. "Why you came here?"

"I already know."

"You do? Did you talk to the Marvins or —"

"I didn't talk to anybody."

"Then how do you know?"

Hannah sat up and looked out to where St. Stephen's spire rose over the town.

"There's this scene in *Hamlet* where the queen has to tell Laertes that his sister, Ophelia, died," she said. "Ophelia was in love with Hamlet, and he loved her too. But then one day he became cruel. He toyed with Ophelia and he rejected her and he would never even say why. In the end Ophelia drapes herself with wildflowers and lies down in a stream to drown. When the queen tells her brother what she's done, it's this beautiful, sad speech. *There is a willow grows aslant a brook* . . . The first time I read it, I started to cry. There was something about it that seemed so familiar. I thought maybe it was because I'd studied the play in school or something. But it wasn't the whole play that felt familiar, it was just them, just Hamlet and Ophelia."

She smiled dreamily.

"I felt like I knew them so well that I knew things Shakespeare didn't even write. Like how, in the beginning, when they were still happy, they used to meet in secret at a cabin with a sky blue door. But there were things Shakespeare got wrong, too."

Her look darkened and she turned away again.

"It wasn't Hamlet who became cruel. It was Ophelia. He loved her and she toyed with him and rejected him. It was Hamlet who was heartbroken. It was Hamlet who drowned. And when Ophelia saw what she'd caused, she felt this pounding deep in her chest, like a second heartbeat, and she just . . . ran."

Hannah fingered the key around her neck.

"No one needs to tell me who I am," she said. "I know."

"Hannah, you can't really know that. You —"

She looked back over her shoulder. The sun was just coming up over Lucy's Promise.

"Tomiko and Crystal have to start cooking breakfast soon," she said. "I like to be there when everybody wakes up."

She slid off the bars and landed on the ground. When we got back to the high school, Hannah climbed to the top of the stairs, but she didn't go inside. She stood there, just under the single bulb that lit the entryway, staring at our reflections in the glass of the front door. The night was soft and quiet.

"I'll tell everybody you said goodbye."

I kicked at one of the concrete steps. "Yeah. Thanks."

I started to move away, but Hannah spun and ran back down the stairs. The next thing I knew, her arms were around me and her lips were pressing into mine. I closed my eyes and it was as if some barrier between us had dropped away, as if we'd both melted into this warm darkness.

"Do you remember the night we saw the fireflies?" she asked.

Our arms were still around each other and our foreheads were touching. I imagined our breath swirling together in invisible eddies between us. I said that I did.

"And then later, when it was just you and me on that trail and the moon was out?"

I tried to say yes, but I couldn't seem to speak. She pressed the flat of her palm against my chest.

"You'll forget that too," she said. "And this."

She kissed me again, and then a light came on inside the school, erasing our reflections in the door. Tomiko and Carrie came out of the auditorium, yawning and stretching.

Snow Cone padded beside them, sniffing at the air. Hannah reached back and undid the leather cord that held her key.

"Here," she said. "Take this."

"No, I can't. You—"

The key twisted and flashed as she tied it around my neck. It settled in the hollow of my throat, still warm from resting against hers.

She went back up the stairs and reached for the door.

"Do you still feel it?" I asked. "The heartbeat."

Tomiko and Carrie saw Hannah and waved, huge smiles brightening their faces. Hannah waved back, and then she looked over her shoulder at me.

"Every day."

She pushed open the door and went inside. Snow Cone barked happily as Carrie and Tomiko threw their arms around Hannah. As they started toward the cafeteria, Hannah turned back to me one last time. The glow from the lights in the hall washed over her, warming her face and her shoulders and her long neck. She smiled, and then she was gone.

I ran a fingertip along the blade of the key, and then I walked away.

28

W HEN I PULLED the phone out of my backpack and turned it on, I was greeted by a dozen old voice mails and text messages, all from Gonzalez, all from the days following the riots. I got him on the third ring, and after a few minutes of assuring him that I was fine and Hannah and the kids were fine, I asked if he thought he could still get me out. He said he could, and then there was a long silence that made me think we might have lost the connection.

"Gonzalez?"

There was a sigh, and then he said one word. "Greer."

I was in the park then, and I sank against the fence that surrounded the basketball courts. "Didn't know you knew."

"Whole thing was twenty-four-seven breaking news out here," he said. "For a few days, anyway. There was some noise about the guy who shot him being prosecuted, but nothing came of it. Chaotic night. He was just doing his job. He felt threatened. The usual thing."

There were other voices on his end. Gonzalez leaned away from the phone and called out to them in Spanish.

"Sorry," he said. "I'm back in the Bronx with my folks for a while. I'll text you the address. You're coming here when you get out, right?"

My hand went automatically to Freeman's letter in my pocket. "I don't know. There are some things I have to do."

"Could really use you, buddy," he said. "Remember that portfolio review at Comic Con?"

I had forgotten about it completely. It seemed impossible to believe that there was a world where things like that were still going on.

"It got me a sit-down with some guys at Marvel, which is awesome, except they want me to pitch projects to them. I'm sitting here trying to brainstorm, and it's like, when nobody cared about my ideas, I had a million of them. Now that someone *does* care, I got nothin'. I need that Cassidy *brain*."

I kicked at the bottom of the fence. "Listen. I better—"

"Yeah. Say your goodbyes, man. I'll have news soon. A few hours from now Cardinal Cassidy will be NYC bound!"

Gonzalez hung up. By then, scores of infected were coming into the park. I threw the phone into the backpack and got moving without any real destination in mind.

As the sun rose, the infected headed toward Monument Park or to the barricades. They gathered into work crews as they went. Some set about carting off the last of the riot debris, others fought back overgrown foliage or fortified the wall that stood between us and the rest of the world. On a tree-lined street one group stood around a vacant lot between two houses that had been cleared and tilled, revealing rich black earth.

"So we put cauliflower here," a man said as he sorted through packets of seeds. "And the broccoli over there."

"But then where does the cabbage go?" asked another.

"What cabbage?" a woman asked. "Where do you see cabbage?"

"Right there."

"That's not cabbage, that's arugula."

"What about the tomatoes?"

"Guys! Hold on, okay? Just give me a second."

The group shifted, revealing a woman in a wide straw hat standing with her back to me, poring over a book. She looked from the garden plot to the book and back again.

"Broccoli," she said, pointing to a spot by the fence and then ticking off three more. "Radishes. Spinach. Cauliflower." She slammed the book closed. "We're planting for a late fall harvest, so no tomatoes."

Everyone moved away to start digging in the spots Mom had indicated. She looked a little less thin than she had the last time I'd seen her. There was a roundness to her face. A glow to her skin.

"Honestly, Sara," one of the women said. "I don't understand what you're even doing here this morning."

"Just wanted to get my hands dirty," Mom said as she knelt in the dirt.

"Yeah, but don't you have to get ready?"

Mom ripped the top of a packet of seeds. "It's a party. We've thrown a dozen of them."

I moved into a stand of trees across the street and watched as she planted row after row and then gently covered the seeds with soil. Eventually, the rest of the crew insisted that she go home and get ready for a party that was happening later that afternoon.

Mom took her book and left the garden, strolling down the sidewalk. I made a slow count to twenty, then fell in behind her. She ended up in the yard of a small yellow house at the end of a cul de sac, the same one I'd broken into that night weeks ago. She crossed the lawn then disappeared into the backyard. It wasn't long before others arrived, singly and in groups, and followed her. Some carried small boxes, others baskets filled with bread or bundles of flowers bound in twine. I watched them for a while, then started to leave. Before I could take more than a few steps, though, a group of men and women swept by me toward the house.

"Where ya going?" one of them called. "Party's this way!"

"No, I'm not — I was just —"

Someone laughed and hooked her arm through mine, pulling me along, even as I protested. Before I knew it, we were in the backyard, and the group dispersed. I knew I should leave but the scene behind the house kept me rooted in place.

The backyard was full of people, dozens of them, mostly

milling around a long table loaded down with food and glass pitchers of water with thick slices of lemon floating inside. Everywhere I looked, there were flowers. Daisies mostly, and sunflowers, bundled on tables and on the seats of mismatched chairs. A man with a guitar showed up and then a woman with a violin. The crowd cheered as they started to play. So many infected in one place triggered this bone-deep instinct — to turn and go, to run, to get away. But then I remembered that I was safe. Immune.

I found myself weaving through the party in a kind of dream. Even though my clothes were ragged and grimy from old sweat and ash and blood, the people who noticed barely seemed to care. It was crowded enough by then that my arm or shoulder kept brushing someone else's. At first, I'd jerk away immediately, but they'd simply smile and go back to their conversations. Once, I passed by a man telling a story, and when he was done the people around him laughed so hard that I felt the rush of their breath against my skin and didn't even flinch. And the smells! Without my mask, I picked out the scents of sweat and soap, of fruit and grass and flowers.

By the time I made it to the other side of the yard my head was spinning. I grabbed hold of the food table to steady myself. There was a pitcher of water nearby. I filled a glass and drank it in one long gulp. It was cold and sharp with the flavor of lemons.

"Mind if I join you?"

I turned at the sound of the voice. Mom was standing just behind me, fanning herself with a folded-up sheet of paper. She was in khaki shorts and a button-up shirt that was covered with embroidered flowers. Her deep brown skin was glowing with sun and sweat. She came up to the table and poured herself a glass of water.

"Did you get something to eat?" she asked once she drained it. "There's plenty. More than plenty. Though, I hope you like tuna noodle casserole. There was so much canned tuna in the last supply drop, we have six of them."

"Sara!"

Mom turned and waved at someone on the other side of the yard. "Jessica! Is Richard here?"

"He's right behind me. He and Jack are lugging the grill."

"He's not going to throw out his back again, is he?"

"Fingers crossed!"

Mom laughed. I put down my glass and started to walk away. "I should probably let you —"

Mom grabbed my shoulder to stop me. "I hate to ask, but do you think you could help me with something?" She pointed up the back stairs to the porch door. "We're giving one of our neighbors a chair we don't need, and since you're the only strapping young man currently present, I thought maybe you could help me carry it down."

"I —"

"Nope! Won't take no for an answer. Come on! It'll earn you an extra slice of cake!"

She threaded her way through her guests and up the stairs. It was cool inside the house, but there was an odd musty smell that made me think of mothballs and lace. I flashed back to the last time I was there. Fred on the ground. Mom screaming. I looked to see if there was any trace of blood left on the floor, but it had all been wiped away.

"Can I get you anything?"

Mom had gone to the kitchen and was pouring herself another glass of water from the sink.

I shook my head. "No. I'm fine. Thanks. Which chair do you want to . . ."

"It's the blue one," she said. "But have a seat. I just need to cool down a second. Hot out there, isn't it?"

I dropped into a chair at the kitchen table, which was decorated with a vase of plastic sunflowers and a set of porcelain dog and cat salt- and peppershakers. Mom drained her glass, then drew aside the curtains over the sink. The sunlight made bronze highlights on her skin. I saw her in an airy dress of yellow and green tatters, gliding across a dark stage. I took the saltshaker and tried to become absorbed in turning it in small circles.

"That was Fred's mom's. He keeps talking about boxing up her stuff and putting it in the attic, but he never does."

Mom moved from the sink and took a seat across from me. She toyed with the plastic sunflowers.

"He has all these old handwritten cookbooks of hers, and he's working his way through them, trying to relearn the recipes. He says when he smells her meatloaf, he comes this close to remembering her."

Mom smiled at me over the flowers. For a second it was as if we were back before the outbreak, sitting at the kitchen table after school, as we had a hundred times before. In the weeks since I'd first seen her, I'd come up with a hundred things I wanted to ask, but all of them suddenly left my head. It had been stupid to follow her.

I bent down and reached for my backpack. "If you show me which chair you want moved, I can —"

"I know who you are."

I froze, my hand suspended over the pack's strap.

"I saw you in the alley that time. And then again the night —" She took in a breath. "The night you came here."

"I don't —"

"It's okay," she said quickly. "I'm not going to — Fred didn't recognize you and I don't think . . . I don't know why, but I don't think you're dangerous. Are you?"

I shook my head.

"Why'd you come here that night?"

Her voice sounded exactly the same then as it did when we were little and one of us had gotten into trouble for something. Dad always yelled, but not her. She'd ask why we did what we did, as if she were just curious, as if we might have a reason and that the reason would matter.

"I thought that man, Fred — I thought he might have taken you."

"Why did you think that?"

I shrugged. What could I say? There was a squeak as Mom's chair moved closer to the table. She took the pepper-shaker and turned it over in her long fingers, studying it as if a secret code had been scratched into its side.

"We knew each other before," she said. "Didn't we?"

I started to speak, but then there was a surge of noise from the party as the glass door to the porch slid open.

"Sara! Everyone all right in here?"

Mom jumped up from the table and ran to Fred as he came into the room. She slipped her arm around him and kissed him on the cheek. "We're good! This is, uh . . ."

"Tom," I said quickly.

"Tom. Right. He worked on the gardening crew with us. He was going to help me get that chair for Mrs. Beamon."

"Ah, so he's a lifesaver then!" Fred crossed the kitchen in two brisk strides and shook my hand. I could feel the waxy scar I had given him just behind his knuckles. "I've had this twinge in my back for weeks and can't seem to shake it. In thanks, we'll send you home with thirty-five to forty pounds of leftover tuna noodle casserole."

He turned back to Mom and clapped his hands together.

"Now! My dear one. My sweet. I'm sorry to say it, but the time is almost upon us."

"Seriously?" Mom whined. "Can't we just skip it and run away somewhere? Come on, it'll be all mysterious."

Fred laughed, and then, when he saw that I didn't understand, he said, "We promised our friends that if they brought their instruments, Sara and I would kick off the dancing. She's nervous."

"I know it's silly," she said. "But I'm positive that I have two left feet. I've never been more sure of anything in my life. I'm going to be a disaster."

"You're going to be wonderful," Fred said.

"I just have to pull myself together."

He kissed the tip of her nose. "Bourbon's in the cupboard," he said. "I'll go stall. Tom, thanks again. Feel free to come over and lift heavy things for me anytime."

There was another rush of noise as he opened the porch door and closed it behind him. I followed as Mom moved to the living room, to a window that looked out onto the backyard. Fred was circulating through the crowd, catching up everyone around him in great bear hugs and then laughing.

"Not long after I met Fred, this guardsman was going door-to-door," she said. "He had a stack of papers, and he was telling everyone who they were. Fred already knew who he was by then, but I didn't. When the guardsman came to our house, I had Fred tell him to go away."

"Why?"

Mom's forehead wrinkled with concentration. "When I try to look into that place, into the time before, I have this feeling that . . ."

She shook her head, frustrated.

"What?"

"There were good things then," she said carefully, as if she were making her way across an old bridge, testing each step before she committed to it. "I know that. There were people I loved, who loved me. But there's something else in that place too, something that . . ."

Mom took hold of an edge of the dusty curtain and crimped it between her fingers.

"I was helping Fred cook once," she said. "I went to chop some carrots, but as soon as my hand touched the knife, I started crying and I couldn't stop. Every time I try to think about why, it's like I can't breathe."

Tears came into her eyes. Outside the window Fred and some of their guests were clearing an area in the middle of the yard. Fred must have felt Mom looking at him, because he turned and waved expansively, like someone hailing a ship. She smiled and brushed away her tears.

"When I was first getting to know Fred, it was like . . . it was like I was walking by a pool on a summer day. I wanted to run right at it and dive into the deepest part without looking. Just to get cool as fast as possible, you know? I think maybe that's how I did things before, but I didn't want to do that with him. I eased in." She smiled again. "As much as I could, anyway. Everything seems so simple now. We're just happy. It's like learning to walk. It seems so obvious once you know how."

Mom swept away the last of her tears and then her hand

fell to her side. I thought she was going to pull away when I took it, but she didn't. Her fingers curled around mine and pressed into my palm.

"You were right," I said. "We did know each other. Before."

Mom didn't say anything for a long time. She didn't move. The air in the house became perfectly still. Outside, her friends seemed to move in slow motion.

"How?"

When I didn't answer, she turned around.

"Will I be better off if I know?"

In that second it seemed like our whole life streamed by. Mom dancing. Mom bent over a garden washed in sunlight, her hands buried in the soil. Mom collapsed on her knees on the other side of your body.

"I don't know," I said. "I really don't."

There was a round of applause outside, and then the musicians started to play. Fred lifted his arms and mimed a waltz, grinning up at the window. I let go of Mom's hand.

"You should go," I said. "You don't want to miss your dance."

Mom looked into a mirror that hung by the window and smoothed her hair. When she was done, she crossed to the porch door, pausing there with her palm pressed against the glass.

"Do you remember a game called Monopoly?"

I nodded.

"We have a tournament every Monday night," she said. "Fred and I and our friends. Maybe you could join us sometime. And then we could talk more. The three of us. I think I'd like that. I think we both would."

A chant started up outside. "Sa-*ra!* Sa-*ra!* Sa-*ra!*"

She smiled. "Guess that's my cue."

"Don't worry about the dance," I said. "You're going to be great."

"Fingers crossed."

The crowd cheered as Mom went out the porch door and waved regally. I watched from the window as she descended the stairs, and then she and Fred moved out to the middle of the yard. At first Mom clutched at Fred, resting her head on his chest as he turned them through the grass and whispered in her ear. But then something seemed to ease in her, and her long legs swept across the grass, her toes pointed. Her chest rose and her head and shoulders fell back, making her body into this perfect swanlike curve. Fred responded immediately. His body straightened and lifted. It was as if the music had moved through the air and into Mom and then, through her, into him. Their bodies melded together and whirled through space, perfectly unmoored, gliding. As they came near the window, Mom looked up at me and smiled a radiant, laughing smile. The strangeness of it was overwhelming. It was her, but not her. It was then. It was before.

There was a buzz behind me. I returned to the kitchen

and took the phone from my backpack. A text from Gonzalez: *Front gate. One hour.*

I stood in the kitchen imagining all the different ways my future could branch out from that single point. Go to the gate and leave Black River. Stay here with Mom and Fred. I saw the three of us sitting at the kitchen table with the Monopoly board between us. We'd play deep into the night and end up draped over the furniture in the living room, talking.

But then how long would it be before Mom asked about our life before? And then, how long until I told her? What good would it do, I wondered, to bring that old world into this one? Would she be any happier? Would any of us?

The music surged. I turned back to the window. The rest of the crowd had joined in the dance, making the backyard into a universe of spinning bodies. I caught one last glimpse of Mom and Fred, and then they vanished into it. It was a future that belonged to them and them alone. I had no right to take it away.

My phone buzzed again. There was one last thing I had to do before I left Black River. I lifted the backpack onto my shoulder and walked out the front door.

A few minutes later I was standing on our front lawn. It didn't surprise me. By then the house's ability to draw me back seemed perfectly natural. I climbed the porch steps and went inside, letting the same invisible hand that had guided me across Black River lead me up the stairs, past your room and mine and Mom and Dad's. I didn't stop until I came to Dad's office.

The door was closed. Covered in months of dust that turned the white wood an ashy gray. I took hold of the cool metal knob. The works inside it creaked as the bolt drew back into its housing. A crack of light appeared between the wall and the door. I let go and it swung open. There was a sigh as the air trapped inside the room was released.

I stepped into Dad's office.

All his things were still there, exactly where he must have left them when he walked out the morning of the sixteenth. I ran my hand along the spines of the books on his shelves. Countless sci-fi and horror paperbacks, box-set DVDs, and comics in tall collected editions. All of them were set back from the edge to make room for the horde of souvenirs he'd picked up at various cons and festivals over the years. Day of the Dead skulls; toy cars; a set of juggling balls; the small, grim army of ceramic superheroes that guarded all of it. Batman. Superman. Captain America. Dr. Strange. Cardinal.

I went to a window and forced it open. A grass-scented breeze swept in, carrying the hum of distant voices. I leaned over the sill and took three slow breaths. When my head cleared, I stood up with my back to the room. I was positive that if I turned around, I'd find Dad bent over his desk like Smaug in his den, head down, his massive frame curled over the computer as he tapped out his scripts.

Of course, when I did turn, there was nothing but a black, armless chair tucked under a desk. Dad's laptop was closed, and next to it was an empty Superman mug, an uncapped fountain pen, and the lumpy ceramic cup I'd made him in the third grade. It was filled with a bouquet of black pencils. The words FOR DAD were badly painted on one side in green and red. I'd given it to him for Christmas, wrapped in the pages of the Sunday comics. I remembered him unpacking it the day we moved to Black River and then filling it with great ceremony. His favorite pencils. A fistful of change. And something else. Something he drew from his pocket and dropped inside. Something that landed with a soft ping.

I dumped the pencils and the change out onto the desk and sorted through them until I found what I was looking for. A key. Thin and delicate. I turned it over in my fingers, then took it to the filing cabinet by the desk. My hands trembled as I slipped it into the lock. There was a click, and the top drawer popped open. It was empty except for a single brown folder labeled

THE BROTHERHOOD OF WINGS
— Volume 5 —
THE HAUNTED PLAIN

There were six manila envelopes inside, one for each of the issues that would make up the final volume. The first two envelopes contained completed scripts and rough sketches.

The next three had general notes and an outline. I sank to the floor, spread the papers out in front of me, and began to read.

Cardinal was bloody and battered, and his armor was falling to pieces when he was exiled to the Gardens of Null, but he didn't give up. He knew that he had the only thing he needed — time. The Volanti wouldn't arrive for another year, and he was determined to be ready for them. He spent the following months scavenging the Gardens for any piece of technology that might help him repair his armor, all the while fending off attacks by radiation-mad gangs of mutants and the vicious Hounds of Null.

As Cardinal toiled in his cave workshop, other exiles living in the Gardens drifted into the story. They were all funhouse versions of the Brotherhood. The fat and jolly, if slightly dim Brother Handcrank was clearly meant to be Goldfinch, and Jumpin' Jerry Johnson was an even younger and more innocent take on Blue Jay. The others were there too — Black Eagle, Rex Raven — all except for Sally Sparrow. Her absence was like a dark hole in the center of the story.

Cardinal pushed the exiles away. He insisted that his work was too important to be interrupted, but it was obvious that their presence reminded him too much of his dead friends. One night, in the midst of a furious radiation storm, a gang of mutants raided the workshop. Cardinal was on the verge of defeat until Jumpin' Jerry and his friends swarmed the cave and saved Cardinal's life. Afterward, as they tended his wounds, Cardinal told them about his mission. In the end he was convinced that he couldn't beat a force like the Volanti alone, and he agreed to make them into a new Brotherhood. The fourth issue ended with Cardinal sitting down at his workbench to begin construction of their armor.

After that, all that was left were notes and scraps of dialogue. The fifth issue was to take place on the day of the Volanti's arrival.

"Gee whiz, Cardinal! What's gonna happen to you when we win?" Jumpin' Jerry asked in a bit of dialogue Dad had scratched out on a napkin. "I mean, when we knock the stuffing out of these jerks, Future You won't have a reason to come back in time, which means you won't be here to train us to beat the jerks in the first place!"

"Easy, Jerry," Cardinal said. "You think about this stuff too much, you'll break your brainpan. I think time has a way of sorting itself. As for me, when we win and the future is put right again, I guess, well, I guess I'll just . . . disappear."

I opened the last envelope. Issue six. Inside, there was nothing but a single sheet of paper. Dad's only note for the final issue was written in a scrawl so dark that it almost ripped through the page.

At the battle's decisive moment Jerry Johnson is revealed to be an advance agent of the Volanti. He betrays Cardinal and the Brotherhood. All but Cardinal are killed. The Volanti land, and the transformation of Abaddon into Liberty City begins. Cardinal, barely clinging to life, lives out the rest of his days alone, trapped in the Gardens of Null.

The page fell out of my hands. It fluttered through the air and landed on the pile in front of me.

29

R. LASSITER'S OFFICE takes up the top floor of a building so tall that when I stood at the windows in the lobby, I could see all the way to where the Hudson and the East River meet at the southern tip of Manhattan. Brooklyn was locked in fog on the opposite shore.

"Mr. Cassidy?"

The receptionist stood at her desk by an open door, a clipboard in her hands.

"This way, please."

Lassiter's private office was full of sunlight that streamed in through a window behind his desk. The receptionist said the doctor would be right with me, then closed the door. I took a seat. Muffled footsteps passed down the hallway outside. My fingers drummed against my leg. I unzipped my backpack and pulled out Dad's folder.

I'd read every page of his notes a dozen times since I left Black River, but I couldn't seem to stop myself from going over them again and again. I thought if I studied every word, every line of dialogue, every sketch, I might find some hint of the person Dad used to be. The one who'd trooped off to the diner with us on Sunday mornings and laughed as we all squeezed into the booth and paid for short stacks and bacon with handfuls of quarters. The one who wrote those early Brotherhood issues in the corner of the living room, while we played video games and Mom cheered us on.

No matter how hard I looked, that man wasn't there. Maybe it was the unfairness of it that bothered me the most. Dad had dreamed about writing *The Brotherhood of Wings* ever since he'd been a little kid, dazzled by old Justice League and Legion of Super Heroes comics. It was his story. It wasn't right that the last chapters were written by a complete stranger.

There was a hum as the air conditioning cycled on over my head. I slipped the folder into my pack, trading it for Freeman's letter. Strange how heavy a couple sheets of paper and an envelope could be. I turned it over in my hands. What had Freeman called his library cards? Letters of transit? I guess this letter was that too. A passport to a different world. Another me.

I put the envelope back and went to the window. This one faced north, looking out over Central Park and Harlem and then past that to where the skyscrapers disappeared. I could just make out a few hills rising in the gray distance. Even though Black River was hours away, I picked out the tallest one and told myself it was Lucy's Promise.

My hand went to the key hanging around my neck. It was

cool and heavy. I closed my fingers around it and shut my eyes.

I was on the bridge over Black River Falls, looking up at Lucy's Promise, its green lap and shoulders. And then I was in the camp, standing in the middle of the four cabins with the trail behind me and the woods all around. I could smell dark earth and rainwater and the papery scent of old leaves. Everything was just the way it used to be, except now it was all so empty and so quiet. The next thing I knew, I was flying off the mountain and over Black River. I saw everyone as they were in that moment. Freeman in his library, shuffling between stacks of books that weren't really books but alternate realities cast in ink and paper. Mom kneeling in her garden, her hands in the earth, Fred by her side. I saw Hannah next. She was standing onstage, surrounded by velvety darkness, a silver crown circling her green hair. The kids were all around her. On the stage. In the wings. Watching from the front row, wide-eyed and grinning. I whispered their names one by one. Makela. Astrid. Tomiko. Isaac. Eliot. Ren. Crystal. Jenna. Carrie. DeShaun. Ricky. Margo. Benny.

Footsteps clicked down the hallway behind me and stopped on the other side of Dr. Lassiter's door. Voices murmured. Someone laughed. I pulled Freeman's journals out of my pack and stacked them on the desk. As the doorknob started to turn, I reached back in for Freeman's letter. Dr. Lassiter stepped into the room. He was younger-looking than

I expected. Tall and thin, with sandy hair and clear gray eyes that reminded me, with a jolt, of Greer's.

"So," he said, laying his hands flat on his desk. "What can I do for you, Mr. Cassidy?"

Dr. Lassiter smiled. The sky over his shoulder was a clear blue. Freeman's letter slipped out of my fingers.

That was almost two weeks ago. Dr. Lassiter and I talked for a long time that first morning. I'm pretty sure he thought the whole thing was a prank until he read Freeman's journals. He got excited after that and told me I needed to stay in town for a while so he could scan my brain and run all these tests on my blood. He keeps saying there aren't any guarantees, but it's clear he thinks he's onto something.

Whatever happens, once he's done with his work, we're going to pack up all of Freeman's journals and give them to this reporter he knows at the *New York Times*. Man, watching that bomb go off is going to be *fun*.

So how's day-to-day life for a human test subject? Not too bad, actually. Lassiter got me a room on the very top floor of one of those midtown hotels that's like a hundred stories tall and has all the cable TV and room service a guy could want. That's where I am now, sitting at a desk by the window, looking out at the city and writing to you.

Every morning I leave the hotel and head to Lassiter's office for whatever tests he's come up with that day. When he's done I go for a walk. I've probably walked the entire island of Manhattan at this point. It's strange being surrounded by so many people again. Having concrete under my feet instead of dirt. Traffic lights and street signs instead of trees. More than once I've lost my bearings and turned to look for Lucy's Promise — as if some part of me thinks I'll find it towering over the Empire State Building or St. Patrick's Cathedral — but of course it's never there, and I have to find my way without it.

I always seem to end up in Brooklyn, at that park we went to the day Mom and Dad told us we were moving to Black River. I get an ice cream, grab a seat on a bench, and write to you. When I'm done, I take out Freeman's letter and try to figure out why I haven't given it to Lassiter yet. I mean to do it every morning, but then every afternoon I walk out of his office and it's still sitting in my backpack. When I get to my hotel room, I put it on my nightstand and fall asleep staring at it.

When I haven't been writing to you, or walking, or getting poked with needles by a mad scientist, I've been helping Gonzalez get ready for the big meeting he has with Marvel. Now that the Guard's out of Black River he's back to the usual one weekend of training a month. In between, he works on his comics and strives to be as civilian as humanly possible. His hair has gone a little shaggy, and he's grown what he insists is a beard, but it's really just these weird patches of stubble.

He flipped when I told him what he was going to be pitching to Marvel. I laid everything out for him not long after I got to the city. Dad's notes and sketches for Volume Five, plus a few additions of my own. He got to work immediately and has barely taken a break since.

It's a clear night and Manhattan is all lit up. I keep thinking about that time we went to see Mom dance — how the four of us walked to that restaurant afterward dressed up in our fancy clothes. Dad kept telling us to keep our eyes open because at any moment we might turn a corner and see Spiderman grappling with Dr. Octopus or Captain Marvel rocketing overhead. You and I both laughed, thinking we were too big for things like that, but we kept watch anyway, because who knew, maybe the world was just waiting to surprise us. I wouldn't have thought I'd feel the same way after all these years, but even now, when I look down at the lights of the city, they sometimes seem to flicker, like a dark form is passing between us, like a winged man is soaring through the sky.

Earlier tonight, I stopped by my nightstand and I picked up Freeman's letter. I stood there a long time, turning it over and over in my hands.

I'd hoped that writing to you would help me make sense of everything, that it'd give me the guts to finally pull the envelope out of my bag and slide it across Lassiter's desk. But it seems like just the opposite has happened. The idea of forgetting everything, even the worst things, scares me more than remembering.

The envelope tore easily enough. I did it once, and then I stacked the halves together and did it again. When I was done I let the pieces fall into the trash.

Anyway, I guess I better get going. I told Gonzalez I'd have dinner with him and his folks and then help him work on his pitch. I'd say I'll write more later, but the truth is, there's another letter I want to write. I think it's about time I left you alone and got started on it.

Love you, brother,
Cardinal

Dear Hannah,

You wanted to know how my dad's story ended. This is what I came up with.

Cardinal retreats to a cave at the summit of Ghost Mountain, a lone peak at the edge of the Gardens of Null. He watches as Abaddon slowly transforms into Liberty City. Its great towers rise and the burnt red skies turn blue. A canal is dug through the Gardens of Null and soon they become green and lush.

Decades pass. Cardinal turns seventy. Then eighty. Then ninety. He becomes stooped and frail. He rarely leaves his cave. He sees no one.

One day a family is picnicking in the meadow that lies at the foot of Ghost Mountain. A boy dares his little sister to climb it and seek out the crazy old hermit they say haunts the caves. He thinks she'll be too scared to do it, but he doesn't know his little sister very well.

Even at seven years old, Sally Sparrow isn't afraid of anything.

She fills a knapsack with provisions, sneaks away from

their parents, and climbs the mountain. She finds the old hermit lying on a bed made of stone in a cold, dank cave. He's shriveled and frail. Dressed in rags. His skin is like tissue paper draped over a frame of bone. Sally's heart breaks. He seems so familiar to her, even though she's sure she's never seen him before. She kneels by his side and feeds him morsels of food from her pack and wets his chapped lips with water from her canteen.

"How did you get here?" Sally Sparrow asks. "What are you doing in this cave all alone?"

Cardinal's eyes are covered in a film of gray. Sally is nothing but a shadow and a warm breath against his cheek. She takes his hand in hers and squeezes. When he speaks, his voice is like the moan of a rusty gate.

"My name," he says, "is Cameron Conner."

He tells her everything he remembers about the world to come. All about the Brotherhood and how the Volanti reappeared after a hundred years to betray and murder them. He weeps as he tells her how he saw the great love of his life, Sally Sparrow, die just before he fled uselessly into the past.

Frightened, Sally runs away, but when she reaches the sunlight and sweet air at the mouth of the cave, she's overwhelmed with guilt to have left the helpless old man on his own. She returns, only to find the stone bed empty. The old man and all his things have disappeared.

The final spread will be wordless. The spires of

Liberty City sparkling in the light of a noonday sun. High above them, the Brotherhood of Wings soars, with Cardinal and Sally Sparrow in the lead, hand in hand.

Hope you like it. Save me a front row seat for *Hamlet*. I'll be home soon.

Love,
Card

ACKNOWLEDGMENTS

SPECIAL THANKS to my pal and official science advisor, Dr. Kenneth Fortino, who was kind enough to set me up with a couple world-class scientists whose advice was invaluable to me as I worked on this book. All my thanks to Laura Thomas, PhD (Research Health Scientist, War Related Illness and Injury Study Center, DC VA Medical Center) and Catherine Franssen, PhD (Assistant Professor of Psychology at Longwood University). Memory is a bafflingly complex subject and you both helped make it just a little bit clearer.

Thanks as well to Martha Brockenbrough, Joelle Charbonneau, Eliot Schrefer, and Roland Smith. Also to Ken Weitzman and Danielle Mages Amato, who were kind enough to give me their thoughts on early drafts of this book.

Huge, heaping helpings of thanks to Sara Crowe, the whole team at Clarion, and my wonderful editor, Lynne Polvino, who were all tireless in helping me make this the best book it could be.